Tia

WALLS,
A Metaphor
(A True Story For All
Caregivers Of Children)

By: Will Lonardo

1

ISBN 978-0-9829769-8-2
eISBN 978-1-938862-30-4

Written by Will Lonardo

Cover by Gipson Studio LLC

Published by Dailey Swan Publishing, Inc

Dailey Swan Publishing, Inc
Bellevue, Wa. 98004
www.Daileyswanpublishing.com

DEDICATION

WALLS is dedicated to life's outcasts, especially the innocent children, who suffer the painful indignities of being different and the loneliness of neglect. May Billy's story enlighten their caregivers to guide the young along the bumpy roads they sometimes travel toward tomorrow.

To my mother, Della, I love and miss you, Mom. You and I took the long way in finding peace between us, but I now envision the crossroads up ahead where we'll hopefully be together one day with my father. And to Kathy, who started me on this literary journey so long ago, I thank you for the love and family you once gave me.

A Special Dedication

IT'S WITH LOVING GRATITUDE
that I extend my appreciation to
Shirley Frederick,
for without her my words may not
have fulfilled their purpose.

JUST A WORD

I was to learn many years later in life of those rich and famous who, as adults, experienced the same mystifying disease that haunted me as a boy. While breaking Babe Ruth's single season homerun record in 1961, Roger Maris developed a mild form of what's called alopecia areata (hair loss). Filming "Dark Passage," Humphrey Bogart was forced to wear a wig when his hair and beard began to fall out suddenly. Rick Smith, a long-time host of PM Magazine in Providence, RI, lost his job and left show business due to the sudden onslaught of his alopecia areata. Schuyler Robbins, once a successful New York model and the original "Marlboro Man," was earning $1 million a year when he fell victim to the disease. Even the wealth of John D. Rockefeller couldn't stave off his bout with the medical phenomenon.

The adult testimonials are endless, but nowhere nearly as devastating as those pertaining to the thousands of children who suffer this or any form of difference. To a child singled out or neglected in any way, the immediate effects are only part of their nightmare. The psychological wounds that often follow sometimes never heal, as the WALLS surround them, first from without, then from within.

WALLS are not merely made of stone, wood, mud or brick, by stone cutters, carpenters, masons and bricklayers. They are also built out of anger, shame, lies, jealousies, guilt, ignorance and fears. These human weaknesses confine many by putting up unseen barriers not only between adversaries, enemies or friends—but often between family members too. We all have hated, envied, loved and hidden in their shadows at one time or another. But how great it can be when the WALLS come tumbling down or we've found the way to surmount them and love one another again.

An elderly Jewish woman told me a long time ago that

everyone should raise a child and write a book before they die. I was a young man at the time, still struggling with the empty bitter feeling in my heart that had haunted me since boyhood. The wise old woman further said that writing about our memories can be self-healing as well as inspirational. "We can all learn from one another's experiences," she said, "especially about our age of innocence. It marks the measure of our strides forward." I thought of her as I completed twenty years of writing WALLS. It's been a slow, cleansing process, and extremely grueling at times to relive what once was. My mother may have laid the foundation of the wall that divided her and me, but in anger, and sometimes rage, I set the stones in place on top of it. The shadows cast from its great height kept me wandering blindly well into adulthood, not knowing how to forgive and forget or find lasting internal peace. For without love in children's lives, they become lost in an unforgiving void of despair, sometimes never coming into the light. It seemed like an eternity finding my way out of the darkness. WALLS is my journey, told to you step by step.

FOREWORD

By 1995 the worst of times turned all that I deemed and had prayed for into heartache. The family life that I had so wanted since my youth was breaking apart, eighteen years of the greatest loves I ever knew. It was a decade already marred by disappointment. A successful career in the arts had grown into a business, but corporate decisions of the heart, instead of my mind, ended a promising future of yet another dream.

It was during those dark days that I began to compile the memories into the book you are about to read. I wrestled with how it should be written, often putting it aside, telling myself I was a nobody and publishers wouldn't print it. "Write your story," a close friend kept insisting. "How you were forced to live as a boy was wrong and needs to be shared. Parents must know that what happened to you should never be the way for any child to grow up."

I wrote the first drafts as fiction in order to give WALLS what I thought at the time would be a better, marketable chance coming from an unpublished author. The story has never been intended to serve as a childrearing sermon or a "how to" Parenting 101 thesis. A third person approach, I believed, could work because of my taking creative liberties to further enhance the storytelling. But the over-exaggerated truths made me feel dishonest to myself and, more important, disloyal to the readers whom I wished to touch.

Years passed, and one day a literary agent's rejection note simply said, "Billy is you. Write the story from your heart just as you lived it. One day a publisher may see the value of what you experienced and why it's best to be told as an autobiography." I had been so caught up in depicting my life in an entertaining (novel-like) way, that I had forgotten its purpose. Thus, six years from when I began, I set about rewriting WALLS in the first person, as me, Billy. My final wish is that what I've written makes a difference by its portrayal of what befell a child's family when love was lost and a mother and son's hearts were broken.

"If you bungle raising children,
nothing else you do in life
matters much."
- Jackie Kennedy

IN LOVING MEMORY OF
The Most Reverend Bishop
David B. Thompson
(Emeritus of Charleston, SC)

"He was my Guiding Comfort,
My Rod and My Staff."
- Will Lonardo, Nov. 2013

WALLS, CHAPTER CONTENTS

ONCE UPON A TIME

Childhood Innocence And Impressionable Years

Mother Della, Dad and Me, when we were family in the good old days.

CHAPTER ONE
IN THE BEGINNING

All was well in my little corner of the world the winter of '47. In the Germantown section of Philadelphia, Pennsylvania, life was good, filled with all the love and security of family and friends around me. The neighborhood called "The Brickyard" was my playground, a magical kingdom for a little boy's curious mind and boundless energy. A child's imagination guided my hands as I built a wall from the ruin and rubble. Brick by brick it got higher, and I felt safe on the other side, playing in the vacant lot next to my parents' tiny neighborhood café. The bad guys wouldn't get me, no sir, not Billy. I was the captain and this was *my* fort. My mother often stood at the B & L's back door watching me, and her presence then was reassuring. All throughout my youth, her small but mighty image would take on contrasting forms as I grew. She could be a pillar of strength for a child to run to or a cold, insurmountable stone wall I would eventually turn from in the shadows.

My parents were decent people whose Italian heritage reflected the hard work ethic of the generations that preceded them. We didn't have much, but our household was always open to anyone who was hungry or had an ear for music from the old country. People were always coming and going. My mother's cooking and Dad's mandolin seemed to draw the whole world to our doorstep. A child couldn't have felt more contented than I did with all the attention I received in those times.

It was cold and blustery in The Brickyard that particular day. I remember being all bundled up like a mummy and hearing the parish church bell toll the hour and off in the distance a factory whistle signaled quitting time. My mother stood in the doorway with arms folded, watching me, her little stone mason. Our family came from a long line of stone cutters, and she'd brag to my uncles that I'd be the best one yet.

11

She opened the door slightly. "Billy, c'mon. Your father isn't feeling well. We're going home." She rapped on the window impatiently. There was a tone of urgency in her voice, but I ignored her at first and continued playing. My wall was more important. I would build walls out of anything, even inside the house with pillows or boxes. They were an obsession with me throughout my early years. Castles, walled cities, old forts or even prisons were intriguing. To see the Great Wall of China in person would have been the ultimate. Still is.

"Billy, did you hear me?" She opened the door wider. "We're closing early. Let's go!"

I continued laying the bricks. It was the best wall ever and I didn't want to stop. "Look at it, Mommy," I said. "Isn't it big? Those bad kids up the street won't knock this one down. It's real strong. Look, I put mud in between the bricks like Daddy showed me."

"Pick up your shovel," she said, her eyes glaring at me.

"Please, Mommy, can't I stay?" I always hated leaving things unfinished, since I was little. Maybe it's a Virgo trait, but I'm still that way.

"No!" She stepped toward me. "Get in here!"

I scooted inside, turning sideways so she couldn't swat me on my rump. I discovered early on how far Della could be pushed. When she gritted her teeth and you could see them, that was a sign of her limit. I'd often tempt fate and go beyond her tolerance when I was little, which eventually cost me dearly. She was tough when it came to obedience; but, hey, I was a kid, and to me that made her a meanie.

My father sounded pretty bad, coughing and spitting up as he clung to Della on the way home. I looked up at him helplessly and didn't see the big strong man I was accustomed to. He was Daddy, my hero, but on that day he appeared frail and sickly. It frightened me to see him like that. By the time we reached the house, he was shaking all over as he stumbled and swayed up to the kitchen door. I remember clinging to his hand as he tried to keep from falling.

My mother unlocked the door, holding onto his arm with

12

her other hand, and the three of us struggled to the kitchen table, where he collapsed into a chair and moaned. "What's wrong with me, Del? I'm getting dizzy." His voice was weak and his complexion pale.

She touched his face, which obviously must have been warm. "You're burning up. That's it. I'm calling the doctor. I should have called him days ago."

I became fearful, feeling threatened and helpless at the sight of his weakness and vulnerability. "You'll be okay, Daddy." I remember looking up at him through teary eyes. He folded his arms on the table and bowed his head as I tugged at one of his pant legs, hoping to see his great familiar smile. He reached out to me, and I wanted to jump up into his arms. That was my father, and it frightened me seeing him that way. I've never forgotten those tender moments, because we never had any more after that.

He struggled out of the chair and rested his hand on my shoulder. "I'm a little tired," he said. "I just need some sleep. Don't worry, everything will be okay." He held me close to him as we walked into the bedroom, where he spoke those special words that make everything right in a child's heart. "You're a good boy. I love you." It was the last time my father would ever say them to me. But I've never forgotten the sound or the feeling of them.

The coroner's report listed the cause of my father's death as pneumonia. The Brickyard neighborhood that night lost its finest citizen, and all of our lives were changed forever. The boys my father had trained to box in the basement of the Precinct Police Station hung out by the house in disbelief for a long time afterwards. I watched them through the window day after day, roaming around like lost sheep with no place to go. Many were without families. Della would just look out at them, cry, and shake her head. It had been important to my father that the boys have a purpose in life, because nobody else seemed to care about them. They were all my buddies.

The lines of people who came to pay their last respects at

the cemetery were long leading up to the gravesite. I hadn't quite understood that I'd never see this great man again, yet I knew he had gone somewhere, and I sensed that nothing would ever be the same. I kept hearing how he had been a friend to so many, and it made me proud. But why was everyone crying? I placed my stuffed dog, Poochie, alongside the gravestone to say goodbye. It was the last thing my father had bought me, and I wanted Poochie to say goodbye too.

The B & L was eventually sold, and my mother went to work in a candy factory. Her twenty-seven-dollar-a-week paycheck didn't go very far and times were hard. My dad's absence made it even tougher. No longer were there the surprises he had often brought home. Gone were the block party gatherings he had organized, and nightly sing-alongs at the house with my Uncle Reno joining him on guitar. Our world had sadly been transformed, leaving a great big emptiness. No other man could fill his void, nor could Della, who didn't possess his loving, gentle ways. It wasn't easy for her to be both father and mother.

My memory about those times became more vivid from the day my father died, as though I was born again out of his death. Della sat by the front room window weeks later, staring tearfully out at nothing as I played on the floor with my building blocks.

"Don't cry anymore, Mommy," I said. Her sadness seemed to go on and on, which was upsetting for me to watch day after day. I was a kid. What did I know about pain of the heart?

She turned from the window, wiped her tears and got down on the floor next to me. "I was just thinking about your father." She picked up some of the building blocks. "What are we making here?"

"Oh, just some dumb old wall. Daddy was gonna show me how to build a house. He said we'd have our own some day." I liked when my father played with me and we went places together. Every chance he got we did something, but those memories were brief. All I knew for sure was that they wouldn't happen anymore.

I never realized then how brave mothers can be for their children when times call for it. There's no doubt how great the sorrow must have been inside her, but she managed a smile and began joining the blocks. "Let's build a house together."

"It's not the same, Mommy," I said, which must've hurt her. But I was only thinking like a kid.

"Well, let's just pretend that it is, okay? He'll be very proud of us. Would you like to live in a big house?"

"If Daddy could be with us." Nothing seemed right to me without my father. I needed the reassurance that somehow we'd make it without him.

We played together for a while that afternoon and built four walls without windows. When it was finished, we sat there and talked about the man who had meant so much and whose presence we were trying to learn to be without.

The words she said to me then I've never forgotten. "Daddy's in heaven now, but he's watching over us. You can still talk to him." And I do, always hoping that I'll see him again one day. Wouldn't it be great when we die to go to some glorious, peaceful place where we're reunited with all those we loved in our lifetimes? I think after suffering the painful losses of each other here on earth, it would be a good thing. Could you imagine the reunions?

The Brickyard Café. That's Mom in the window, arms crossed and watchful.

15

CHAPTER TWO
MOVING ON

In 1948, after much coercing from my mother's upstate relatives, we packed up our Brickyard memories, bid farewell to everyone and left for the little town of Easton. It wasn't easy to leave what had been the only home I knew, but Della hoped things would be better for us in her hometown.

We settled in with my kind Aunt Margaret and nasty old Uncle Sam. Theirs was a grand corner house with a tree-shaded backyard and plenty of rooms to play hide and seek in with my three cousins. It was all there: the aroma of home cooked Italian food, music from "the old country" like my father used to play, pretend boxing with cousin Tony, and the front porch atmosphere of the neighborhood people. Aunt Margaret was the family matriarch in every sense of the word and also my godmother. She was my favorite and a shining example of what made a big family close and important, especially when in need of each other. Saturday nights were family time in the great house. She had ten other brothers and sisters, and if someone didn't show up for food and fun they'd hear from Aunt Margaret. She kept them all together, and we cousins enjoyed every moment. I know *I* did. It's where my dreams of having a big family one day began. Aunt Margaret was like my father. The more people the merrier. Of course, Uncle Sam wasn't too thrilled about the weekly gatherings, and he'd storm off to bed early, cursing everyone. He was the first person I'd know with such an ugly disposition, and I think of him every time I come across someone like that. Just as I had puzzled over my uncle then, I often wonder what makes people that way. But maybe it's the naïve little boy still in me who never gives up looking for the goodness that's in the worst of us. There'd be many times to come that certain moments would challenge those beliefs.

The newfound lives for my mother and me at first seemed to be a God-sent answer to prior sadness. For several months we all lived in harmony. Della began working in a pants factory, and we settled down once again to a warm, secure lifestyle. It was during that time that I came down with the dreaded childhood infirmities of measles, mumps and chicken pox. But I had great recuperative powers and before long was back doing what little boys do best, raising hell. Curiosity, imagination, adventure and downright playing hard were my fortes.

Then one day the good times all came crashing down. It was apparent from the start that Uncle Sam had not been enamored with the new living arrangements in his house. He wasn't a fan of children, not even his own, and was unpleasant and cantankerous, forever grumbling about life. I was hiding in the kitchen pantry from my cousin Margie when the fireworks started. In the dark confined closet I trembled in my boots as I listened to the thundering voice of the little man, my uncle.

"Margie! Stop slamming the doors!" Uncle Sam yelled.

"I can't find Billy," she said, slamming another in the next room.

"What did I just tell you?" He got up from the kitchen table where he had been reading the paper. "You better find him before I do."

"Oh, calm down, you old grump." Aunt Margaret entered the room. "Let them play." She was forever intervening on behalf of her kids with the house ogre. I could never quite figure out why he was always so unpleasant. It was such a happy house, except for him. He'd leave for work in the morning cranky and return at the end of the day in the same foul mood.

"Where's the boy's mother today?" Uncle Sam snarled. "It's Saturday."

"Della's working. She needs the extra money."

"Maybe we should charge more rent for watching her wild Indian," he said and sat back down. "He's always underfoot."

"Billy, where are you?" Margie called up the steps from out in the hallway. "Did you see him, Mom?"

"I'm not telling. That wouldn't be fair, Sam, now would it?" Aunt Margaret was a loving, kind woman who unfortunately had married a bullfrog. I'd try to make him laugh sometimes, but he'd stare right through me.

"Tell her anyway. Damn kid," Uncle Sam grumbled.

"Weren't you a child once? Now you leave them be, Sam. Hear me?" Her old-fashioned ways were contrary to most Italian households, and she wouldn't shrink from any man. Italian wives usually kept their place back then, but not good old Aunt Margaret. She'd frustrate the hell out of him and I loved it.

"What are you going to do, hit me with your soup ladle?"

"Don't tempt me, Sam."

I was trying hard not to move in the pantry's cramped space, as I cheered my aunt on. The next thing I knew, the pots and pans were falling all around me. That's when the volume of Uncle Sam's voice went up.

"What the hell was that?!" he barked.

"Probably mice," Aunt Margaret said.

His chair banged into the wall and the next thing I knew the doorknob jiggled. "Must be big mice. Maybe I should set some traps." The door swung open and there stood Uncle Sam in a rage, all five feet of him. "Okay you mice, now I got you!" He grabbed me by my hair and scowled. "Here's our little mouse."

"Let him go!" my aunt yelled. "You're hurting him."

Cousin Margie came running into the kitchen as Uncle Sam yanked me out of the closet. "Look at the mess you made in there, you little ..." He pulled my hair harder until it made me cry. He'd probably be up on child abuse charges nowadays. But that's the way it was back then.

The pantry was in shambles. Pots, pans, all sorts of food stores, flour and canning jars were strewn about.

"Aunt Margaret, tell him to let me go," I pleaded. "Please, Uncle Sam. I'm sorry. I didn't mean it." I squirmed every which way to free myself.

"Stand up!" Uncle Sam shouted, shaking me.

"Let him go, Daddy." Margie tugged on her father's arm. "We were only playing."

"Turn the boy loose," Aunt Margaret said, coming at him and waving the soup ladle. "Shame on you. He's only a child. He didn't do it on purpose. Now, let him go or I'll bop you one."

"Stay out of this, Maggie!" Uncle Sam yelled. "I'll teach him! He's not going to upset my house."

"Daddy, don't hurt him." Margie kept tugging on her father's arm. "It's my fault."

Uncle Sam shoved her aside and loosened his belt, holding onto me with his other hand. I strained all the more. That wasn't the kind of treatment I had been accustomed to. My father's ways were much different. When I misbehaved, all he had to do was stare at me. There was never any physical exchange, and when it was all over he'd smile or wink.

"You're not my father!" I said.

"I'll show you who I am." He raised his belt in the air, while Margie tried to pull me away. It turned into a tug of war, and I was the rope.

"What's going on here?" Della said, slamming the kitchen door behind her. "What are you doing to him?"

Uncle Sam was surprised to see her and immediately released me. "I'm disciplining the boy. Look at the mess he made in our pantry."

"What was he doing in there?" Della asked, looking at Aunt Margaret.

I felt like the cavalry had charged to save the day. "I was only hiding," I said. *Get him, Mommy*, I cheered to myself. *Beat him up.* He was the meanest person I knew, and I hated him. There hadn't been anyone before him that I feared or disliked so. It was a new feeling. His ugly little image remained with me for many years. Whenever I'd be confronted by a person of small stature who was a bully type, Uncle Sam would always come to mind. It's like they have a need to compensate for their lack of size. There would be one in particular later on in my life, sort of a Napoleon character.

"The kids were playing hide and seek." My aunt grabbed Uncle Sam's belt and stared him down. "So he hid in the pantry. Nothing serious. Just a few broken jars."

"I didn't mean it, Mommy. Uncle Sam scared me and I fell."

"The boy's always upsetting things around here." Uncle Sam held onto his pants as he spoke. "He's always underfoot and getting into things. This can't continue. Things have to change."

"Like what, Sam?" Aunt Margaret asked.

"Either your sister gets him in line, or..."

"Or what?" Della took my hand.

"He needs a man to teach him," Uncle Sam said.

"You're not that man. He's my son and I'll do the disciplining when and if he needs it. And you keep your hands off of him."

"You baby him too much." Uncle Sam sat down at the table. "This house has been upside down since you moved here."

"Well, I'm sorry you feel that way."

"He didn't mean that, Della," Aunt Margaret said, always the peacemaker.

"Like hell I didn't. Someone had to tell her."

Della walked me out of the kitchen into the hallway, pulling me along behind her.

"See what you've done?" Aunt Margaret jabbed Sam with the ladle. "Now say you're sorry."

"I'll say no such thing. That boy has been a spoiled brat since his father died. He wouldn't have tolerated his behavior."

My mother stopped abruptly and spun around. "My husband allowed Billy to be a child. He never once had to scare him into being good. All your kids are frightened to death of you. Look at Margie over there. She's afraid to move."

"That's my business."

"And Billy is mine. I'm sorry we're in your way." Della held her head high and continued up the hallway. She was a hard person to deal with when somebody annoyed her.

After that incident, my mother and I found ourselves unwelcome in the grand house on the corner. Aunt Margaret tried her best to keep peace, but before long it became obvious that we were going to have to move on. Uncle Sam put us out of his house, and once more we were on our own in need of a place to call home. Many years later when he was dying from tuberculosis, we visited him at the TB sanitarium. The bullfrog had become gentler by then and eagerly welcomed all visitors. It amused me as a kid to see how friendly and harmless he had become.

The fall of that year had been another time of new beginnings, and we settled into an attic room in a house on the main street of town. From the two small windows high above the street, our tiny room, or "castle in the sky" as I called it, looked down on what I pretended to be our kingdom. The room barely accommodated one bed, two chairs, a dresser and a cedar chest. A short hallway led past a dark storage room and narrow staircase. With the security of my mother's presence and some imagination, that rather cramped living space became my entire world. I imagined it being everything and anything I could think of: a cavalry fort with high, impenetrable walls, a king's castle, or the old B & L Steak Shop. It was my private playground.

Della tried to be all things to me, and I did cherish the moments we had. She'd pick me up from Aunt Dorothy's after work, and we'd have dinner together somewhere and then return to our little room. It would be many years before I learned to appreciate how hard it had been for her to be both a mother and a father.

Aunt Dot, another of Mom's six sisters, was also married to a tyrant. She was a tender, sweet lady, and I thoroughly enjoyed her. But, unfortunately, my presence there wasn't always welcomed by Uncle Nick. Too much boy for him, I guess. Needless to say, we didn't frequent the relatives, which left Mom and me pretty much to ourselves. But that was okay. I didn't need anybody else.

Back in our "castle in the sky," we'd settle down for the evening, which usually ended with listening to the radio or her telling me a bedtime story. She liked to tell spooky ones, like the night King Kong kept looking in our windows. Everything seemed perfect as I best remember, and we'd fall off to sleep side by side, sometimes behind my wall of pillows.

In 1949, at the age of six, I started kindergarten. The days began bright and early with Della taking me to St. Anthony's before going off to work. When classes were over, Sister Francis would take me over to the convent, where I'd remain in the care of the good sisters until early evening. I enjoyed being with Sister Francis and the other nuns. But like most good times, those special visits would soon come to an end.

I didn't see Sister Francis again until many years later, when she visited Easton from her new parish in Florida. The memory of that tiny woman dressed all in black has never left me. She remains an image of gentleness, wisdom, caring and how people should be kind toward one another.

The next year I entered first grade at a different school, which presented my mother with a new problem. Someone had to be sure I got home safe and sound. The temporary solution would involve yet another family member who in short order became frustrated with the responsibility of me. I'd occasionally roam off somewhere, not to be found. Little did I realize then that I was fast becoming my own worst enemy. I had energy to burn as a youngster and a tremendous curiosity. Nosey, some called it.

Della often had to work Saturday mornings for extra pay. But in spite of all the promises made by my cousins to watch me, I had become a burden that no one cared to lighten for her. So on occasion I'd be left in our castle in the sky to my own diversions. What trouble could a seven-year-old boy possibly get into?

I had beautiful curly brown hair then, and the temptation to cut it was too much to resist one particular Saturday morning. What I intended to be just a trim turned into a total disaster, setting off a chain of events that would drastically change my life once again.

Upon returning home, my mother entered the room and stopped abruptly. She studied me for a moment with her arms folded. "What did *you* do?"

"Nothing," I replied, standing in front of the dresser

mirror sheepishly looking at her reflection, while trying to hide the scissors. She had the icy look in her eyes that I was growing quite accustomed to seeing. I believed that I was doing a good thing allowing her to go off to work by watching myself. After all, how bad could a haircut be? It saved money. Besides, the fact that I heard other parents say they would never leave their kids alone made me feel special that Della could. Boy, was *I* ever wrong.

"What do you mean nothing?" Della gestured toward the bed and dresser. "Look, there's hair everywhere but on your head." She walked around the bed, took the scissors from me and picked up some of the long, curly locks of hair. "What do you call this?"

"Hair?" I timidly replied.

"Why did you cut it?"

"I don't like it. The other kids make fun of me. They call me cutie because it's long and curly."

"So, you just decided to cut if off," she said. "Just like that."

"It'll grow back." I ran my fingers through what was left of my hair. "Won't it?"

"In a month or two." Della picked up more of the curly locks, holding them in front of my face. She glanced at them and then back at my head. "I can't fix what you've done. What am I to do with you?" She sat down by the window, sighed and stared outside for the longest time.

"I'm sorry. I won't do it again. Honest." I remember worrying about what was going to happen to me. She was obviously upset and was contemplating my fate.

"I can't trust you alone, not even for a few hours. You're always getting into something. If we can't find you after school, you're somewhere getting into trouble."

"I'll never cut my hair again. I promise. You can even let it grow down to my feet." When you're a kid who's been bad, you'll promise anything to not be punished, and I would've given up candy at that moment.

"Come here." Her eyes softened as she reached for me.

"It's okay. You're just too young to be left by yourself."

"Really, Mommy, I'll be good." I couldn't seem to keep out of trouble, and Della's tolerance of me was obviously wearing thin.

She gave me one of her hard embraces, something my mother didn't often do. Showing affection was difficult for her. It always was and always would be. "It's not your fault. I shouldn't leave you alone anyway. You're only a little boy."

Della glanced out the window and then stood up. She thought for a moment, then walked toward the doorway. Something told me I was in big trouble that time. I could see it all over my mother's serious face.

"Where are you going?" I asked.

"Stay put," she said, attempting to rearrange my butchered head of hair. "I'm going to make a phone call. Clean up your mess."

"Who are you calling?" That was the question for the ages in my short lifetime. I asked it often in those days.

"Your Uncle Joe," she answered and left the room.

I dreaded those phone calls she made to my uncle when I had done something wrong. He was the one whose advice she took, which most times meant some form of punishment. My curiosity soon got the best of me, and I sneaked down the steps. The phone was on the first floor, just inside the front door. I listened for a moment, then on all fours crawled along the banister to the head of the staircase. The house was silent and Della's voice carried up to where I lay on the floor.

"Joe, I don't know what to do with him anymore," I heard her say, and then there was a long pause. "But he's just a little boy."

I listened intently, not knowing the nature of their conversation, but it didn't sound good, and as I would soon find out, it wasn't.

"Philadelphia!" Della exclaimed. "But that's so far away. I don't think I could do that to him."

The words I managed to hear that day were unsettling ones, and I remember the cold feeling they sent through me, except for the word 'Philadelphia.'

"Maybe you're right, Joe," she said. "I guess it wouldn't hurt to check the school out. Where is it? It sounds like a good place, but it's so far away. I have to do something. Okay, get me some information and call me back. Goodbye."

I turned and quickly tiptoed back upstairs to the attic room. My mind was filled with apprehension and questions. Their conversation had sounded like plans were being made to put me far away in some desolate place for bad boys. I promised myself I'd be an angel from then on, so there'd be no reason to get rid of me. My mother wouldn't do something like that to me anyway. I was only a kid, and she loved me.

Della talked to me about the possibility of moving back to Philadelphia, not far from the Brickyard. A place where I'd go to school, and she wouldn't have to worry about me while she was at work. It sounded fantastic. I hugged her for all I was worth in my excitement. "When can we go?" I asked over and over. I knew in the end that she wouldn't let me down. We were a team. Much to my unpleasant surprise, I couldn't have been more wrong.

Sister Francis and my kindergarten days. That's me, lower left.

CHAPTER THREE
HAIL GIRARD, ACCLAIM HER MANHOOD

Fall arrived and with it came the excitement of yet another change in my life. We were moving back to Philadelphia, my hometown, a place where memories were sweet and secure. *Finally, something good has happened for us*, I thought. Unlike the Brickyard house, our new home was a magnificent boarding school set in a lush, isolated community within the big city. On a prior visit with Della for pretesting and interviews, Girard had overwhelmed me from the outset, especially the ten-foot wall that surrounded the beautifully landscaped fifty-acre campus. Even hearing the school anthem for the first time with Della at my side had sent a rush of pride through me. I imagined all the new things we'd do there together. "You're gonna be proud of me," I said when told I had been accepted at the school. "Just like the words in their song about being a man. You'll see. I'll be just like Daddy. A real man."

Girard was founded in the 1800s by Stephen Girard, a prominent philanthropist. Born in France, he left home for the sea as a cabin boy, eventually settling in Philadelphia. In time he grew to be a wealthy merchant and banker, giving freely of his time and money to many causes. The lives of underprivileged, orphaned or fatherless boys concerned him greatly, and before his death, with the bulk of his estate, he established Girard, our new home.

Della and I stood next to one of the small lodge buildings that guarded either side of the main entrance to the school campus and looked up at Founder's Hall just beyond the circular gardens. The structure was an architectural wonder, an exact replica of the Greek Parthenon. Its magnificence dwarfed everything that surrounded it. I stared in awe of the multicolumn building for a moment, then turned toward the high ornate metal gates. They were massive. We had finally found a safe and beautiful place to call our home.

"Good afternoon, ma'am and young sir," the lodge keeper

said. He was attired in a gray uniform and politely touched the bill of his train-conductor like hat as he approached us. "I'm Carl. We met a couple of months ago when you were here. Remember how curious your son was about our wall?"

"Walls fascinate him." Della shook Carl's hand. "He likes to build and draw them all the time."

"I think he likes gates too." Carl walked over to where I was examining the immense lock. The walls and the gate had impressed me about the school right from the start. They gave me a secure feeling, especially with my mother there too.

"We're supposed to meet Mr. Swagg here," Della said.

"Yes, ma'am. He'll be along shortly."

I pushed and tugged at the big old gate but could barely move it. "Boy, the key must be big for this. We'll be real safe living here, Mommy. There's a wall and everything."

Carl showed me the skeleton key. "It's not like your normal house key."

At that moment a long black car came around the circular gardens and pulled up by the lodge. Mr. Swagg, a very dapper man, stepped out and approached Della. He was a gentlemen's gentleman. I remember feeling comfortable around him right away, from the moment he tipped his tweed six-panel hat. "Good day, Della," he said with a warm smile. "Welcome back."

Mr. Swagg was the head housemaster in charge of the Westend where all the new boys lived. A soft-spoken and kindly man, he was nattily attired in a bulky cardigan sweater, neatly pressed brown pinstriped slacks and oxford penny loafers. His thick-lensed, brown-framed glasses slid off the bridge of his nose as he spoke.

"It's good to see you again, Mr. Swagg." Della shook his hand and they talked softly for a minute or two, while I was preoccupied with Carl at the gate.

Mr. Swagg took hold of her arm and they joined Carl and me. "Hi, Billy," he said. "How are you?"

"Do you lock the gate at night?" I thought back to my toy jeep being stolen from our home in The Brickyard soon after my father died.

"Tighter than a drum," Carl patted me on the head. "You're safe here."

Everything was perfect at that moment, and I couldn't wait for us to move in. We had been through so much, and this seemed to turn all the bad things right. It was a new day. "It's so neat here, Mommy, isn't it?"

Della turned away and walked toward the car. She had an uneasy look on her face, but I didn't think much of it at the time. I was too wrapped up in the newness of everything.

"Well, what do you say, son?" Mr. Swagg put a hand on my shoulder, which I found very comforting. "Let's get going. We have a lot to do."

Carl held the car door open for us, and I eagerly jumped in. "You come and visit me sometime," he said and tapped on the window. He stepped aside and waved as we drove off.

"We will see him again, huh, Mommy?" I smiled and waved back. What a nice man, I thought. There were finally people who actually cared about us.

The tree-lined main street extended from end to end through the heart of the school grounds. Marble and granite buildings, some with ivy clinging to them, were generously spaced among walkways lined with trees and green velvet landscaping. Some of the hallowed halls were named to honor Stephen Girard's life work, such as Banker, Merchant and Mariner. It was a self-contained, campus-like village that sat right in the middle of an all-black neighborhood in the city. I was taken in by the sheer magnificence and contrasting splendor of the place, which certainly stood out from its surroundings.

It had been a rather long day of admission and indoctrination procedures. By then my curiosity and enthusiasm had swelled in anticipation of seeing where Della and I would live. My mother would finally no longer have to worry about me when she went off to work, and I felt good about our lives as we rode down to the Westend. The complex of buildings was comprised of six Georgian style mansions in a square, overlooking the largest playground I had ever seen. What else could any kid want? I remember thinking how lucky we were to be in such a fantastic place and together.

CHAPTER FOUR
KNICKERS, KNEESOCKS, BEANIES
AND A NAKED HEART

Mr. Swagg walked up ahead as we passed through the classic portico colonnade entrance onto the spacious courtyard. Della took my hand and gave it a gentle squeeze. "I forgot how impressive this place is," she said.

"That it is." Mr. Swagg pointed toward the far end of the playground with the pipe he never seemed to smoke. "It's well laid out. That wrought-iron fence over there makes it the boys' own safely enclosed little world."

"It's like a little village for little people. What do you think, Billy?" she asked me. "Did you ever see such a big playground? And look at all the fun things you can do."

I broke away from her once I saw the swings, slides, seesaws and sandbox. "Can I go play?" There was even a small baseball diamond and hopscotch blocks painted right on the macadam surface.

"Maybe tomorrow, son." Mr. Swagg pointed to one of the buildings. "Let's go see your new home. Miss Hart is waiting for us."

"Who's she?" I asked.

"Your governess," Mr. Swagg responded. "You'll like her. She's very nice."

"What's a governess, Mommy?"

"She'll look after you when I'm gone," Della said, nervously fidgeting with my hair. "I won't have to worry anymore about you running off."

So many had watched me, or should I say, tried to up to that point, and I wondered how Miss Hart would compare. I already was hoping she'd last, because none of the others had, and this was an opportunity I sure didn't want to ruin for us.

"Here we are. House D." Mr. Swagg opened the French doors. "Your new home, son."

House D's very large white living room had a high ceiling,

a fireplace at one end with a wide staircase at the other. The tall French doors and windows let in the reddish glow of the sunset, casting reflections across the highly polished wooden floor. An antique cherry-wood secretarial desk was positioned along the opposite wall by a grouping of little desks all in a row.

I stared at the miniature wooden desks and chairs and immediately wondered which one was mine. They kind of reminded me of the seven dwarves' cottage in *Snow White*.

The rest of the room was beautifully appointed. A big brown leather couch and matching high wing-backed chairs were arranged around the fireplace on a Persian rug. It was a cozy setting accented with paintings, bookshelves and a pendulum clock mounted on the wall.

Mr. Swagg closed the door behind us and motioned to the fair-complected blond woman who was speaking to some people by the fireplace. I watched Miss Hart closely as she approached us. There was a warm friendliness about her that seemed to brighten the room. She wore a white puffy-sleeved blouse, loose-fitting yellow sweater vest and a tan plaid straight skirt. I wasn't too sure yet what a governess did, but that was okay. She made a good impression on me from the start, especially with her welcoming embrace.

"She's pretty, Mommy," I said.

"Why thank you, young man." Miss Hart smiled. "And you're very handsome."

Mr. Swagg stepped forward. "Miss Hart, this is Della Lonardo and her son, Billy."

"My, what a curly head of hair," she said, touching the top of my head.

"It's grown since he chopped it off." My mother fussed with me and my hair more than usual that day. "I left him alone one morning when I went to work. You should've seen the haircut he gave himself."

"Kids can do the craziest things," Mr. Swagg commented as he opened the door. "You'll have to excuse me. Lots to do on admittance days, but I'll be back." He winked at me and left. It didn't take long to like Mr. Swagg. I felt at ease around him from the start, because he appeared easygoing and kind, just like my father was.

Miss Hart closed the door. "Tell you what, Billy." She put her arm around me. "Why don't you go with your mother over to the couch. That's Mrs. Ward with Kevin and Mrs. Scalzo with Benny over there. They're new boys too. I'll be right back. I must check on the other boys upstairs. They're supposed to be taking showers. But you know boys. Maybe while I'm gone our seamstress will fit you."

I looked up at Della, puzzled, as Miss Hart walked away. "Fit me for what?" I inquired. Everything was happening so fast, and my curiosity had me anxious for what was next.

"New clothes," She took my hand. "You're getting an entire new wardrobe. Isn't that wonderful?"

"What about my own clothes?"

"We didn't bring them, remember?"

"You didn't bring yours either. Are you getting new ones too?"

She grabbed my hand and hurried me across the room to meet the others. *Wow*, I thought, *a new home, new clothes, and new friends*. I couldn't imagine what else would be new, but I was ready for it.

"I can't wait to see our room," I said. "I hope it has big windows like our old house at The Brickyard." Della wasn't excited like I was and pulled me along as if she was in a hurry. That's when I began sensing that something was wrong. She seemed nervous, and I could always tell her mood changes. There were only two, bad and good.

Miss Hart returned a minute or so later, just as Miss Seagles, House D's seamstress, entered the room. "And how are my new boys doing?" she asked, fussing over us like a mother hen, which I really liked. Della never did do that sort of thing.

"Excuse me, Miss Hart, dear." Miss Seagles' voice trembled as she peered over her granny glasses. She was an elderly woman dressed in an old-fashioned ankle-length frock and apron. "I'm ready now for the boys. My, aren't they precious, the little darlings."

Kevin, Benny and I glanced at each other, trying hard not

to laugh. To us she was comical looking, what with her constant blinking and jerky steps when she walked.

"Perfect timing," Miss Hart said. "Why don't you three run along with Miss Seagles and get fitted. Meanwhile, I'll take your mothers on a tour of the house."

"Can't my mother come with me?" I asked, taking her hand.

Della leaned forward and whispered in my ear. "Go on with the other boys. I'm anxious to see how nice you're going to look in your new clothes."

"Okay, but hurry back, Mommy," I said. "I want to see our room." It had to be bigger than our castle in the sky, I thought, judging by the rest of the school. My eagerness for us to settle in at that point was making me rammy. The days had never looked brighter and so promising for us since my father's death.

When we returned from the seamstress wearing our new clothes, Mr. Swagg stood by one of the wing-backed leather chairs speaking with Miss Hart, while our mothers sat poised on the couch waiting to see how their sons looked.

"Don't they just look fine in their new clothes?" Miss Hart straightened our ties and fussed with each of us. "I love knickers on a boy with a white shirt and tie. It makes them look so proper and gentlemanly, don't you think?"

"The beanie caps are a nice touch," Mrs. Scalzo said.

"Yes, they look so adorable." Mrs. Ward hugged her son.

"Do you like your new clothes?" Della asked. "You look so handsome in them." Her voice sounded strained, and she appeared to be sad to me.

"Be happy, Mommy." I touched her face, thinking of how sad we had been for so long. I remember her not smiling much, and I wanted her to.

"My little man," she whispered.

"Can we go see our rooms now?" I glanced up at Miss Hart, noticing that nobody was smiling. It didn't make sense to me at the moment that everybody looked so glum.

Mr. Swagg nervously cleared his throat and glanced at his watch. "Well, gentlemen," he said, "It's been a long day. I bet you're tired, right mothers?"

The other mothers glanced at their sons and nodded. I couldn't figure out why nobody looked happy. This was supposed to be a good thing, but it sure didn't seem like it to me.

"Growing boys need their proper rest." Miss Hart broke the silence in what was becoming an uneasy moment.

"Us old folks too." Mary Scalzo put her arms around Benny. "C'mon, give Mom a big kiss."

"Me too," Mrs. Ward said and rubbed her nose on Kevin's. "It's getting late. Della, you have a two-hour bus ride ahead, don't you?"

"Uh, yes, I do." My mother looked down at me with sadness in her eyes, and it was then I realized that something was very wrong.

"Well, I am afraid you mothers will have to say your goodbyes now." Mr. Swagg went to the French doors and opened them. "It is late. I'll stop by in the morning, Miss Hart, to see how the boys are doing." He bowed slightly and gestured toward the doorway. "Ladies, whenever you're ready, I'll accompany you."

Mrs. Ward and Mrs. Scalzo held their sons' hands and walked to the door. No one said a word. Mr. Swagg and Miss Hart were noticeably uneasy as they glanced toward my mother, and I was trying to understand.

"It was nice meeting you moms," Miss Hart said. "Now, don't be worrying about your sons. They'll be fine."

Benny and Kevin hugged and kissed their mothers one last time, then waved as the two women disappeared out the door. Benny's lips quivered, and Kevin looked lost. Miss Hart put her arms around their shoulders. "Don't worry. Before you know it, you'll see them again."

"Mommy, where's everybody going? You're not leaving too?" I grabbed hold of Della's arm. She wasn't going out that door if I could help it.

She hesitated, speaking softly. "I have to go home now."

My mind couldn't comprehend what was happening. The

new life I had imagined for us was being turned upside down and I didn't know why. "But, this is our home now!" I cried out as my heart sank. "Isn't it?"

Della took me in her arms and tried to soothe what was already an obviously upsetting and embarrassing situation for her. "It's for the best, Billy. They can do more for you here. Really, they can," she said. "Besides, you'll make lots of new friends like Benny and Kevin."

"But you told me..." I couldn't find the words. "I thought we'd both live here!"

"I'll write to you all the time."

"I don't want letters! I want you!"

There were no words that mattered, all I knew was that my mother was leaving me. *Grownups aren't supposed to lie*, I thought. I couldn't believe what was happening. How could she do this and not have said anything before, it was all so wrong...so very wrong.

"Calm down, son. You'll see her again." Mr. Swagg gently separated us, but I squirmed loose and rushed back into her arms.

I remember how weary and distraught Della looked as she said, "He was so happy to be moving back to Philadelphia... and now I'm leaving him."

"Please, Mommy. Take me home. I promise I'll be good!" I clung to her with all my might. "I won't stay here without you!"

"Della, I'm sorry, but it's best if you leave." Miss Hart pulled me close to her. "I'll take good care of him."

"Billy, you be good for Miss Hart." Della waved and quickly slipped out the door.

That final glimpse of my mother sent me into a screaming rage. "No! Come back, Mommy! Please don't leave me here!" It was an indescribable feeling. Not even when my father died had I felt that empty inside. There was nobody to love me anymore, and for the first time the fear of being alone crept over me.

Mr. Swagg followed her, closing the door, and a palling silence fell over the room. I tugged, kicked and struggled, all the while staring angrily at where my mother had just stood. I desperately tried to understand. *It must all be some game*, I puzzled. Any moment my mother would reappear and everything would be the way it was intended. I remained focused on the door, but it never opened. The seconds ticked by and my hopes faded with each passing minute, while Miss Hart tried to calm me. Benny and Kevin kept their vigil at the window, straining to catch one last glimpse of their mothers. It all felt like a nightmare, so unreal. Parents don't desert their children.

"Well, it's just the four of us," Miss Hart said. "Let's sit down and get to know each other." She held my hand and led us to the couch.

I reluctantly obliged her. "I'm not supposed to be here alone. Mommy lied to me." *Why did she do that?* I wondered. Most of my life I refused to accept my mother's reasoning, until just a few years before she died. As for why she never could be truthful to me about many things, I'll never understand.

"I'm sure she didn't want to," Miss Hart said as she brushed my hair back from my forehead. "Sometimes grownups have reasons to tell a fib now and then."

"I don't care. It's not right. I'll run away." I've never forgotten the crushing pain of that moment. It hurt so badly that I could hardly breathe. In my child's mind it made no sense to be given to strangers when there was family back home. I sat there crying, stunned by it all.

Miss Hart wiped my tears and put her arms around all of us. "You'll make a lot of new friends here. All of you will." She managed a friendly smile, trying to disguise her own sadness for us.

I jumped from the couch and bolted for the door, screaming for Della as I flung it open. Into the night I stumbled, across the expansive playground, and ran for the main road, never once looking back. My legs pumped faster and faster as I looked up ahead, hoping to catch sight of my mother. In the darkness, the trees along the roadside seemed to bend over, trying to thwart my way. I called out over and over, "Mommy, don't leave me here! Where are you? Take me with you! Come back, I'm scared!" My voice echoing off the granite buildings was the only sound in the night. It was surreal, like living a nightmare, a nightmare I would relive repeatedly in my sleep and countless dark waking moments. That empty feeling has haunted me on and off throughout most of my life, even now as I write these words, or on occasion during a late night dream.

My heart pounded as I turned the final bend in the road. Up ahead the main gates came into view. They no longer appeared inviting to me as before. Instead they loomed as towering cold monuments of metal, keeping me from the most important thing in my life. I slammed into the ungiving gates, crying out into the darkness. "Mommy, I'm here! Please come and get me!" I stared across the street as a trolley car paused then moved on. Della was gone. She had deserted me behind those walls with all my fears. The horror of a new life, all alone, had begun.

Every emotion ran rampant and coursed through my desperate mind and body. Anger seesawed with hurt in a frenzy of tears and confusion. The madness of it all made no sense. Why was I left there? What's a young boy to think abandoned so far from home? There was no place to turn but inward. I looked in every direction, but where was I to go in that strange and uninviting place?

As I stood back from the gate I caught sight of the lodge-keeper standing there. Carl waited patiently with outstretched arms. "It's okay, Billy," he said. "Don't be afraid."

"Stay away from me," I gasped between sobs. I wasn't about to trust any adult then, nor would I for many years to come. They were all in this conspiracy as far as I was concerned, so I kept my distance.

Carl took a few steps toward me. "I won't hurt you. You know, I was a new boy here once just like you, and *my* first night was rough too. But it'll be okay, you'll see."

The closer he got, the more frantically I looked for a way to escape. I remembered the door inside the lodge that opened to the city streets. The old man wasn't fast enough to catch me.

Nobody back home could either, when I didn't want to be caught. I never did like being confined, not unless I was behind my own walls and there I would always feel safe well into my adult years.

"Were you really a new boy here too?" My voice wavered as I walked toward the lodge building with the intent to run when I got near the outer door.

"Yes, I was, a long time ago." Carl was soft-spoken and his manner was gentle. "Both my parents had died."

"My father died too, a couple of years ago." I planned to distract him by talking friendly, but he was wise to me and blocked my way when we got inside.

Carl watched my every move. "Now, now, don't get any ideas," he said. "It's mighty lonely out there. What do you say we have a piece of hum mud. It's ginger cake. You'll love it. We make it right here in our own bakery. It looks like a mud pie."

Now he's trying to bribe me, I thought. "What's a hum?" I asked sarcastically.

"Hum is short for hummer. That's what you are now, a hummer. It's a slang word. Home, hummer, get it?"

The wall and the gates appeared to be getting higher and more intimidating as I looked out the window. "Why is there a wall here?" I tried to get around him, but it became obvious there wasn't going to be any escape that night.

"Oh, it's just a protection thing, separates the school from the city."

I no longer felt the same way about the wall or the gate as I had earlier that day. They weren't friendly anymore, and I saw them as a barrier, not something to feel secure behind. The more I stared at them, the more frightened I became and doubtful that I'd ever see my mother again.

Carl put his arm around me. "That big old wall out there will keep you safe. Somebody will always be here for you, like Mr. Swagg, Miss Hart, or even myself."

"My mother and me were supposed to live here together." That's all I kept thinking about. "She lied to me."

"I'm sure she doesn't want you here any more than you

want to be. She probably didn't have a choice. But trust me, this is a good place."

A car pulled up and Mr. Swagg got out. He breathed a sigh of relief when he entered the lodge. "Whew, am I glad to see you, son," he said. "Sorry I couldn't get here quicker, Carl. I didn't know he had run off." He took out his pipe and filled it with tobacco.

"You should have seen him, Mr. Swagg, coming around the circle. He charged into that gate like it wasn't there. I thought for sure he'd climb it."

"Good thing it was closed, huh?" Mr. Swagg puffed on his unlit pipe while searching his pocket for a match. "Or he'd be back upstate by now."

I was still feisty and determined. "You can't keep me here. I'll run away. You'll see. Your dumb old wall won't stop me."

Carl squeezed my arm. "He's a tough little guy, Mr. Swagg, but the boy's really scared. Let me know how he's doing, would you?"

"Well, I guess I'd better get him back." Mr. Swagg took me by the hand. "We wouldn't want Miss Hart to get in trouble because she's missing a boy."

"Do I have to go?" I liked being there with Carl, and the fact that I could see through the gate toward the corner where my mother had last stood also gave me some comfort. It was a false hope that she'd reappear and take me home. In the coming months I'd spend hours dreaming up ways to escape. My commitment to running away would become an obsession, a solemn promise to myself, and I never once feared the consequences. It wasn't right what they did to me, and I knew that some day I'd show them all.

On the drive back to Westend not a word was spoken as I continued to hope that I'd see my mother somewhere in the darkness. Maybe she was still out there. It was so hard to accept that she had deserted me, and the heartache was a wound I never thought would heal.

The reality of being on my own set in immediately. I pleaded over and over to anyone who'd listen that this all had been a mistake. As the weeks went by my anger grew and I cried myself to sleep most nights. Sometimes Kevin and Benny would join me by the dormitory window and we'd stare out over the wall at the city. It was during those hours that I felt most alone. At times the wall would close in on me and I could hear my mother's voice calling out. "Billy, Billy, I'm not far," I'd hear her say. "Come to the wall so that I can see you." In my most dreaded nightmares, I'd climb to the top, but always fell back into nothingness.

CHAPTER FIVE
A FAILED ESCAPE

Life in a boys' school, circa 1950s, was definitely not a solitary existence. From the moment we got up, the clock controlled our lives. We ate, slept, played, bathed, studied and even went to the toilet in groups. Our clothes were like period costumes on a Hollywood *Boys Town* movie set. We wore pants gathered at the knees, socks that sometimes reached our thighs supported by black garters, extra wide neckties on baggy dress shirts, Buster Brown shoes and, of course, the beanie cap. The bedtime nightshirt was an adventure to sleep in, especially when it gathered up around your head and your naked rump stuck out. Those were the accepted fashions of boys' school life in those days.

It was hard for me to fit in from the start, because I honestly believed that being there was all some big mistake. Aside from Kevin and Benny, I stayed pretty much to myself. I'd find a secluded spot on the playground or in House D and talk to the little picture of Della I kept in my pocket. Before long a few of the boys got to calling me Baby Billy and Mommy's Boy. Their comments made me all the more uncooperative. But they also drew me closer to Miss Hart, and I'd follow her around sometimes like a lost little lamb.

Dormitory life at the Westend wasn't quite as bad as the older boys' cattle barns at Lafayette or Good Friends buildings. But it was a far cry from sleeping with my mother in our tiny one room castle in the sky. Many a night I reached out for the security of her warmth and those bedtime stories she'd tell, only to hug my pillow and pretend. Ironically, many decades later Della would tell those same spooky stories to my daughter.

In time life got as normal as one could hope for, given the circumstances. Benny, Kevin and I became close friends, and we'd share our sorrows in whispers during the night. But the tearful sounds of lonely boys soon turned to devilish nocturnal laughs and plans of retaliation or escape. Place a bunch of boys in an oversized bedroom, and they'll eventually conjure up mischief of some kind.

There were many frustrations to deal with as a newbie. For varying reasons we were all unwanted new boys thrust together in a place no one was actually fond of. Competitive energies often ran high, fights were frequent and daring challenged the norm. After a day of rigid discipline, the nights sometimes encouraged the foolhardy and beckoned inquisitive spirits. Left to a boy's fertile imagination, House D became much more than it was during the supervised daylight hours.

The six granite mansions were identical structures consisting of two separate dorms; a large, white-tiled, 30-sink washroom and shower area; a dining room with kitchen; a sitting room with fireplace and thirty desks; plus a tiny upstairs efficiency apartment for the governesses. The houses were totally self-sufficient, and except for the connecting porticos, they stood completely independent of one another.

The Westend complex seemed to me like a well-enclosed fortress on three sides, except for the portico entranceway from off the main road. During the first month or so living there, I often spent my playground time sitting under its colonnade staring up the road thinking of Della and recalling the life I had once lived at home, along with my childhood curiosities that usually got me in trouble. Occasionally in front of the Westend I noticed delivery trucks and other vehicles coming and going nearby, toward the back of the school. Some returned while others didn't, which led me to believe that there had to be a back gate just down the road. Eventually this set me to wondering about a possible escape from my walled-in existence.

I began to develop a rebellious attitude by then, becoming contrary to rules and regulations, and would at times defy authority to attract the wrong kinds of attention. My purpose was to force the school into not wanting me, but Miss Hart and Mr. Swagg had the patience of saints, and I guess it might have been because I really wasn't a bad kid. It was just my devilish way of showing them that I didn't belong there.

It was on a Saturday afternoon in late October of 1951 when I decided to make my break to freedom. I had great expectations of success for my sad heart of hearts. The only real plan I had if I got beyond the wall was to run as far and as fast as my legs could carry me. If I reached Girard Avenue and then on down to Broad Street, I thought, making it to the Broad and Erie Bus Station wouldn't be too difficult. That was where my mother and I had arrived from Easton twice before. Of course, at the ripe old age of eight, how possibly sound was my logic? But my stubbornness drove me on even back then, the same as it has over the past twenty years it's taken me to share my story with you.

As I sat there that day counting the spending money I had saved from Della's letters, it was taking me a while to get up the courage to run for what I hoped would be my way out from behind the oppressive ever-present stone wall. What didn't help was when Dr. Freedman's extremely large shaggy sheepdog, Luther, appeared from around the far side of the school Prefect of Study's house, which stood next to Westend. Luther was an overly friendly dog, and if he caught sight of anyone on or near the property, all of his one hundred plus pounds would come bounding toward them. It had happened to me before, and he played rough. My dream seemed impossible as I watched him roam about on the front lawn. His lousy timing was not only interfering, but as I was wearing my best clothes for the trip home, the last thing I needed was to roll around in the grass with a slobbering animal.

I was watching Luther closely when Kevin and Benny came up behind me. "We figured you'd be out here again," Kevin said, bouncing the soccer ball he had with him.

"How come you have your Sunday clothes on?" Benny sat down alongside me on the portico steps. "We're not supposed to wear our good shirt and tie on the playground."

"I snuck out through the dining room after lunch," I replied. "Miss Hart didn't see me leave, and the tie was in my jacket pocket. I'm going to run away today. I told you guys I would. Remember what I said about the trucks?"

"Yeah, but are you sure there's a gate back there?"

"Those trucks, and cars too, they're going somewhere, Kevin."

"What if there's a guard back there?" Benny asked.

"If I can't get out, I'll just have to come back."

"But what if you're caught?"

"So? What can they do to me? I'm already in a jail."

"Put you on bread and water maybe."

I was very nervous and impatient at that point, hoping Dr. Freedman would come out and take Luther back inside. That's when Kevin's soccer ball gave me an idea. "Hey, how about kicking the ball over on the lawn near Luther? It might distract him when you and Benny go for it."

"Uh, I don't think that's a good idea, Billy," Benny interjected. "That dog is bigger than I am."

Kevin looked to see exactly where Luther was. "What if he doesn't see the ball? He's way over by those trees on the other side. I don't know if I can kick it that far."

Nothing was going to stop me from at least trying to run away that day. "Call him before you're ready to kick the ball," I said. "That should get his attention."

Kevin shouted at the top of his lungs, "Luther, here boy!" With Benny behind him, he booted the soccer ball, and the two of them charged after it.

Meanwhile, I was off and running as fast as I could down the road. I never looked back as I turned the corner near the metal shop, which was right before the Mechanical School Building and the wall. About thirty or so yards up ahead of me I saw an eighteen wheel tractor trailer and a smaller truck that was backing away from it. That's when I got my first look at the towering high green gate. Unlike the main gate at the other end of campus, this one was constructed of two immense solid wooden doors that to my horror were slowly closing as the larger truck gunned its engine and started to drive through the opening in the wall. My heart sank as I felt my hopes of freedom being dashed to an outer world I missed so much. I caught a quick glimpse of the row houses across the street and imagined the families who lived in them, as an empty feeling crept over me.

Well, so much for my first escape attempt, but I vowed

then that there would come another time and place somewhere on Girard's campus when I would try again. Looking back on it now after all these years, I sort of chuckle to myself about the determined daring and innocence of an eight-year-old who wanted to be home with his mother. I often contemplated after that day how far I might have gotten. As for Kevin and Benny, when I returned, they were still wrestling with Luther, trying to get the soccer ball away from him.

CHAPTER SIX
A BOYS' HOME CHRISTMAS AND HAIR GONE BY FOR A WOULD-BE KING

The first year for a "newbie" was exceptionally rough, because Girard felt the adjustment period to the school should not be inhibited by outside influences. No visitations from anyone were permitted for six months, which made for my first Christmas without family. There were other House D boys in the same position, but that didn't make me feel any better. I missed my mother. Not being home around the holidays added to the loneliness and magnified the despair for all of us. I would often take Della's letters to bed, clutch them close to me, shut my eyes and let her scent on the paper help me to fantasize she was near.

Miss Hart did her utmost to ease the sadness of those early months and remained continuously supportive, but to no avail. I couldn't adjust to the place, or to the lie that had been told by Della that had left me there without her.

The school's code of conduct was still strictly adhered to without any special preferences given. When the older boys departed for home one week prior to Christmas, those of us left behind felt the void in our lives even more.

The days had been filled with play and the nights with fireside stories read to us by Mr. Swagg, or an occasional movie. Of course there was The Lone Ranger on radio, which also made for a special treat in Miss Hart's room. The privileges were better during those weeks. We were allowed to sleep later in the morning, and free time was extended. Even the meals were more varied and abounded with fare fitting of the season. Morning mail call was the highlight of each day with excitement and anticipation of presents from home.

I never quite understood the reasoning behind a new boy not being able to have any personal contact with family or friends for a period of time. The days were interminable. Nevertheless, there some of us were that Christmas. The loneliness became a dreaded fear lurking inside me. Miss Hart did everything imaginable to ease my pain. She'd even take me on long walks to the front gate to visit with Carl. The view of the city through the open gates was compelling, and the urge to run was always there.

Christmas Eve I sat in front of the fireplace daydreaming of home and the way holidays used to be. I wasn't feeling particularly well that day, and it went beyond homesickness; ever since my failure to flee out the back gate, depression had set in, and the walls appeared to grow higher and higher.

"Billy, a couple of packages arrived for you this morning," Miss Hart said as she sat alongside me, playfully trying to coax me out of my stupor. "I bet they're from your mother."

"How come I couldn't go home for Christmas?" I asked.

"We like our new boys to get used to the school for a while. We're your legal guardians now you know."

"I don't understand. It's Christmas. Mommy and me are always together."

"But you're not alone," she said. "I'm here with you, and there are the other new boys, like Kevin and Benny."

"It's just not the same." How could it be?

"Don't worry, your mother will be able to come visit you in a couple of months. Now c'mon, let's open one of your presents." Miss Hart placed the larger package in front of me. "I'll stay here with you."

We never opened presents on Christmas Eve back home. Instead, my mother and I would make a day of it together in town. She'd take me to a movie matinee and then dinner. Afterwards, we'd walk back through the neighborhoods to our castle in the sky and look at all the Christmas decorations along the way. I remember how I envied those families who had homes, but our room wasn't so bad. Della always had it cheerfully decorated and we were cozy there together. "Mommy and me never opened presents until Christmas morning," I said, pushing the box away from me.

"Well, let's make this a special Christmas. There'll be more surprises tomorrow." She started to unwrap the outer paper, and I reluctantly joined her.

As I removed the large stuffed toy dog that reminded me of Poochie, I began to cry, because my father had bought him for me. When he was stolen from our house the time we were robbed, it was like I had lost a friend. "Stuffed toys are for little kids," I said angrily.

"That's not true." Miss Hart petted the dog then embraced me. "Nobody's too old for stuffed animals. I have a Teddy bear. Look, this guy's so cute. He'll be good company for you. You can name him and keep him on your bed."

"All I want is to be home with my mother." There wasn't anything or anyone that could've changed that then. Della was on my mind constantly, and the longer I couldn't see her the more tormented by it all I became. I was angry for what she had done, but being with her would've been better than living behind those ever-present walls. They were suffocating me, and I wanted to run away from them as far as I could.

The spirit of the season was truly a part of Girard's cloistered campus. The halls were indeed decked with holly, and House D had its very own Christmas tree trimmed by the fireplace. We gathered around it late Christmas Eve, sipping hot chocolate as Mr. Swagg read from *Grimm's Fairy Tales* and Miss Hart led in the singing of carols. Early the next morning we were up for a special Christmas Day breakfast, followed by chapel services, a Charles Dickens afternoon movie with cartoons, and an evening listening to holiday radio shows while enjoying eggnog and gingerbread. When tucked in bed later that night by Miss Hart, I prayed for a return to Christmases remembered, when Santa Claus delivered presents to all good little boys.

New Year's was just another day far from home, and soon the lucky ones returned from their vacations. Holiday revelry reverted back to the daily humdrum routine of boys' school life, and my thoughts of home intensified. Unlike the others, I couldn't come to grips with the circumstances that had so drastically changed my world. I was still trying to understand my mother's deception. How could this have been a good thing for me when I was hurting so much inside? There was no forgiveness in my heart, and I didn't want to look for it either.

Months passed by and I tried to grow accustomed to my fate. Throughout the daytime my thoughts and energies were expended in school and play. But left alone at night, my prayers, hopes and dreams all focused on one image, home! Those were the hours devoted to imaginary conversations with Della, pleading with God for deliverance and, of course, my dreams of escape from inside that dreaded wall. At times I dreamt of being back on the streets of Easton running with old friends, or just treasuring make-believe free moments. The nights were my peaceful times of withdrawal and would remain so for years to come.

Science has yet to fully comprehend all of the mind's powers and its countless mysteries, but my heartbreak and the anguish of being abandoned had already set in motion a physical phenomenon that would change me for the rest of my life. I've disagreed in part with the medical community over the causes of what was about to happen to me. But one thing I do know for sure is that it was sheer horror when it struck.

I awoke one morning to find my bed strewn with an unusual amount of hair. With such a thick growth of curly dark brown hair, I initially passed it off as normal shedding. But day after day the hair loss became more unpleasant, and an alarming amount of it began to appear on my comb, brush, towels and even clothes. Then one day as I was grooming for breakfast, I remained in the washroom after the others had left. I looked in the mirror and ran my fingers over my scalp. Panic immediately struck me. There, in my hands, was more hair! I lightly tugged and with ease removed a small clump. What was happening? I could see one bald spot and then another. Why was my hair falling out? What will the other kids say? Could I hide it? In those few brief moments, the ugliness of it all terrified me. I desperately cried out for Della. But she wasn't there, nor would she be, and that was the worst pain of all.

I turned from the mirror and wanted to run far away, but

to where? Through tearful eyes, with strands of fallen hair stuck to my lashes, I saw Miss Hart enter the washroom and ran to her. "Miss Hart, look." I showed her the hair on my hands. "My hair is falling out! Please let me go home. I want my mom."

She held me tightly, fumbling for the right words to say. "What? Let me see. Oh, I'm sure it's nothing to worry about, Billy. It's probably only some scalp infection, or something temporary like that. Nobody will notice. You have a nice head of hair, more than most kids."

"You're just saying that." I looked up into her blue eyes. "I'm gonna be bald and the other boys will laugh at me, won't they?" I said. "Now they'll really think I'm a baby."

"I'll let you skip a haircut for now, until you're better. How's that? It will be our little secret. But first thing tomorrow we'll go to the infirmary together. You'll be fine."

"It's real bad, isn't it?"

We stood in front of the mirror for the longest time, while she combed through my hair and tried to put me at ease. "There's only two tiny spots here. I can barely see them. Nobody will ever know. It's our little secret. We'll just keep your hair long for a while. Okay?"

There would be no medical explanation the next day, or hopes of a cure, but treatments for something they knew nothing about began immediately. My hair was kept short for the ghoulish ultra-violet procedure which had me sitting in a dark room with goggles on, and then a greasy ringworm salve that stank was applied to my scalp. So much for being inconspicuous. To this day, alopecia areata still remains a mystery, and my heart cries for those who have it, especially the thousands of innocent children.

The disease was extremely deceptive from the beginning. It seemed to toy with me both physically and mentally. The random behavior of it was strange and puzzling, with no set pattern. As one bald spot would grow in, bringing temporary relief, another would appear. Its malicious nature was mystifying and naturally aroused the curiosities of the other boys.

The horror that had suddenly begun early spring of 1952 made adjusting to my new life in that walled-in place all the more difficult. My only contact with Della up to that time had remained through her letters, but she never mentioned my hair. By then I began to feel as though no one cared. It was the first time that I thought of death and the peace it might bring.

When it seemed my life couldn't get any bleaker, I was told by Miss Hart one evening at bedtime that my mother would be coming to see me. When that day finally came, it was a cold, drizzly morning, and I was sitting on the playground swings in anticipation of Della's arrival. No one else was on the playground at the time, and my eyes were glued on Westend's portico entranceway. The second she appeared, I ran as fast as my legs would go. "Mommy! Mommy! You're here!" I shouted, nearly knocking her over when I reached her. That was the most we had ever hugged and kissed each other.

We spent the day at the Philadelphia Zoo, which wasn't that far from the school. It was a good day together, but as it got later the reality of going back brought out the resentment in me, and the tension between us mounted. Watching the other parents with their children didn't help either. They'd all go home together, but I wouldn't.

"Can't I go home with you, Mommy?" I asked. "Please."

"I wish you could," she said, brushing through my hair with her hand. "Your hair looks good. It's a little short but still curly. The school wrote to me about it. Miss Hart did too. You're lucky to have her. She really cares about you."

That was the first time that day she had said anything about my hair. "You left me and you're going to again. I don't call that lucky. Besides, you don't know anything about my hair. The bald spots come and go. You didn't even mention it in your letters." It was obvious that my comments made her uncomfortable, but I didn't care.

"We'll be seeing more of each other starting next fall when you move to the Junior School Building. That's good, isn't it? You'll be coming home once in awhile."

"Not until Thanksgiving." I wasn't going to let her off the

hook so easily. "Big deal. And then I only get a week at Christmas and Easter to be with you."

She squirmed a bit. "Don't forget the two weeks in summer."

"That's not enough," I said. "And then I have to come back here and say goodbye to you all over again."

"That's unfair of you to say. This hurts me too, you know."

"Lying to me wasn't fair. It's horrible at the school. I hate it there." I turned my back and started to walk away from her. "Why can't I be home with you? Nothing is like it was before."

"I can't leave you home alone…you know that." She draped her arms over my shoulders from behind me. "Let's not ruin the rest of our day together by arguing."

It was so unlike her to show any kind of affection or feelings, and to me it seemed phony. As I watched the lions pace in their outdoor enclosure, I wondered if they thought about escaping their walls. I had already tried to run from mine. Watching the other children with their parents didn't much help either, for I knew they would all be going home together.

We parted that day happy for having seen each other, but the distance between us was now even further than just the miles on a map. How sad it was for the both of us back then, being alone without each other.

A brief visit from Mom in the early Girard days when visits weren't often.

CHAPTER SEVEN
THE LITTLE LORD OF FOUNDER'S DAY

On May 20th every year, Stephen Girard was honored. Even President Truman once visited the campus to pay tribute to Mr. Girard and his contributions to Philadelphia and the nation during colonial times. He helped the United States government finance the War of 1812 and played an important role in founding the Second Bank of the U.S. Girard was also a noted philanthropist and gave generously of his time and money during the yellow fever epidemic in 1793. The boys' school was eventually founded with the bulk of his estate, establishing a trust fund that to this day maintains Girard and the free education it affords the students.

My first Founder's Day Celebration would prove to be extra special. For years the school had been recognized far and wide for its great soccer teams. That Founder's Day, for the first time, a soccer king was chosen from the "newbies" at Westend to march in the 1952 parade.

I awoke that Saturday morning with the same expectations of every other boy who enjoyed special occasions. We all knew of the historical significance and the lavish festivities of that day. Thus, all of us looked forward with eager anticipation of it being a day most unlike any other Saturday inside our walled community. Seated at the breakfast tables, everyone gulped his food and excitedly chattered about the day's activities, the highlight of which was the great parade, followed by the Annual Alumni Soccer Game.

Toward the end of breakfast, the dining room French door opened, and in strode Mr. Swagg carrying a soccer ball. The joy on his face was contagious. He smiled and said good morning, then went over to the head table and whispered in Miss Hart's ear. She stood up and clapped her hands in reaction to whatever the secret was. "Attention, boys," she announced. "Mr. Swagg has some wonderful news he wants to share with us." Her exuberance added to our expectations, and everyone began to talk excitedly.

Mr. Swagg walked around the dining room in that casual stride of his until we quieted down. He had a relaxed way about him at all times. Even when angry, he'd get his point across without scaring the daylights out of you.

"Well, gentlemen," he said, "do we all know our school's alma mater, *Hail, Girard*?"

"Yes!!" came the unanimous reply. It was one of the first things a Girard boy learned, along with the *French National Anthem* and *The Star Spangled Banner*. Stephen Girard's French heritage was reverently respected by all "hummers."

"Well, boys," Mr. Swagg continued, "let's hear you sing *Hail Girard* so loud that Mr. Girard can hear you at Founder's Hall. As a matter of fact, if you wake him up, that will be quite all right too!"

We sang in perfect unison. Mr. Swagg and Miss Hart applauded at the end, and then he placed his hand on my shoulder. In a gentle voice he complimented me on how well I had sung, and then asked me to stand up. For a moment I thought he was going to want me to sing solo. Instead he handed me the soccer ball.

"As you know, boys," he said, "our school has one heck of a soccer team. Not only is the sport a tradition here at Girard, but many of our teams have become legendary in the city over the years. Unfortunately, our opponents wish we didn't even exist, but it is a game that our school bases much of its pride on. After today, you new boys will know why soccer is one of the first things we teach you. Now, this Founder's Day our school president, Dr. Cooper, has decided to make one of you our honorary Soccer King for the entire celebration."

Mr. Swagg turned me around and grinned. "Well, son, I know you can sing our alma mater, but do you know how to kick a ball?" I was stunned by the question and stood there not knowing what to say. I had played with the "little hummers" earlier that fall but hadn't felt that I was any good. "Tell you what, Billy," Mr. Swagg continued, "let's go outside and see how good you are."

Out on the playground Mr. Swagg established an imaginary goal, with himself as the goalkeeper. He paced off a few yards. "Okay, Billy, try to kick one past me. C'mon, score a goal!"

My first few attempts were bad, but on the third try I kicked one to the left side. The ball sailed over Mr. Swagg's outstretched arms as he attempted to block it. A cheer went up from the House D boys. Whether he could have stopped it or not didn't much matter to me that day. I was so proud, and for once I wasn't getting gawked at because of my hair problem. However, some of the boys later on let their jealousy be known. The name ringworm soccer boy was popular for a while.

Mr. Swagg gathered everyone around, handed me the ball once more and placed his hands on my shoulders. "Billy, that was a great goal. You'll be a good soccer player one day for Girard. How would you like to be our Soccer King today and represent all your buddies in the parade and at the big alumni game this afternoon too?"

There hadn't been too many glorious days for me at Girard, but that Founder's Day was special. Oh, how I wished Della could have been there to see it. I was not only given a crown to wear, but I suited up in the same uniform the varsity wore. The parade was a major event of the daylong celebration leading up to the alumni soccer game. There were bands from all around the city, including Mummers string bands, drum and bugle corps, high school marching bands and Girard's own Steel & Garnet Contingent. What a day to remember that had been as I marched in front of the varsity squad carrying the game ball. We marched up the main road, past all the brightly decorated campus buildings, around the circular flower garden in front of the main gate, alongside the multicolumned Founder's Hall and onto the velvet green soccer field. The music rang in my ears as the May flowers spread their fragrance and the colorful pageantry filled my senses with a sight I've never forgotten. Girard was a fine school with a reputation for student excellence, steeped in a grand old tradition of high ideals and discipline for young boys. I stood proudly on the playing field that day as the vast crowd sang *Hail, Girard*; and, if only for those brief moments, I was a true "hummer."

My hair loss had remained spotty and continued its hide-and-seek ways. It would grow back entirely at times, only to start falling out somewhere else on my head. The kids weren't too ruthless during those early times, but on occasion someone would make a wisecrack or call me a name. Those brief encounters were only overtures of what was to eventually become an everyday occurrence.

A year passed and I was finally permitted other visitations from Della and even some vacation time at home. It wasn't much, but I eagerly anticipated the moments as if they were my last. Each time we left one another I feared not seeing Della ever again. My brief stays at home unfortunately always ended in a repeat of that first day Della had left me at Girard. I never wanted to return to the school and often thought of running away the night before I was scheduled to go back. Little did I realize then that each time Della left me behind, another brick of vengeful hatred toward her was added to the wall between us and to a wall of distrust of women in general.

In the summer of 1953, I reluctantly bid farewell to Miss Hart and Mr. Swagg. The time had come to move up the main road from Westend to the Junior School Building. I would miss those two dear friends who had been so patient and good to me. They were loving people and truly cared about us kids.

"I wish I didn't have to leave you, Miss Hart," I said, standing in front of the Junior School building with my suitcase. "Thanks for walking up with me. Can't you come in too?"

"I'm afraid not, Billy. You'll have to do this on your own. You're older now and this is where you belong. You'll like Miss Klunk."

"Is Miss Klunk a nice lady like you? The older boys say she can be real mean when she's mad. They call her Bulldog."

"Just be good, hear me?" She gently fussed with my hair, which made me think all the more about how much I would miss her. "And don't you call her that name. It's not very nice."

"What about my hair? It's harder to cover up the bald

spots. Will she help me comb it too, like you did?"

"Miss Klunk knows all about you. I've spoken to her." Miss Hart put her arms around me and continued to play with my hair for what would be the last time. "It's okay. She knows everything. She's your governess now. But if you want to talk to me you know where I'm at."

"You don't think I'm a big baby, do you?"

"No, no, I don't. I think you're a very brave young man."

I didn't want to let go of her. "Will you come to see me?" I asked. "Please, I'll miss you."

"I'll miss you too. Now go on inside to Section 1."

Miss Hart had been special, and I watched her walk down the main road until she was out of sight. I had made it through those early times because of her, and I'd never forget what she meant to me. But once inside the Junior School building it was like starting all over again. Even though I had made friends with a few of the boys, it didn't matter. Everything was new, and my protector, Miss Hart, wasn't there to comfort me. I found Section 1, where I was to report, and peered past the doorway. There weren't any House D boys that I recognized and I started to panic.

"You there, boy! Where do you belong, young man?" the woman in black called from behind her desk. "If you're supposed to be in Section 1, you've found it. If not, you better get someplace in an all-fired hurry. I'm about to call the roll."

Welcome to the Junior School, I said to myself. Right then I thought of running after Miss Hart or finding a place to hide.

CHAPTER EIGHT
A BULLDOG'S BARK, THE PUNISHER OF EVILDOERS, AND GOOD FRIENDS?

Third grade normally is an exciting time for kids, but for me it had marked advanced changes in the alopecia areata, which began to put a strain on my friendships. Even Kevin and Benny weren't as close to me as they once were. My hair loss became more active, and as the kids got older their harassment increased, sometimes becoming downright vicious. No one ever explained to them what I had or even disciplined those who taunted or mocked me. Instead, I was left to their torment, and there was no running home to Mommy. When I couldn't take any more, I'd lash out in retaliation. Punishment for rule violators was very strict at that age, and I often found myself walking the yard for fighting. It was no ordinary size yard either. The entire asphalt playground took in three baseball diamonds, a covered sandbox as big as a house, three outdoor basketball courts, plus an area with swings, a jungle gym, seesaws and slides. Many times walking off a punishment I experienced its expansiveness on cold winter days or in the blistering heat of summer.

Miss Klunk, our new governess, was a far cry from the gentle, caring Miss Hart. Nicknamed "Bulldog" by the boys because her features reminded them of her bark, she was moody, unpredictable and feared. I never understood how this woman ever got her job because it was obvious she didn't have the patience for kids.

The new residence was different from the warm and cozy confines of House D. The homerooms were on the first floor, washrooms in the basement, dining rooms in the middle building; and the dormitories, along with huge shower rooms, were on the third floor. The large dorms accommodated up to thirty-five beds, and Miss Klunk's room was adjacent with a connecting door. She'd come storming down the aisles many a night with flashlight in one hand and paddle in the other to physically reprimand someone.

I found myself rudely awakened from a deep sleep one night by the cracking sound and stinging pain of wood on my bare bottom. Some of the boys had been fooling around, and when Miss Klunk entered the dorm, she must've thought I was in on it. The more I cried and questioned the beating, the more physical she became and the louder we yelled at each other. The ultimate insult to her was when she grabbed my hair and some of it stayed in her hands. "Ugh! Hair! You wretched child," she screamed, trying to free herself of the strands that were clinging to her. "You little faker. Get out of that bed," she continued. "You're a mess and a sneak. Don't think for one minute that this hair problem of yours will keep me from punishing you!" She grabbed my nightshirt and dragged me out of bed. "I'll show you, you insolent little beast. Get out in the hall. Go on. Get out of my sight."

When some of the others laughed, she banged her paddle off the metal bedpost with a fiendish gesture and shouted, "If any of you think it's funny, you can join him! One more sound and this entire dormitory will walk the yard! Now hush up...all of you!"

Miss Klunk a moment later walked up to me in the dark hallway and turned the flashlight on in my face. "You don't fool me," she said. "I know your little games. You think because you're different you can get away with everything."

I was scared. "No, I don't, Miss Klunk." I couldn't imagine what she was going to do next. But having been reprimanded by her before, I was prepared. I had a reputation by then for being a troublemaker. I simply didn't care at times and was being bad merely to impress my tormentors, hoping they would like me.

"What am I to do with you?" she asked, in a softer tone of voice. "At times I feel sorry for you because of your problem, but I can't allow you to disrupt my section. You think I'm tough. Wait until you get to Good Friends and Lafayette Hall. Hopefully your hair will grow in by then. We want you boys to mature into fine young men. Not sneaks and troublemakers."

"But Miss Klunk, I was asleep," I said, pleading with her.

"Shush." She waved the paddle in my face. "Just keep your nose to the grindstone. Don't agitate things if you know what's good for you. Now get back to bed."

She had never backed off before, and it took me by complete surprise. "But, but you ... you told me to stand in the hallway," I stuttered.

"Go on before I change my mind." She grinned as she turned away, shaking her head and mumbling to herself.

My personal relationship with Miss Klunk after that incident was highly unusual compared with that of the other boys'. I'd like to believe the woman just didn't know how to cope with my unfortunate hair loss situation. I guess she was no different from anyone else on campus in that respect, because nobody knew what I had. It wouldn't have surprised me if she thought I was contagious or something. Some of the boys already felt that way. But if she'd catch any one of them hassling me, they'd get smacked for it. Who knows, maybe it was just another reason to punish someone. The funny part was, she'd glance at me afterwards as if my approval mattered, then would turn away. One day toward the end of the year I approached Miss Klunk in our homeroom to thank her, and she couldn't retreat fast enough to get behind her desk. Her moves were jerky and awkward when she was nervous, but I held my hand out to her.

"Troublemakers," she said, fussing with the things on her desk. "They shouldn't be talking to you like that. Boys. They have no manners." She went to take my hand, but changed her mind and grabbed for the coffee cup. "Whoops." Over went the cup, spilling coffee on everything. "Now look what you made me do. Go on with you. Get back to your desk."

I never did quite figure out Miss Klunk, but I sure tried every chance I got. When I'd do something wrong, she'd give me her scary, penetrating glare, huff, and move on. I could tell how much my presence must have frustrated her. It didn't take long for the bullies to notice Miss Klunk making an exception of me, for which I became known as her scurvy pet.

The third and fourth years at Girard were the strangest of times as I tried hard to fit in anywhere and with anyone. My thoughts of freedom and home persisted, but the wall was always there. In spite of it all, I became an honor student and a rather decent athlete, playing baseball and soccer.

One night just before summer vacation, Miss Klunk and I had a rare but final talk. It was an incident that I'm positive confused her, and it puzzled me as well. There was this boy, Brian Lehroy, whom I had befriended. He was a very bright kid and somewhat of a loner himself. I wasn't being too picky as far as friends because there just weren't many in that section like I had at Westend with Kevin and Benny. We were all getting older, and that was the age when the taboos started, like hanging around freaks, oddballs or anybody who was different.

Brian and I would sometimes sneak into one another's beds during the night. It was good to be close to someone, and I felt comforted by having him around. We'd talk for hours and then separate before falling asleep. Well, at least that happened most nights, until...

"What are you two doing?" Miss Klunk asked and shined her flashlight in our faces. "Get out of there, young man," she said to Brian. "Get in your own bed. Billy, come with me."

When some of the boys laughed, she quickly reprimanded them. That paddle of hers dished out a lot of abuse, day or night, and she seemed to wield it with great joy.

"How long has this been going on?" Miss Klunk closed the door behind her. She immediately began fussing with things in the room.

"What do you mean, Miss Klunk?"

"Don't play dumb with me, you and the other boy."

"But Brian and I are good friends."

"That doesn't mean you can sleep together."

"We were just talking."

"You both were sound asleep. Not unless you were faking it, like that other time."

"We must've dozed off."

She looked at me in a different sort of way than before. "I don't appreciate your lies. I overlook a lot of things because of your..."

"He's just about the only one who talks to me."

"Not all cuddled up together at night and in the same bed. It doesn't look good."

"Why?"

"You know very well what I'm talking about."

"I'm sorry, Miss Klunk, I don't."

"Just don't let it happen again. You're going to be ten years old."

"But we were only sleeping."

She tried to show me how we looked by wrapping her arms around herself. It was funny watching her. "You were close. Holding on to each other, uh, like...," she stuttered.

"We must've done that in our sleep. The bed is too small for two. We didn't want to fall out."

"No more. Do you understand me?"

"Yes, Miss Klunk," I lied, because at that age it didn't make any sense to me what she was talking about.

"I've never known a boy like you."

"I'm the same as the others except for my hair."

"Will you be going home for summer?"

"Part of it. My mom works."

"I won't be your governess this coming fall."

"Yes, I know, ma'am." I didn't know whether to be happy or sad at that moment. Actually, it didn't much matter because I'd be back, and I didn't care who my governess would be.

Miss Klunk sat down, then stood back up. "You and I didn't get off on the right foot." She roamed about nervously, straightening things, picking up objects and placing them down somewhere else. "I tried, you know," she said, pausing in front of the dresser mirror to look at herself. "Wait until you get to Good Friends. Huh, you'll learn real fast there. So don't be sleeping with other boys, if you know what I mean...you do, don't you? Young men don't do those things."

I yawned. "No, uh, I mean yes, Miss Klunk." At the time, I really didn't know what she meant. But years later I thought about Brian Lehroy and those nights together. I can't quite explain the feeling I had for him except to say I enjoyed his company. And when an illness kept him in the hospital, I was sad and missed him very much. When he returned, I was so happy to see him. But it was a different sort of warm feeling, like I hadn't experienced with another boy. Miss Klunk never spoke to Brian about the incident. Who knows, maybe I had become special to her. It would trouble me for many years until at the age of thirty-six I would finally make love with a woman.

I went home that July during Della's vacation and came back to Girard at the end of the month. I dreaded those return trips and often wished by some miracle the bus would break down or not even show up. Della did the best she could to make my stay at home as pleasant as possible, but the time went by way too fast, and before long I was on the road back.

We usually arrived early at the Broad and Erie Bus Station, which gave us an hour or more to be together. She'd then take me to a nearby restaurant and afterwards we'd do some shopping. With my arrival time back at the school fast approaching, we'd get on the Broad Street Subway to Girard Avenue, and from there the trolley car shuttled us the rest of the way. Every step closer sent my stomach to churning. Carl, the lodgeman, would always greet us, then Della and I would walk to the building. After saying our goodbyes, I'd watch her go up the main road until she was out of sight. That repetitive scene was like a sad movie that leaves you hoping for something good to happen before it ends, but it never did.

GOOD FRIENDS

Miss Henson was my new governess at the Good Friends building. She was a tall, stately, middle-aged woman who could be stern if need be, but in a very caring way. She was a heroine of sorts to the boys, being the first governess ever to permit television viewing one night a week after showers. Every Wednesday at eight o'clock in the evening, provided everyone was good, we'd all file downstairs from the third floor in our nightshirts to watch the new *Walt Disney* show in the TV room. That was a big thing and the highlight of our week. It didn't take much to please a bunch of boys' home kids who'd be getting ready by nine o'clock for lights out.

I was feeling mighty low one Wednesday after supper and had asked Miss Henson for permission to write a letter home instead of watching Walt Disney. I sat at her desk in the dimly lit homeroom, hunched over close to the desk lamp. The gloomy setting made it perfect to write my letter to Della. That day had been a particularly bad one with the other boys, and it inspired my words.

Dear Mom,

I'm sorry I haven't written sooner, but I've been real busy with school work and stuff. You'd like my new governess, Miss Henson. I didn't want to watch the Walt Disney show, so she let me write this letter instead.

Kevin and Benny haven't talked to me much since they came back from vacation. I guess they're afraid of what the class bullies would say if they hung out with me. I miss doing things with them like we did at Westend, but I'm getting used to it. I'm doing real well in class, and starting next week I'll be a table captain in the dining room. They only pick the best students to do that.

"How's your letter coming?" Miss Henson said, entering the room.

"Okay, I guess." I sat up straight and rubbed my eyes. "But I'm not done yet. I got a lot to tell my mother."

She walked over to the desk and stood behind me. "It's late. The other boys are going upstairs now. You can finish it tomorrow."

"I'm tired anyway," I said and started to pick up my pencils, paper and a few drawings I had done.

Miss Henson leaned over the desk. "I see you drew some pictures. You're a good artist. You should send them home."

Those pictures weren't intended for anybody to see, and I reached for them. "Oh, they're just some scribbles."

"Hmmm." Miss Henson picked one of them up. "What's this a drawing of?" she asked.

"Uhh, a wall," I said.

She pointed at a figure in it. "Who's this person standing alone on the wall?"

"Me." I wasn't prepared to explain what I drew.

"Now, I'm just curious." She looked closely at the drawing. "Are these birds on one side of the wall flying over a house?"

"Yes, ma'am. That's the house my father said we'd have someday."

"And what are all these creatures on the other side?" she asked. "There's a lot of them."

"Bad people."

Miss Henson caressed my cheek tenderly and gave me a gentle squeeze. "I see. Well, let's put everything in the drawer for now and get you to bed. You can finish your letter tomorrow."

Miss Henson went out of her way to make our homeroom look and feel as cozy as possible, unlike the cold drabness of Miss Klunk's section. We spent a lot of our free time in those homerooms, especially in winter. Each boy at that age still had his own desk where he kept all his personal belongings. From time to time we'd find a treat or some little trinket left there by Miss Henson. Drawing paper, crayons and pencils were usually what I found.

"How are you doing today, Billy?" she asked one afternoon, pulling up a chair next to my desk.

"Okay, I guess." I looked up at her and could tell that she knew I was lying. "I wish they'd stop calling me names."

"Do you want to tell me who the boys are?"

I continued to draw. There's that code about not squealing when you're young, and I never did. I always hoped I could get on their good side by not pointing a finger at anybody, but it never worked. I so wanted to be a part of the "in" crowd, but I never had a chance for that to happen.

"I understand," she said with a warm smile and a wink. "How about making me some pictures I could put up on the bulletin board. Maybe Section 15 can start their own little art gallery, and you'd be the first."

"Me?" I never wanted to draw attention to myself, so I was reluctant.

"Yes, you. Why not? You're the best artist we've got."

"What should I draw?"

"Anything you'd like."

We had a friendly relationship, not a motherly one like Miss Hart and I had. Miss Henson's caring about me and her stable influence were comforting, kind of like a grownup big buddy. She tried hard to get the others to accept me. But unfortunately her special attention on my behalf had an opposite effect, and once again I was called a brown noser. It only furthered my confusion and not understanding why I couldn't get the others to like me.

I had dealt with it the best way I knew and spent my time reading, drawing, writing home or playing alone. My letters that year grew more desperate, lengthy and imaginative, but also ignored. I'd draw incessantly, sometimes creating fictitious worlds with all sorts of characters, then act them out, creating entire make-believe scenes and playing all the parts.

One day on the playground, Mr. Caine, the assistant resident housemaster, approached me. I was Sir Lancelot that day and had just finished jousting with the Black Knight. Riding up on a make-believe white stallion, I was about to be honored by King Arthur when Mr. Caine spoke. "Whoa there, partner. And who might you be?"

"Excuse me, sir?" He took me by surprise. Usually even the young assistant housemasters didn't bother with me. They didn't know what I had any more than the boys did, and I guess it was best to stay clear of me altogether.

"What's your name, my good man?" he asked.

"Uh, Billy."

"I mean the person you're supposed to be. Are you a cowboy?"

"I'm Sir Lancelot."

I explained how I would take some of my favorite heroes and create pretend situations for them. Sometimes I'd even use actual historical figures like Magellan and imagine exploring or discovering new worlds along the wall. Mr. Caine listened intently for a while before he said another word. I remember our conversation well, because he was the first grownup to show me a way of feeling better about myself through my imagination.

"Oh, King Arthur's favorite. Tell me then, Sir Knight, doest thou always ride alone?"

"Most of the time."

"You have a good imagination. Did you ever act in a play?" he asked.

"No, sir, I never really thought about it," I replied.

"You'd be good." He adjusted my baseball cap. "How would you like to be in our school play? The title is *Story Book* and it's about famous characters from out of literature. We'd dress you in a costume and there'd be an actual script to learn, along with props to work with. Would you like to try?"

I hesitated for a moment. "I don't think so, sir."

"Why not?"

"Because, well, because I'd be on stage and all the kids would make fun of me."

He placed his hands on my shoulders and knelt down. "I don't think that would happen. Storytelling is great fun. You see, in a play you take on the role of another person. You wouldn't be Billy, and if you act the part well the audience would accept the other character. Besides, I wouldn't permit them to misbehave in my theater anyway." He stood back up and smiled. "So, what do you say?"

Mr. Caine was a tall, willowy man and the drama teacher for the high school students. His campus image was quite noteworthy and very thespian. The sweater most often draped over his shoulders on cool days made him seem worldly to me. He certainly was impressive standing there as high as the trees peering down with a broad and friendly smile that gave me a sense of security around him.

"Robinson Crusoe," he said.

"Excuse me?" I looked up at him.

"Robinson Crusoe," he repeated. "That's the character I

want you to play. Do you know who he is?"

I stammered, "Uh, yes, sir. He was marooned on an island with some native guy named Friday."

"You're perfect for the part."

I hesitated once more. "Do you really think I'd be any good?"

The show *Story Book* was performed a month later for all the elementary school kids. It was a musical that depicted famous storybook characters presented in separate vignettes. My sketch ran about five minutes with dialog between me and the native, Friday, plus a closing solo number. I worked hard on my performance and enjoyed every minute of it. It also gave me time away from the other boys. And even better, I was someone else besides me. There were many times I didn't want to be me, or even alive in that place.

Mr. Caine and I remained buddies for a time, but then he left the school that summer for another position with a theater group in California.

The year finally drew to a close and I gladly left for vacation that July. My thoughts at home never strayed far from what awaited me once school would reopen in the fall. The hateful pattern of abuse had become almost constant. All that summer vacation I dreaded going back, and I repeatedly tried to convince Della to take me out of the school. But the days came and went without any hope of staying home permanently.

There weren't many boys left at school during the month of August, and the few there spent time at crafts, watching movies or going on an occasional field trip. It was somewhat peaceful then. The troublemakers were gone, and one or two of the remaining boys didn't mind playing with me when there wasn't anything else to do. My peace of mind inevitably ended all too soon, and once again I prepared for the onslaught of the much dreaded new school year.

My friendships had slowly dwindled away that year as I became balder. Name calling and taunting soon evolved into more vicious behavior by some of the boys. The class bullies would either intimidate the others to join in or convince them to ignore me. Rumors rapidly spread that what I had was a contagious disease. The name calling was painful to bear. That "sticks and stones will break my bones" saying didn't work for a ten-year-old. Scab! Baldy! Buff head! Buffalo Baldy! Skin head! Freak! Germ! On and on, most days the verbal abuse was unrelenting. I wore my baseball cap to cover my shame everywhere I went. There were even times when I'd come indoors and intentionally forget to remove it. Soon the cap not only became a nuisance for the teachers but also an obvious target for the troublemakers. They made a game of trying to steal it, destroy it or rip it off my head and play "monkey in the middle" with me.

One day on the playground, four boys got the hat from my head while I was shooting hoops on one of the basketball courts. One of them pushed me down. "Where's your wig, Robinson Crusoe? What's the matter, huh? No Mr. Caine to protect you anymore?" Butchie McGraff, a redheaded boy with freckles, had been my main tormentor, and he seemed to be everywhere, sometimes even in my dreams.

"Come on, Butchie, give me my hat," I shouted at him while his buddies laughed and ran around me. "Let me alone. I wasn't bothering you."

"Sing for us, Scabhead," one boy called out and made faces at me.

Another one poked me with a stick. "Hey, Butchie, let's bury Baldy's hat in the sandpile," he said.

"Yeah, it's probably got scurvy and that stinky stuff on it," the third boy chimed in.

"Say goodbye to your hat." Butchie taunted me and kept waving the cap in my face. "Let's go, you guys. The last one in the sandbox buries it."

They were all around me like buzzards, and I wanted to run and hide. But as I watched them race to the sandpile, I decided to fight and took off after them. The rage inside me exploded as I flung myself into Butchie like a guided missile. "I hate you! I hate you! All of you!" I screamed. The next thing I knew I was on my back and blood was running down the side of my face. The stick had struck me just above my left temple. Blood spurting everywhere, I summoned up all my strength, and with all the violence stored up inside me, pounded on Butchie's face, ripping and clawing at his hair. I wanted to tear every strand of it from his scalp and make him bald! His face was a bloody pulp, oozing with red delight from his nose. "I'll kill you!" While I frantically grabbed for the stick, the others began punching and pulling me off him. The adrenaline flowed and I swung at or kicked anyone near me like a madman.

Mr. Nichman, the resident head housemaster, was generally a good-natured man, except when his boys were misbehaving. "Okay, gentlemen, break it up." His pot belly bounced as he jumped into the fray. "Settle down, Billy, let go of him!" he shouted. "You others get back." I continued to punch and kick until there was nobody within reach. Mr. Nichman's thick glasses dangled from one ear, and what neatly arranged strands of hair he had were standing on end, but somehow he wrestled us apart. It was lucky for Butchie that day (and me), because if I had gotten my hands on that stick, I could've beaten him to death. The violence inside of me was festering and already growing out of control.

We were a sorry sight, all bloodstained and tattered, including Mr. Nichman, who was huffing and puffing. He tucked in his shirttail, put his hair back in place and smoothed down the funny little mustache he was always grooming. "Well, gentlemen, what was this all about?" he asked.

"They took my hat, Mr. Nichman," I said, "and buried it in the sand."

"So that's what this is all about." He grabbed one of the boys by the collar and shoved him forward. "Fetch it, boy, and give it back. Apologize. All of you!"

It was great hearing those wiseguys say they were sorry. He made them repeat it louder several times, then led us through the crowd of gawking onlookers, straight to the infirmary.

Mr. Nichman and I became rather good pals after that. He took a special interest in me throughout the rest of my stay at Good Friends, a place whose name I still don't understand.

He'd let me come up to his room sometimes to watch TV or just talk. On "Pepsi Days" if I didn't have ten cents, he always made sure I got a soda. One time after inviting me to his office Mr. Nichman presented me with a brand new pair of roller skates. "I just thought you might like to get around the yard quicker," he said and smiled. He was a good man and, like Miss Hart, Mr. Swagg, Carl, and even Miss Henson, helped me keep some semblance of sanity.

My personal troubles with the boys didn't improve the rest of the year. As time went on, more and more of them wouldn't bother with me. The fear of catching what I had kept most of them at a distance. The rest were leery because they didn't want to get involved with the trouble that seemed to follow me everywhere.

During supper one evening, I was table captain again, and it was my job to make sure that the portions were equally distributed around the table.

"Don't touch my food, scab boy. I'll serve myself," one of the boys said. The insults went back and forth between myself and him as well as the others at the table. I had asked not to be a table captain, but as usual no one listened. Before long our ruckus had attracted the wrong attention.

The dining hall master of that meal happened to be the much-feared Miss Linstrom, whose mere presence seemed sinister. She glided over to our table like a mountain lioness after her prey and paced around us several times. I can still clearly see her, attired in a high, lace collared silk blouse accented by a big cameo pin at the neck, with matching earrings and strands of pearls. Her pale, overly made-up wrinkled face was framed by an updo of blue-gray hair. A floor-length black skirt completed the regal ensemble. "That's enough, boys. You will all oblige me tonight after showers. Outside my room." She glared at each one of us, turned and padded toward some other disturbance.

"But Miss Linstrom," I called after her, to no avail.

Miss Linstrom punished ten frightened boys that night after showers. Her means of disciplinary retribution in itself had been a legend on campus. We all knew what lay ahead. One by one we'd file into her den, where she'd lift nightshirts and introduce bare bottoms to her infamous "rhinestone punisher of evildoers." The wooden handmade paddle not only had an air hole at the business end, it was also studded with rhinestones!

"Good evening boys," she said as we stood with our noses to the wall outside her room. "Have we been waiting patiently for Miss Linstrom? I assume we all know why we are here tonight. Disobedience must be corrected at an early age. Unfortunately, there are those who only learn by a firm hand. After tonight, I hope you all appreciate my words and there will be no further shenanigans. I would consider any recurrence an insult to my good friend here." She smacked her side with the paddle. "The punisher of evildoers."

Terror was on the face of each boy as we stood in silence. The hallway clock slowly ticked off the minutes as the time drew nearer to pain. We stood shoulder to shoulder, our noses pressed ever harder to the wall, nervously awaiting the roll call of the doomed.

Miss Linstrom ordered the condemned to respond quickly when their names were called. One by one we were invited in to meet the rhinestone enforcer. What made it worse was hearing the vicious cracking sound that accompanied the cries, whimpers and screams of each victim.

I was the last to be called and nervously approached the doorway as Jayson Rogers was coming out. He was crying uncontrollably and still holding up his nightshirt when he went by me. In the light coming from Miss Linstrom's room, I could see traces of blood on his rear end. This was the ultimate form of physical child abuse in those days, and we lived in constant fear of it.

"Young man, stop staring at him," Miss Linstrom said. "He deserved what he got. Now get in here and get what you have coming." Her haunting eyes glared at me in the dimly lit room, and I trembled in her presence.

Fear had completely overtaken me. "Please, Miss

Linstrom," I begged. "This wasn't my fault. They didn't want me touching their food. What was I supposed to do? They were calling me names. That's why I don't want to be a table captain."

She grabbed my arm, snickered and pulled me up to her face. "Listen, little man!" she shrieked. "As table captain you have a responsibility. If you can't control your table, don't continue to argue back with them. You should have come to me before it got out of hand. I appointed you captain because I thought you had more sense than the other boys. Obviously I was wrong. We want only leaders at the head of each table, not whiners."

I desperately continued to plead for some reasoning, but to no avail. She spun me around and, with a sadistic look on her pale face, flung up my nightshirt and delivered five painful whacks. Then, spinning me around again, she placed her hand over my mouth and angrily muttered through clenched teeth, "Now, not another word out of you! Go to bed. Get out of my sight or I'll fix it that you can't sit down at all."

I lay in bed awake for hours, trying to rationalize what had transpired. The storm outside that night matched the one brewing inside me. I knew the day would come soon enough when I'd have to confront the others who were at that table. Through my lonely thoughts, tears and sobs, I heard the threats of revenge called out to me. "Tomorrow you're mine, Billy Boy," a voice uttered in the dark. "You're gonna get punched for every whack I got."

"Yeah, baldy," another called out. "That goes double from me. You better say your prayers."

"You'll pay, scab," someone else said.

"Oh, where have you been Billy Boy, Billy Boy," Butchie sang softly. "Oh, where have you been, ugly Billy ..."

The fear that lullaby instilled in me sent chills up my spine, and it wouldn't be the last time I heard it. From then on, even sleep wasn't an ally.

As the year wore on, my hair loss took more of its toll on me and my friendships, and soon there were only a few boys who'd be seen with me, provided a bully wasn't around. The more I was alienated and became distraught over it, the more the hair loss seemed to react negatively to the stress. Obviously my strange appearance made me an oddity and someone to stay clear of or mock. At times it was tough to avoid any confrontation, and there was no place to escape to nor anyone to help me.

Even my short stay at home that summer wasn't without empty feelings at times. Della had found herself a boyfriend. Jim Mahony was a divorced man with his own daughter, whom, oddly enough, he never spoke of. But he seemed nice enough to me in the beginning. I guess he had to be for Della's sake. I saw him as competition for the little time there was with my mother. He did stay away pretty much though while I was there, which I considered decent of him. But on the day I was to return to Girard with Della, he joined us at the bus station. I couldn't help but think how happy he must've been. The kid was leaving. My mother and I were having our normal spats that came with every departure. They'd usually begin a few days prior as I'd be counting down the final hours. It was one thing to be going back and another to have to ride a bus. There wasn't a trip that I didn't deposit my innards along the highway somewhere, on myself or next to a fellow passenger.

There was time that day for Della and me to visit awhile back at school, so we sat on a park bench across the main road from Lafayette Hall, the building I'd live in that year.

"Some scary looking place, isn't it?" I said, gazing at the ancient-looking structure. "Lucky me. I get the rest of the summer to get used to it before the animals return, all my tormentors."

"Maybe they'll be different this year," my mother said, trying to comfort me, or perhaps herself. "You're all older now. Can't you try and get along?"

"You know, Mom, you don't have any idea what it's like in here, do you? Look at me." I removed my baseball cap. "Does this look like I'm having fun?" She tried to look away as I stuck my face in hers. The hairloss at that point had gotten bad. One entire side of my scalp and most of the back was bare. It wasn't a pretty sight. There was no way of running away from something like that, and I felt further trapped by being somewhere I didn't want to be. "Why don't you listen, huh?" I yelled. "Why?"

"We just spent a wonderful month together," she said.

"Two weeks, Mom! You worked the other two...remember? Besides, you had your boyfriend. How come you never mentioned him before in your letters?"

"Do you like him? He likes you."

"He has no choice because I'm you're kid. I bet if I was home all the time he'd be different."

Her patience with me was wearing thin. "We'd still need someone to watch you while I work."

That was a worn out excuse that I had grown tired of hearing. I didn't need a babysitter anymore. Hell, I was a grownup as far as I was concerned. "Why don't you say the truth for once? You don't have time for me, especially now with him around."

"I don't want to hear anymore." She stood up. "I have to go."

"Sure, leave. You do that good. Pop wouldn't run out on me. You don't deserve a son."

Della raised her hand to smack me, but stopped. "I'm sorry you feel that way. I do love you, no matter what you think. You make this so hard." She gave me an awkward smile and walked away, never once turning around all the way up the road.

"For who?" I yelled after her. I wasn't about to believe any of this had been hard on her. It wasn't the way I saw it. This had gone on for over five years by then, and if there was any remorse in her at all, I don't remember ever seeing it. And if she was just being strong for me, I didn't buy that either. Della had gone and got herself a boyfriend, and to me that merely proved how unimportant I was to her. All any of it did was further feed the growing anger that steadily raged on inside me.

CHAPTER NINE
GENERAL LAFAYETTE'S HOUSE OF HORRORS

Lafayette Hall, named after the famous French Marquis, was one of the original buildings on campus. The structure was very old and medieval in style, which gave its ominous, castle-like presence an air of foreboding. The setting was perfect for the horror show I experienced during my sixth-grade year.

It didn't take long for my antagonists to begin. I was the token outcast and a target for every kind of abuse one could imagine sixth graders capable of. There was no escape from it, because we lived together twenty-four hours a day. I spent the daylight hours in constant expectation and fear of new hells. It mystified me that after six years nothing was ever done to put an end to all the abuse. Oh, there were some half-hearted attempts made through reprimands of one sort or another, but no one ever attempted to explain my hair loss to the other kids. I did, and for the most part they'd laugh or simply ignore me. It served to further my resentment toward authority and everyone who stood in the way of my freedom, freedom from the wall around me. And the one I was building in my heart. If only someone could have seen what was causing this and the path it had set me on.

In spite of it all, I concentrated even harder on my studies. I was determined to be the best student possible, and that school year, academically, would be my finest. I wanted to prove to my taunters that nothing could deter me. Taking formal art classes for the first time, I used art as a means of escape and release from anger. Just like Mr. Caine had said, "Use your imagination."

Mr. Hector was my section housemaster and history teacher that year and encouraged me to draw as often as possible in my free time. He was a shy but highly intelligent individual, and my classmates made light of his quirky and aloof demeanor. Our head housemaster, Mr. Kugler, would even sometimes have to pry Mr. Hector out of some book he had buried himself in. "Mr. Hector, if you please!" Mr. Kugler would shout. "You have young charges who need your attention. C'mon, sir, you're not at the university." The other boys would laugh and tease him, throwing things at his back when it was turned. I felt sorry for him. Mr. Hector was a sweet, gentle man, and I found his tenderness very comforting. We spent a lot of time talking about art, art history and even life itself. But, unfortunately, our friendship suffered its share of scorn and ridicule.

"Remember to always try to smile at your detractors," Mr. Hector said to me one afternoon after class. "It confounds them. I learned that at an early age when my peers heckled me."

"Why did they make fun of you?" I asked.

"I was different, an ugly sort. And too smart for them, I guess."

"That's a dumb reason."

"Not for kids at your age." He handed me my book report. "Excellent work, by the way, the highest mark in the class."

"Oh no, now I'm gonna hear it for sure. They already call me a baldheaded brown noser since you and Mr. Kugler made me one of the class officers." I had even become afraid of being the best I could be.

"That's sheer nonsense. You earned it. Besides, your book report content was well researched and written. And, I might add, the drawing of Magellan on your cover is quite good, your finest drawing yet."

"Thank you, Mr. Hector, but don't announce the scores like you usually do. Please. I don't really want to be treated special. I just want to be liked by the others, that's all. I hate being called names." I pointed out the window to a group of boys standing around outside. "They even call you names."

"I hear them. Pencil head, flipper feet, and what's that new one, 'The Thing,' isn't it? Where does that come from?"

I looked at him sheepishly. He was a rather oddly shaped person, with big feet and a tiny head on his large, bottle-shaped frame, hairy too, especially on his knuckles. I turned toward the window.

"C'mon, Billy, you can tell me. I'm just curious."

"Yes, sir. They got it from that movie we just saw. You know, the one about that creature from space buried in the ice."

"Uh huh." He chuckled nervously. "Well, I do have big feet. But I've been called worse. I'm also a little hairy too, don't you think?" He stooped over. "And my arms are longer than most people's." He swayed from side to side and dangled his arms toward the floor. "But I can't drag my knuckles on the floor."

I bit my lip, trying not to crack a smile. Some of the boys at Lafayette did call him Hairy Hector, or The Missing Link. "Don't the names bother you?"

"When I was younger it did. Not anymore."

"It hurts when they call me names."

"They'll eventually grow up and stop. Trust me. Just remember what I told you. Don't let them know it gets to you. Hold your head high and be proud of who you are."

I already was. Mr. Hector put his hand on my shoulder and we walked out of the school building together. Across the road were some of the boys we had just talked about. I recalled wishing that they'd all drop dead right there, or even better that their hair would fall out.

As we walked past them, Mr. Hector smiled, pointing in their direction. "Good afternoon, gentlemen," he said.

I looked up at him and then at his hands. He sure did have hairy knuckles, but he was my friend and I liked him. "They'll think I'm kissing up to you for sure,"

"It's unfortunate we, I mean your teachers, governesses and housemasters, can't possibly provide the individual attention that children need. We can only do our best."

"I had a family. But after my father died, my mother's relatives didn't help us like they said they would. So here I am."

"And so we all are," he said. "How about I treat you to a soda?"

The school began a new series of experimental treatments

on my scalp, under the direction of Dr. Howard at the infirmary. Several times a week, after breakfast, Nurse Hood would place me under the ultraviolet light, which was immediately followed by the application of some new specially prepared ointment. The treatments accomplished one thing. My head became a blazing inferno, with a horrible stench that followed me the rest of the day. The only outcome from the greasy mess was a different name called me, "Stinky." It smelled worse than the other salves, and even I couldn't stand it.

The large medical building on Girard's campus was fully equipped and professionally staffed. It housed a clinic for daily patient treatment, a complete dental facility with a full-time staff, and a hospital wing for in-patient care that also had an operating room. Dr. Howard, who was responsible for the health of fifteen hundred boys, ran the entire complex. Twice a year each boy was given a complete dental exam and once a year a total physical. The dentist was never a treat, but because of beautiful Nurse Hood we boys loved the physicals. She was a young registered nurse in the hospital wing and always assisted Dr. Howard with the physicals. The formfitting uniforms she wore made her even more alluring, which I guess helped make Nurse Hood my first teenage crush, along with probably every other thirteen-year-old there. But I was already backwards and shy when I would see girls at home, because of my hair. So I kept my private fantasy about Nurse Hood to myself.

At that age we were just becoming sexually aware of certain bodily functions and the shapes of females. Erections sometimes occurred at inopportune or embarrassing moments, such as in Coach Boggs' swim class while he taught the backstroke. He'd yell, "Periscopes up!" Swimming naked among other boys was okay, but being in the buff while Nurse Hood was around wasn't. Dr. Howard had a sadistic remedy for a boy with an erection during a physical examination, and it struck fear in the hearts of many a young man. In my case, the entire event was uncomfortable, because I hated being nude in front of anybody. My head being half naked was enough.

I experienced firsthand the infamous Dr. Howard chop

that year as a sixth grader. We arrived at the infirmary and were sent to the rear of the building where Nurse Hood greeted us. She looked and smelled extra nice that day as everyone followed her into the larger ward where we prepared for our examination.

"Okay, gentlemen, you all know the routine," she said. "Remove your clothes, take a blanket and I'll be back shortly to line you up for Doctor Howard."

Nurse Hood's "shortly" was always momentarily, and she returned while most of the boys were still naked or just covering themselves. She passed from one boy to the next, putting everyone in alphabetical order and adjusting their blankets. Then, clapping her hands to get all the talkers' attention, she began the preliminaries. "Do any of you have any colds or injuries that the doctor should be aware of?"

There were a few colds and one pulled muscle, mine. I raised my hand. The preceding week I had strained a hamstring in a soccer game, and my thigh was still a little stiff, even though I had gone to the hospital for treatment.

"Billy, step out of line and let me see you walk toward me," she said. Most of the mobility in the leg had returned, but I still favored it somewhat. After her next comment, wolf whistles, moans and howls went up from the other boys. "Let me see it. C'mon, don't be bashful."

As I stepped forward to open my blanket, I accidentally stepped on the front of it, pulling it off my shoulders and onto the floor. The room instantly resounded with laughter as I clumsily tugged on the blanket.

"That's enough, boys. Keep it down," she ordered, bending over me to help. She placed the blanket around my shoulders then asked if I could just stick my leg out for her to see. Talk about embarrassing moments.

"Show her the middle one, baldy!" came a wisecrack from one of the boys. Once more the room erupted into laughter and whistles.

Nurse Hood chose to ignore the comments and went about her careful examination of my thigh. At that age it was far more embarrassing than it was arousing to have a gorgeous nurse feel your leg, although the view of her kneeling in front of me did cause a slight stir in my young hormones.

She stood back in front of me, closed the blanket and made one more medical observation that brought the house down. "There's still a slight stiffness in that muscle." It took her a few minutes to settle everyone down, restore order and get us back in line. A few boys had tears in their eyes and stomach pains from laughing so hard. "You boys are naughty," she said. "Now quiet down and listen for when your name is called."

I remember how embarrassed the erection made me feel as I entered the examining area. There it was, sticking straight out at attention and saluting the good doctor.

Dr. Howard's bedside manner was brief and right to the point. He rested my penis on the palm of his left hand, informed me that the organ looked healthy, and then made one quick karate chop with his right hand. The little soldier went to at ease instantly. The doctor was all business and continued the examination without further comment.

When he finished, he turned toward Nurse Hood, who was sitting behind a very flimsy see-through screen, and matter-of-factly said, "Billy's hair loss persists, the right leg hamstring muscle is healing and he could use some weight on his bones. Other than that, I find him healthy ... extremely so!" With the last two words he looked briefly at my soldier and saluted. I nervously retrieved my blanket and noticed the frown on Nurse Hood's face as she said goodbye. During my teenage years when I started to doubt my manhood, I always thought of how Nurse Hood had made me feel that day.

Lafayette Hall was a paradox to me, and I experienced every kind of emotion imaginable. *The Addams Family* would have been quite comfortable living in the antiquated mansion. It, too, had an atmosphere of weirdos, nasties, and mental cases. The zit age had struck. Little boys turned into teenagers and suddenly felt that they were men. It was a metamorphosis without butterflies emerging, not one. The lines were drawn, and if a boy didn't follow the crowd he just didn't exist. If you were studious, you were a "brainy" or a campus scholar. That group usually stayed close-knit and was only bothered when a bully needed help with homework or a test. The brains would almost always accommodate the demands of the tough guys. There was no escape or going home after class hours, which made anyone a moving target at any time, even in his sleep. The athletes also had their clique and usually coexisted with the "brainies" and the "toughies" without much of a problem. As for me, I really didn't fit anywhere. No one had the guts at that age to be a friend to the "scab." I presented an awkward problem for all of them. I was an honor student, captain of the middle school's student safety guards, selected as a class officer by the faculty, first string goalkeeper on the youth soccer team and first baseman for the school's little league team. I was everywhere, doing everything, and hoping to be accepted by someone. I wanted to belong in the worst way, but none of my efforts afforded me the acceptance I yearned for. In some cases all the good I did merely caused an opposite effect with my classmates. I just couldn't win for trying.

Sometimes I would go to extremes out of sheer desperation in order to gain recognition from somebody. In class I would share test answers, which on occasion caused reprimands for cheating. On the playing field, I was always giving the other guy credit, cleaning soccer shoes or oiling baseball gloves. At Lafayette Hall, I'd even volunteer for cleanup jobs to help someone with their punishment detail. It was pretty sad. There wasn't anything I wouldn't do to have a friend, like even removing the spitballs intended for my head from off Doc Dennis' blackboard so he wouldn't see them.

On one occasion I made an exceptional fool of myself. Big Joe Costello was a good looking South Philly Italian who had one hell of a head of black hair. Everywhere he went his band of groupies were with him. Besides his Elvis Presley hairdo, I admired his coolness and the rebel in him. What would it be like if I was in his inner circle? I used to think maybe the class bullies wouldn't mess with me.

I was straightening up the washroom one evening and paused in front of one of the mirrors. The hair loss had been somewhat dormant for a time, and I wasn't losing any more than I had already lost. On the left side of my head, except for the sideburn and a few clumps at the nape, everything was gone. I noticed that if I cocked my head at a certain angle, it appeared that I had a full head of hair. It was a thrilling vision for me, and my spirits soared with the momentary hopes of all my hair growing back. I just happened to be standing in front of Joe's mirror when my fantasies were triggered. With Joe's brush, I began styling what hair I had, just like his. I wet the brush and applied Vitalis, then repeatedly swept back the right side until it finally stayed in place. The look was called a DA or Duck's Ass. In my case it was more like a half-ass Duck's Ass. Using my comb and applying more Vitalis, I styled the top like Joe's and curled the bangs down over my forehead. For the final touch I squeezed a greasy gob out of the BrylCreem tube and slicked back the right side one more time. This gave the hair an added shine. Fussing over what hair I had was fun at the time. It also spurred on an imaginative role playing of being Big Joe. Lost in make believe and dreams of hair glory, I was completely unaware of the intruder who had entered the washroom.

"Hey, you. What the hell are you doin'?" came words from the one voice I didn't want to hear. "You tryin' to be a pretty boy or somethin'?" Joe's manner of speech and inflection were kind of like a boxer who had taken too many blows. He slowly sauntered toward me along the row of washbasins, glancing at himself in every mirror. None of his cronies were with him, but it didn't matter because he was intimidating enough. He grabbed the comb from my hand and sat down on the adjoining sink. "You're usin' my stuff. How come? Who the hell gave ya permission, boy? I know I didn't." He poked me with the comb. "What's with the new do? You going somewhere special?" Then, using the comb for a pointer, he added, "You know, if you had more hair, it wouldn't look too bad."

I stood there speechless while Joe stared at me, the sink,

and the stuff I was using. I thought for sure he was going to throw me up against the wall and drag me around the washroom like a mop. Instead he got up, slowly circled around and sat down on the other sink next to me. He sniffed the air and tapped my head with the comb. "Whew, you sure smell pretty, boy. How much of my shit did you use? Your hair's stiff as a damn board."

I nervously watched every move he made before I stuttered a few words in self-defense. "My hair is growing back and I want to train it like yours. I'm sorry I used your stuff. I'll pay you for it. It's just that your hair always looks so cool. I thought if I used your hair tonic and things it would be easier. I didn't mean any harm. Believe me, I just want my hair to look like yours when it grows in. That way I'll only have to train one side. I'll pay you for what I used. I'll pay you tomorrow. I'm sorry, Joe, I didn't think. Don't be mad. Please."

He pressed the comb over my mouth. "Whoa, shut up already. Calm down. Relax, don't get your ass in an uproar. I ain't gonna hurt ya, boy." Big Joe stood up, tossed the comb down and looked in the mirror. With one hand he arranged a few misplaced strands of his hair and firmly gripped my shoulder with the other. "Tell me something, is what you got catchy? I mean, if I use my brush and comb, am I gonna catch it?" He tightened his grip, making it clear he wanted the truth. "Don't hand me no bullshit now. I want a straight answer. Because if I find out ya lied to me, I'll kick your ass."

My answer was simple, because it was the only thing the doctors were sure of about what I had. "No, it's definitely not contagious," I said. "The school wouldn't let me live with you guys if it were. You don't have a thing to worry about. Honest."

Joe released his hold on my shoulder, smiled, stepped back from the mirror and walked around to the other side. He punched me lightly on the arm and said, "Cool. I believe you. Now, clean up my area here and put my stuff back. The next time you want to use it, ask." With that he started to walk back along the washbasins. Halfway to the door he stopped, turned and took a few steps toward me. "You're all right, kid. Good luck with the hair training bit. It'll look great when it all grows. I'll see you around."

I remained frozen as he slowly shuffled out the door. I couldn't believe how nice the big guy was to me. He reappeared at the doorway. "Yo, Billy. We didn't talk tonight. You got that? I have an image to live up to," he said and then vanished.

I ran out of the washroom and called to him. "Hey, Joe, thanks, big guy! I'll see ya around."

He gave me a thumbs up and kept walking. If there was a list of some of the boys I'd like to see again, Big Joe would be on it. But I learned many years later that he never finished at Girard.

That year was full of surprises, both good and bad. There were a few highlights that stood out in my mind. Such as the Bowie knife I won as a Boy Scout (Troop 411, Daniel Boone Patrol) for special achievement. Unfortunately, I'd be arrested for wielding it in a family dispute years later. Then there was my mother's boyfriend, whose presence always puzzled me from the beginning. I saw him as another distraction between Della and me. And, of course, the family philanderer, Uncle Frank, had visited me on two separate occasions at the school. Years later he stole my father's valuable diamond onyx ring right out from under our noses. Our family never changed, and neither did my life. The wall was always there, and the one inside me grew even higher.

The year stumbled along, with each trying day blending into the next. The torment from the others never ceased right up until vacation time. One night in the dormitory just before lights went out, the uglies sang to me. When I think back on it, I guess it was their farewell summer song to me. They were imaginative but not funny.

"Hey, Stinky," one of them called out. "When's your girlfriend Nurse Hood gonna stop rubbin' that smelly stuff on your head? It smells like shit."

"Hey, maybe it is," another boy said.

"Yeah, wouldn't that be funny?" a third one commented. "A miracle cure made of shit."

I didn't say a word and continued hanging up my clothes in the locker next to my bed. Mr. Hector's advice worked sometimes, but I had had my fill by then and was ready to rip into anybody. It's not easy when there's no one around to help you out or take your side, like a grownup. They knew they had me riled that night as I threw the last thing into the locker and slammed the door.

"I don't see anything funny about it," another said. "I sit near baldy in class."

"What are you bitchin' about?" another chimed in. "Try eating next to that smell."

I turned around and glared at him across the old, barnlike dorm, with its creaky wooden planked floors and rows of beds and beat-up metal lockers. The whole appearance of the place disgusted me. It was a fitting dump for what went on there. I reached back into my locker, brought out the belt to my pants and wrapped it around my fist.

A few of them sang off-key. "Oh, where have you been, Billy Boy, Billy Boy. Where have you been baldy Billy."

The dormitory lights blinked off and on, but the chorus continued. "He's been to find some hair, 'cause his head stinks up the air. Dreadful sorry, Billy the scabhead hummer."

Once more the lights blinked, but I wrapped the belt tighter around my fist and stared around the dormitory. The taunts got louder as I raised my fist. In the back of my mind I remembered the sandbox fight a year ago, and I wanted at them more, especially Butchie McGraff.

A whistle blew and the lights blinked rapidly. "That will do over there! Lights out." Mr. Kugler stood in the doorway. He was a tall and lanky bespectacled Norman Rockwell character if there ever was one, dressed in his red plaid shirt and blue work pants with brown suspenders. It was a down-home-on-the-farm look, and mighty scary. The whistle was clenched in his teeth, but we got the message. "It's bedtime," he said, entering the dorm. "Not unless some of you would prefer to stand in the hallway. Do I have any takers?"

"No, sir, Mr. Kugler," everyone answered.

"Very well then." He glanced at the belt wrapped around my fist and motioned me back to my bed. "You boys have radio privileges tonight. Don't ruin it for yourselves right before vacation. Goodnight. And please, let's do make it a quiet one. Not one sound from any of you."

The laughter from *Fibber McGee and Molly*, *Allen's Alley*, *Amos 'n Andy* and *Duffy's Tavern* on the radio seemed to temporarily sooth the savage beasts around me. Those old shows were great, and their characters carried me every night beyond the walls to happier places. I'd lie there in my bed and drift off into a world of make believe.

July finally arrived, and it was time for me to head home for a month away from the madness. Route 611 was a highway that had two personalities as far as I was concerned. It was a gentle friend heading home and a road of foreboding on my return. Every landmark and rolling turn of the two-lane highway was ingrained in me. The two-hour bus ride was a slow transition from out of hell into heaven. I couldn't get home fast enough. When I travel that road today, it churns up the memories of being happily homeward bound one way and angry as hell the other. It was my personal Jekyll-and-Hyde highway.

The taxi ride from the bus terminal went past all the familiar sights but didn't head for our castle in the sky. That's when Della chose to tell me about another one of her well-kept secrets. She had moved into the very same building my Aunt Dot lived in. All my young life I had never been told of anything important that either had happened or was going to. When I asked why she hadn't written and informed me, her reply was, "It's a surprise," which proved to be one of the understatements of all time. We climbed the stairs of the Walnut Street apartment building to the second floor, but instead of continuing down the hall to my aunt's door, we stopped in front of another door at the head of the landing. The four-story building was huge, consisting of three apartments plus a drugstore on the first floor corner and a good-sized yard, bordered by extremely high hedges and flowering bushes.

Upon entering the apartment, I immediately noticed a few familiar pieces of furniture I hadn't seen since our home in Philadelphia. I followed her through the living room and past a master bedroom, which was just off the kitchen area. The bathroom amused me when I saw the men's shaving stuff on the shelf. "Thanks for the aftershave lotion and razor, Mom," I yelled into the next room. "But I don't have much of a beard, yet. When I reached the kitchen, there stood Jim Mahony, my mother's boyfriend, peeling potatoes over the sink. The big Irishman was dressed in work clothes and slippers and looked quite at home to me. "Uh, hi, Jim," I said in my stupor. "What are you doing here?"

"Jim and I were married. We're a family now." Della took me by the arm. "Isn't this nice? You got a new home and a ... a stepdad too."

"It's good to see you, boy," Jim said. "How was your bus ride?"

He mumbled something else too, but I didn't hear it because I was in shock. It always seemed as though my mother thought that what was most important in her life didn't much matter to mine. There were no shouts of joy, hugging or even congratulations. I was stunned.

"Well, say something. Aren't you happy? Isn't this what you've wanted ... home, a father and your own room? Jim and I planned this for a long time. We wanted to find the right place for all of us."

I could only think of one thing to say. "Why did you keep this from me?" They both turned my stomach.

"We wanted you to have a real home to come to on vacations."

"Where's my room?" I asked.

Della pointed toward the door on the other side of the kitchen. "Up those steps. I hope you like it. It's big. And it has three windows."

"Congratulations," I said. "I hope you two will be very happy here together."

"Aren't you being a little ungrateful, son?" I heard Jim say as I climbed the stairs.

"I'm not your son."

"We should've told him," Della said. "Oh, I'm sure he'll get used to it. Wouldn't it be nice, Jim, if he *could* stay with us and not go back?"

"The boy's in a fine school, Della. Leave it be. Maybe he can stay home longer next summer."

I was more thrilled about having a room to myself than having a stepfather. It was a spacious converted attic that covered the entire top of the building. It had three windows, facing north, east and west. Each one had a panoramic view of the surrounding neighborhood—my very own, but temporary, castle in the sky.

A rare happy moment together for mother and son.

CHAPTER TEN
A BRIEF SUMMER'S INTERLUDE

My stepfather was a big, beer-guzzling Irishman with an emptiness inside him when it came to kids. He was previously married and had a daughter he never spoke of, nor even saw. That coldness in his character caused a lot of grief for Della and me. He was simply not enamored with having any children around him, no matter whose they were.

I didn't venture far from my new surroundings those few weeks in the summer of '56 because I feared the neighborhood kids would discover my hair loss. So I cowered in the big yard behind the tall hedges and also made friends with the neighborhood's shoemaker, whom my mother had introduced me to. Sam's shop was where I'd pass a lot of my time watching him repair shoes. He was a jolly, good-natured man with funny stories to tell and the latest gossip to share. His shoe shop was a gathering place, sort of like what the Brickyard's B & L Steak Shop had been. If you hadn't heard the latest town gossip, you'd sure hear it soon enough at Sam's, even if it wasn't accurate. As the neighborhood regulars would come and go, so would the town's latest scandal, told differently every time.

My stepfather wasn't pleased with my hanging out in the shoe shop, or hiding in the yard for that matter. "Why doesn't he go up to the playground?" he'd say. "Meet some kids his own age. What is he, a sissy boy?"

"He's afraid, Jim," my mother said one night at the dinner table. "Let him be."

"What's he afraid of?" Jim stopped eating and glared at me. "Look at him. He's got to toughen up. It's not good for him being around grownups all the time or hiding behind the bushes in the yard."

"He's scared the kids will make fun of him."

"Nonsense. They'll never notice with his baseball cap on."

"What if it blows off?"

"If they laugh at him, he'll have to stand up for himself.

Nobody will bother him after that. They all pick on each other once in a while. That's what kids do. I beat up a kid one time for calling me names. He never did it again."

I both hated and feared Jim. The last thing I wanted to happen in the short time I was home was to be fighting with him or anybody. "I just want to be left alone when I'm here," I said. "You don't even know how it is back at school, and I sure don't need more of it."

"How do you know what these kids around here are like? You have to grow up and face this big old world sometime."

"I do. Every day. And I do it alone."

That was the first time I stood up to Jim, and he didn't like it, but Della stepped in before the big man said another word. "It's different for him around here," she said. "He doesn't know any of the children. Nobody's ever seen the hair problem he has. Can't you just leave him alone? He's only home a little while."

"We'll see." Jim left the table, went into the living room and returned with the newspaper. "What about this day camp the YMCA has for kids?" He opened the paper to an advertisement. "This would be good for him. They go on day trips and do things with them, like arts and crafts, swimming, museums..."

"But he won't know those kids either," Della said.

"That's my point. If there aren't any from the neighborhood, what will it matter?" He crumbled up the newspaper in disgust. "Stop babying him! He's going!"

Within two days, there I was at the YMCA, just where I didn't want to be. Della had bought me a new cap just for the occasion, a sea captain's hat, which I hated. I reluctantly waved goodbye to her as the cab pulled away. Some vacation it turned out to be that summer. I wondered why I even bothered to come home. Before she had married Jim, at least she and I spent time together.

The YMCA day campers went to an amusement park that day, which was fortunate for me because it didn't appear odd to be wearing a hat outside. On the way there in the bus I got to know a few of the others and everything seemed fine. I was very dependent on wearing hats in my younger years. But when the wind blew I'd get nervous. That particular day had been sunshiny and calm, until the roller coaster ride. Up and up the cars slowly climbed the steep tracks until we reached the very top, and then down the other side we zoomed. The rush of wind whipped the hat from my head and sent it sailing out over the ride and far down below. I felt naked and embarrassed, but the boy with me just stared in awe at my partial baldness. When we pulled into the starting area, the ride operator noticed me right away. Alopecia areata in its patchy stages is not a pretty sight. He simply asked me about where my hat had blown off, closed the ride down, and went off toward the towering wooden structure along the tracks and disappeared. When he returned with my hat, he placed it on my head, smiled at me and returned to his job. I thanked him and quickly walked back into the park with my new-found friend at my side, who never said a word about how I looked.

That incident made me wonder why there was such a difference in attitude toward me between the kids and grownups at home and those at Girard. It's a thought that to this day on occasion still passes through my mind. But after it happened, I knew without a doubt that somehow and in some way I would leave Girard at any cost, even if it meant living with Jim.

CHAPTER ELEVEN
TRANSGRESSIONS OF THE YOUNG/NO PLACE TO HIDE

Della's marriage to Jim didn't alter the one thing I wanted changed most in my life. But I swore on the bus ride back to Girard that summer that this would be the last year I'd be confined inside those cold walls.

Banker Hall, in my mind, would be the final residence building for me. Its head housemaster fit the school's strict regimen perfectly. Coach Boggs was a former Marine drill instructor and a tough but fair man. He was a true image of a poster Marine, six feet tall, with a V-shaped torso rippled with muscles. A high and tight, closely cropped head of hair and a firm, square-cut jaw made him the ultimate leatherneck in a boy's eyes. Life was lived by the numbers with Coach Boggs. You snapped to when he wanted your attention; a coin bounced off the bed during his dorm inspections; and lockers were dumped if they weren't squared away.

Years later, my son and daughter would be astonished when they visited Girard with me and learned what it was like growing up there back in the day, especially the stories I'd tell about the strict regimen we lived by with Coach Boggs. Although they showed love for Nana Della, there was a resentment against her, which unfortunately at the time would reopen old wounds for my mother. After all, they were only kids trying to understand, no different than I had tried when I was their age.

Coach Boggs was without a doubt the ideal housemaster for our age group, as we were now old enough to be in the battalion. Our military indoctrination as new cadets rounded out the curriculum for all the remaining grade levels. We were now considered young men, and the "batty" or battalion served as an integral part of an older student's life.

My classmates, unfortunately, hadn't acquired any common sense with age and their harassment continued. That year would be the most painful of all. Each trying day had me longing for the solitude of night, when devilish boys hopefully fell fast asleep. Those were the only peaceful hours I had. They were a time to think, to cry, to pray and to hope. I thought of home and why I couldn't be there with my mother and Jim. My prayers for a miracle would often turn my tired eyes to tears before slumber and then the sweet dreams of faraway places.

I was practically bald by midyear, and my head became a shiny target for all forms of abuse. The endless barrage of insults and indignities intensified my resentment and hatred toward everyone. From one moment to the next, I never knew from what direction the abuse would come.

THERE WAS NO PLACE TO HIDE

Doc Dennis was the stereotypical absentminded professor. The building could have come crashing down around him and he would not have noticed. But once Doc realized it, he'd set about working on his theories of why it occurred and how it could have been avoided, after the fact. He was an amusing character to watch and extremely intelligent when it came to the scientific world. We had him for study hall one year in his lecture hall classroom, that consisted of risers with desktop chairs that faced down toward his teacher's platform, which was a maze of beakers, glass tubes, vials, a Bunsen burner, wires plugged in everywhere and a huge sink in which he continually washed his hands. It looked like a mad scientist's laboratory.

My desk was down front on the lowest level, where I spent most of my time watching Doc Dennis fiddle with his experiments. He rarely looked up over his bifocals, except if someone asked a question, and then he'd mumble some goofy answer and return to whatever he was doing.

Something hit me on the back of my head one particular study hall, and stuck there. When I reached to remove it from my bare scalp, the soggy wad or little ball of toilet paper came off in my hand. When I turned to see where it had come from, another one hit me on the side of my head and still another glanced off my cheek. The next thing I knew I found myself in a barrage of spitballs coming from different directions behind me. A few of them sailed over my head and stuck to the blackboard, while another one landed on Doc Dennis's lab coat. But he never noticed a thing, not even the laughter going on.

There were spitballs stuck all over, including the blackboard, where chalk written formulas were. I don't recall who the guys were, except that they were a few of Butchie McGraff's followers. But it didn't matter who they were, because I was usually outnumbered. I then did a very strange thing. I got up from my desk with a science book in hand and went to Doc Dennis to ask him some trumped up question about a homework assignment. He didn't acknowledge my standing there at first, so as I waited I began removing the spitballs from the blackboard. When I returned to my desk, I looked up at the guys who sat behind me and gave them a thumbs up, because I thought I had done a good thing. They proceeded to pelt me with more spitballs.

The harassment seemed endless at times and I lived in fear of it daily. How could I escape it? There just wasn't any way I could avoid or hide from it. Even simply walking from place to place I'd often hear some kind of name called out at me, or find a note on my bed with a ridiculous message on it like, "Hey Baldy, your mommy doesn't even want you" or "Buffalo Billy is ugly." The Buffalo word referred to how my head would shine when the nurse put the ointment on it. Their sick imaginations would run wild and stupid but always feeding the anger growing inside me.

"Hey, scab, don't serve our table," a boy called out from behind me, as I waited tables one day in the Dining and Food Services Center.

"Yeh, skinhead, we don't want your germs," another said.

"Baldy should wear gloves," someone else commented.

I ignored them and continued to place the large food platters on the tables. Waiting tables was a detail we all had to perform at some point when we were older. It was a thankless job hustling food and serving the gluttonous whims of a dining hall full of hungry boys. And there were no tips. It was even more nerve wracking in my case, because most of them didn't want me handling their food for fear of catching the hairless disease. Even my fellow waiters and kitchen help were leery of me.

I had just finished serving a table and was pushing the food cart to the next one when there was a loud crash of shattering china behind me. Someone had deliberately knocked a large meat plate to the floor.

"Whoops. Hey, Baldy, you dropped something," one boy said as the others laughed.

"Waiter." The table captain raised his hand and smirked. "We need another plate of meat." It was none other than Butchie, the same boy I fought with in the sandpile at Good Friends and who also had led the chorus in Billy Boy back at Lafayette Hall. His twisted mind kept revising the lyrics. The Banker Hall version went something like,

Oh, where have you been, Billy Boy, Billy Boy?
Oh, where have you been baldy Billy?
Have you been to seek your hair?
For missing strands that laid you bare?
Oh, poor dreadful sorry ugly Billy.

At times Butchie was like having a personal bully. And that day in the dining hall I could have tangled with him. But I didn't say a word and began picking up the meat and broken pieces of china. The others meanwhile kept up their taunts and laughter.

"What the hell is going on here?" Coach Boggs said with a thunderous roar. "Who made this mess?"

"It was an accident, sir," I replied.

The boys around us giggled, and Coach Boggs pointed at Butchie. "This is your table, mister. If you think it's so funny, you clean it up. Billy, go get them another plate of meat." The coach glared at Butchie and his cronies. He was aware of what actually had happened, and I thanked him quietly to myself. There were those occasional moments of retribution, but not enough of them to satisfy me.

Athletic activities that required close physical contact with the others were unavoidable and created all sorts of other uncomfortable situations. The boys' lack of understanding of my disease had made it unacceptable to them for me to use the same athletic equipment or even be in a swimming pool with them. It wasn't every boy who had felt that way; but, as always, a few controlled the minds of many.

The first part of the year was gymnastics, with the winter months devoted to wrestling, and spring to track and field. Girard's physical education program was very demanding, and the requirements in order to pass were tough. By year's end we were expected to know the basic fundamentals of all three sports. Wrestling presented the most awkward situation, because no one wanted to have bodily contact with me. Coach Bradley tried his best to ease their minds, but to no avail, so he'd often practice with me himself. My hair loss remained a medical mystery, and being the only one with it made me a physical oddity in a close environment of cautious and cynical minds.

Swimming class was even weirder. The students were convinced I might contaminate the water, so most often I'd be alone in the far end of the indoor Olympic size pool. But in spite of the adversity I became a pretty good swimmer and even beat some of them in races. Unfortunately, that only made the ridicule worse. Coach Boggs said to me one day, "Swim teams should shave their heads, less drag in the water." He gave me that toothy smile of his. "They're jealous."

"The hell with all of them," I said to myself one day, and took to forging medical excuses from the infirmary to get out of the classes altogether. That's the one time when the disease had served my purpose well. No one ever questioned, let alone understood, the technical reasons I would make up. I firmly believed back then that neither the instructors nor anyone else really cared if I participated anyway. To them it simply meant that they wouldn't have to deal with my disruptive bald presence.

My dislike for Girard festered within me as those long days

slowly passed by. The things I had once loved to do became insignificant, and I quit the soccer and baseball teams that year. Once again it hadn't seemed to matter much to the coaches or my teammates. I was a decent athlete, yet no one asked me to stay on, maybe because then they didn't have to explain the freaky-looking hairless kid to the opponents. Being bald like I was in those days was uncommon, especially for a teenager.

The disease had altered my life in so many ways by then. I had become a true loner, and very insecure about myself. There wasn't a soul I trusted. As if being fourteen was tough enough, that was the age the boys would display their most vicious patterns of cruelty. It wasn't all my classmates who treated me that way, but those who didn't would keep their distance from me. I guess with some it was fear of the disease, and others, fear of the tough guys who might ridicule them.

Ironically, some years later, one of my tormentors came to Easton seeking my forgiveness. His guilt for what he had been a part of wore him down. It was obvious that he had built his own wall over time, from which only my forgiveness could free him. I'll never forget our brief encounter that day as long as I live.

"Can I come in?" he asked, standing humbly in the doorway. "Please."

Louis Stewart was one of many faces I hadn't forgotten. I saw the mischievous boy in him, trying to become a man.

"The school gave me your address. I hoped you still lived here." His eyes desperately searched mine hoping for some sign of welcome. He was nervous and fumbled for words. "I won't stay long. There's something I have to say, or, uh, get off my chest."

I listened to him intently as we sat across from one another in the living room. He had come a long way in hopes of finding peace between us, and I admired him for it. He went on and on at great length, speaking of the wrong he regrettably had been part of. His sincerity and remorse moved both of us to tears.

When Louis left, we hugged and promised one another to

keep in touch. Sadly, our paths never crossed again, but I often think back on what that healing day must have meant to him. It took me many more years to feel that (and now I wish I could see him once more, just to reassure him) it is okay. There's a list of guys I've always felt that way about, of course, headed up by Butchie McGraff. What a reunion that would make. I dreamt about it then and still do, but I eventually grew to appreciate that what some people might want to remember, others may wish to forget. Oh well, life does go on ... doesn't it?

CHAPTER TWELVE
THE DIE WAS CAST

As Christmas vacation approached that year, it was apparent to me that in the four months since school began I had already dealt with all the humiliation I was going to. I firmly believed that I could no longer be held responsible for my actions. People were either going to finally hear my cries or I would make sure no one ever forgot how they all had ignored me for so long.

Once again my arguments fell upon deaf ears, and the response from Della was empty as before. "Billy, it can't be as bad as you say. The school wouldn't tolerate it. You're very fortunate to be there. Girard is the best boys' school in the country."

"If what you tell us is true, they'll get to the bottom of it," Jim said. "Don't worry, it will be taken care of."

That's all I ever got, promises. Their words were meaningless and empty ones by that time. I had heard it all before.

Della no longer traveled with me on my return trips to Girard, which made my leaving even tougher. I was convinced that nobody really cared. Revenge was on my mind as the bus slowly pulled away from the terminal that gray January day. I glared at my mother through the cold, frost-covered window until she was out of sight. The rage in my heart fueled the bitterness in my mind and turned hopes into insane desires. By the time the bus passed through Girard's main gate later that day and stopped in front of Founder's Hall, I had made a solemn promise of my own to escape from those forbidding walls. Everyone would pay for deserting me, I had vowed.

My old friend, Carl, the lodgeman, was taking the flag down in the circular flower garden. I hadn't talked to him since summer, and my frame of mind sure needed a boost at that moment. He never failed over the years to cheer me up when I was down. But that day was a challenge for him, because I was even colder and gloomier inside than the winter weather.

"Help me fold old glory," he said and handed one end of the flag to me. "I haven't seen you in quite a while. How was your vacation?"

I set my suitcase down. "Different ... and way too short as usual. But lucky me, I have a stepfather now you know...or maybe you don't." I had forgotten to tell Carl the last time I saw him. It didn't seem all that important for anybody to know. "How about that for a surprise, huh? He told me if I'm good maybe I can stay home all next summer. It's the only nice thing he said to me. We've already gone at it several times."

"So, your mother got married?"

"Yep. Never told me until I got home this past summer. Nice of her. She got hitched and didn't say a word to me that she was going to. I never even knew that my Aunt Margaret had died either." It was things like that which drew us further apart back in those days. They made me feel like I didn't matter at all.

"What's your stepfather like?"

"A lot different from when Mom and him dated. He's pretty scary as a matter of fact. A big man, and he likes his beer. I feel that I'm in the way around him. Every day he's on me for something. In the summer I had to go to the YMCA day camp. But Mom seems nuts about him."

"Give it time. You both have to adjust to each other. Maybe she got married hoping to bring you home for good eventually. You never know."

"I doubt it, Carl." He was always the optimist. I handed him the folded flag and looked around in disgust. That would be my seventh year at Girard, and I didn't foresee a change in any way. "Jim wants me right here where I'm at. I overheard him say it one night to Mom. Besides, the school wouldn't release their guardianship of me. Not until I graduate, or I make it difficult enough for everybody."

Carl tucked the loose flap of the flag into the triangular fold, glanced at his watch and then at me. There was a deep look of concern in his eyes. "You've been here for what, going on seven years now? And you still hate it? I hoped that'd change."

"It'll never happen," I said, knowing full well his disappointment. For years he had told me that as the boys got older my life would get better living with them. I never believed him. "Every day's a nightmare, Carl. I don't know what the guys are going to do to me next. I'm the school freak. How many bald kids do you know?"

"Well, you better get to where you're supposed to be before they mark you absent." His face was etched with concern for me, and I loved him for it.

I picked up my suitcase and smiled. "Hey, maybe one day that'll happen." The thoughts of my freedom from Girard were uppermost on my mind, and that conversation with my old friend made me all the more determined.

"Don't talk nonsense," Carl replied.

"You never know." I waved back at him. "See ya around campus."

I was determined that there would be no next year, and I would bring all of it to an end. My loud complaints to the school's administration seemingly echoed off the surrounding wall and returned unanswered. All the doors were knocked on and every ear that would listen was pleaded with. My letters home for help became a daily ritual, as did my pleas to all the antagonists. I had reached a point of total frustration with no direction to turn. It was as if I had been cornered or backed into the wall, and there was no way out but over it.

CHAPTER THIRTEEN
THERE'S NO WALL HIGH ENOUGH

I had received a blue pass one day, requesting my appearance in Mrs. Hill's office. She headed up student relations and had been asked to look into my situation. It had only taken seven years for somebody to formally recognize the fact that I might have a problem. Her solution was for me to begin regular visits with the school psychologist. I couldn't believe that they had sent me to a shrink rather than try to understand what was in my heart. The whole thing was such a joke to me. Then and there I decided to take matters into my own hands.

I sat in the outer office for a counseling session one afternoon when I noticed an entire box of absentee passes. The school used a color-coded pass system. Blue meant a faculty or administration excuse from class, yellow meant dentist and pink was for the infirmary. Within a couple of weeks I had an ample supply of each and began diligently practicing the art of forgery. Before long, if there was a class or function I wanted to miss, I would simply write an excuse. It didn't take much for me to discover that my condition made it acceptable to be seen walking here and there out of class. I was careful not to overdo it and reserved the passes for when I needed the peace most.

Coach Boggs was his usual cantankerous self one morning as I stood on Banker Hall's front steps feeling sorry for myself and contemplating where I'd roam off to that day.

"You better move your butt!" he barked. "Let's go, boy! You'll be late for class! Double time!"

I held up the blue pass I had forged. "I have an appointment with Miss Hill, sir, in student counseling."

"Another pass? You're missing a lot of classes these days."

"Yes, sir," I said, loving the lies I was living. They kept me away from the daily routine of things, and that's all I cared about. I didn't want to be a part of anything anymore, not in that place.

"Well, what are you waiting for?" He played the role of a

Marine and stepped forward, took a wide stance and placed his fists on his hips in a forceful manner. "Get off my steps, boy! Go on."

My wanderings took me to the far end of the campus that day, where the president and vice president of the school lived. I liked it there because it was secluded from the rest of the campus. Sometimes I brought my sketch pad and drew for hours. The two homes were magnificent, and the library building, which was also an elegant structure in the Greek style, stood nearby. It was fun to draw and pass the time away from all the madness.

Chester Pursell was a big, clumsy sort of kid who didn't bother with anybody. His tall, awkward size and slow, jerky mannerisms made him another outcast that no one wanted to hang around. Most of the boys were afraid of him anyway, including myself.

"Where ya going, baldy?" he asked, standing by the library.

I ignored him and kept walking. He took a few long strides and caught up to me. "Hey, wait up," he said. "Where you headin'?"

"None of your business." I walked faster, but he easily kept up with me. "Leave me alone," I said and pushed him away. I didn't even care what he did to me, but I'd put up a good fight if he started something.

"C'mon, slow down, baldy." He stood in my way, towering over me. We must have looked comical in our standoff, me and the giant, but I wasn't about to back off, not to anyone, anymore.

I looked up at him. "Don't call me baldy," I said.

"I was only kidding." He stepped aside and looked down at me with his big, droopy eyes. "Really, I'm sorry."

"Sure you are. Get lost," I uttered sarcastically and walked away. When I reached the bend in the road, I turned and sure enough Chet ran after me. I felt bad for how I treated him, but I had gotten to the point where I just didn't care anymore.

"Come on, wait up." Chet reached out his hand to shake mine. "I didn't mean it."

I looked up at the big lummox. "Forget it. I just want to be left alone."

"Let's shake. I'll never call you a name again, promise." He extended his hand further. "Can I just walk with you?"

"What for?"

"There's nothing back here but a few houses and that damn wall."

"I know. But it's quiet." I shook his hand. "This is where I come when I want to be by myself. I like all the trees and stuff. It's nice scenery to draw, and the wall is kind of hidden."

There wasn't anyplace outdoors on the campus that you didn't see the wall. I guess just being alone and pretending to be free was my reason that day for being a jerk to Chet.

"Shouldn't you be in class?" he asked.

"How about you?" I replied. "Where are you supposed to be?"

"I'm cutting today."

"You're cutting class? Why?"

"Just because."

"Aren't you afraid of getting caught?" I asked.

"Nope. I got a library pass. See?" His pass was white. "Neat forgery, isn't it? It took me a week to get Mr. Becker's signature right."

I laughed and showed him my pass. "Miss Hill. Not bad, huh?"

"Where did you get a blue one?" he asked.

"I got a box with every color. White, pink for the infirmary, yellow for the dentist, and blue is an office excuse. I Stole them from the administration office."

"If we get caught we're dead."

"Who cares. I hate this place. The more trouble I cause the better. I want out of here."

"Me too. It really sucks here. Especially battalion, I don't want to be a soldier. I hate marching. I'm bad at it anyway. Everybody laughs at me."

"You are kind of clumsy. Now you know how I feel."

"Yeah, somebody should beat the shit out of Butchie McGraff and his buddies."

We joked back and forth the rest of the day while cutting classes, but not lunch. God forbid Chet should've gone hungry. The topics we covered included everything about each other, like what and who we hated the most. But running away was at the top of both our lists, especially when I learned that his mother lived in West Philly and we could get there in a day's walk.

For the first time I had a really good buddy, A big one too. We became practically inseparable that spring, which created further tension between me and the others. When Chet and I were together, the boys kept their distance. He certainly was intimidating, which made my life somewhat simpler but complicated his. It was like having an older brother watching over me, but I felt bad because of the price Chet had to pay.

One morning at breakfast Chet found a threatening note under his plate. It stated that if he continued to be my friend, we'd both be beaten up after shop. The Mechanical School Building was at the opposite end of the campus, across from Westend. The huge facility housed carpentry, electrical, metalworking, welding and the auto repair shops. The back of the building had an alley leading to the rear gate, the front faced Westend and the side overlooked the coal yard. There were a lot of places for the boys to jump us along the way back to Banker Hall. When the dismissal bell rang, everyone cleaned up their places and began filing out of the building. I met Chet out front and we cautiously proceeded up the main road. The Armory was only a little way from Mechanical School, where we immediately caught sight of the enemy. There were six of them, and they came out onto the road with, of course, Butchie McGraff in front.

"Hey, scab, how's dumbo?" Butchie shouted. "Look, guys, it's baldy and the beast."

"Aren't they cute, skinhead and his dopey girlfriend," one of the others called out.

Another danced around us. "What do you two creeps see in each other? You're both ugly."

Chet and I kept heading straight up the road as the group

encircled us. They continued calling out insults, but we didn't say a word. With our backs to each other, we just kept moving. One of them got too close, and Chet grabbed him in a flash. "What's the matter, jerk? Now what are your asshole buddies gonna do? C'mon. Not so tough now are yas?"

"Leave him go, Chester." Butchie held up his hand and they all froze in their tracks.

Chet pinned the boy's arm tightly to his back and put him in a half nelson. "Come and get him, bigshot. He's your buddy. You clowns wanted to fight. Okay, we'll start with this creep," he yelled. "Billy, you want the first shot? They won't try anything. They're chicken."

I had never seen Chet so angry as he was that moment. He kept challenging them as we approached the Junior School building, dragging the boy along with us. "Well, tough guys, who wants some of this? I've been waiting a long time to kick somebody's ass."

"Wow, strong words for a dummy," another boy commented.

"I'll show you who's dumb." Chet glared at him. "Make your move."

"Yeah, Butchie. C'mon, you and me! Right now!" I yelled. The rage in me was about to explode. I wanted so badly to settle it once and for all, right then and there, but Butchie backed off. "What's the matter?" I said. "No guts?"

Butchie's mouth made up for his size, and he sure knew how to agitate people. He always had all the answers, but not that day. "This ain't no fair fight," he yelled. "You got the zombie on your side. Maybe some other day."

I stepped toward him with my fists raised. "Let's go, redhead. You're first, and then I'll take yas all on, one at a time." I started jumping from side to side like the crazy person they thought I was. The memory of how my father's boxers moved in the ring came to mind. "Nobody'll stop me this time…remember the sandbox?"

The others moved in closer to Chet, but he applied more pressure to his hostage's arm. "Don't get no funny ideas, you idiots. Don't tempt me."

"Let me go. You're hurting my arm!" The boy started to panic.

"Tough! You're breaking my heart. How does it feel, huh? Maybe I should let Billy pound the hell out of you for all the times you guys picked on him."

The kid screamed as Chet tossed him from side to side like he was a toy. "Call Billy a name now, c'mon, I dare you."

"You two are nuts, Billy," Butchie said, cautiously stepping back.

Chet yanked on his captive's arms harder and angrily shouted. "Chickenshits! You guys had enough? Now, get the hell out of here, you losers! Go on, punk." He shoved the boy aside with ease and the kid took off up the road."

My smile must have been ear to ear as I hugged Chet. For the first time I had had the upper hand, and it was fun to watch the bullies squirm, especially Butchie.

Chet and I were ten minutes late by the time we reached the D & S building for lunch that day. We ran inside and up the steps, where we were greeted by Coach Boggs. "Where the hell were you two?" In our fright, we didn't notice the other six boys lined up against the wall. "You two clowns get over there with the rest," he ordered. "Now, all of you face the wall, and I want to see noses touching cement."

Our punishment was extra duties for the next two weeks, no movies and, with toothbrushes in hand, we all had to scrub the shower and washrooms before bed every night, including the toilets.

The name calling and taunting finally stopped, but Chet's oddball status grew. It was as though neither of us existed. I often suggested that he stay away from me, but his loyalty was steadfast. He wanted us to remain best friends for the rest of our lives. I loved him for it, but inside I cried for him as much as I did for myself.

We soon began to seriously plan our escape. The more we talked about it, the more possible it seemed. Our first objective was to find the best place to scale the wall. It was late April, and the weather had warmed enough that it didn't look odd for us to be outside snooping around. The perfect spot we eventually found was alongside an old equipment shack built onto the ten-foot high wall. Not only did it have a drain spout in the corner that could be easily climbed, it was also out of view from any buildings. The other good news was a tree on the opposite side that would make our descent a piece of cake.

On the morning "freedom rang," we forged passes to get out of school and rendezvoused in the catacombs of the Junior School building. The thought of finally going over the wall was exhilarating but a bit scary. We huddled in the boiler room until everyone was in the dining halls, then sneaked through the back door of the basement theater. Once backstage we slipped out the freight entrance and ran for the wall. Like two highly seasoned S.W.A.T. guys, we scaled it in no time, crossed over to the tree and climbed down. "Freedom!" was the first word out of my mouth as I looked up at the wall and shook my fist. "I told you we'd do it." What a feeling that was. The birds in the tree flew off across the street, and I raised my arms in victory.

"C'mon, Billy." Chet grabbed me. "Let's get the hell out of here before somebody sees us, like the cops."

"Nobody will catch me now, Chet. I ain't going back in there. Never."

We ran through the streets of North Philadelphia, laughing and joking, free as birds. Our plan was to head for Chet's mother's, break in when she was at work, take some money and food, then make our way upstate. It was as though we were fugitives from the law, looking for a safe hiding place and then moving on. Every time a police car went by we'd look for somewhere to hide, or just pretend to be neighborhood kids. The weather had cooperated, and everything seemed to be going well as we approached the Philly Zoo. We were crossing through Fairmont Park near the railroad bridge underpass when a police car pulled up alongside us.

"Hey you two," the policeman called out. "Come over here."

We walked over to the patrol car, trying extra hard to be nonchalant. "Don't look nervous," Chet mumbled.

"Why aren't you in school? Today's no holiday."

Instant excuses had become second nature to me as a result of skipping all those classes. I had grown accustomed to making up stories, so I pointed to a row of parked chartered buses. "We're on a class trip, sir."

The officer seemed pleasant enough as he got out of the car. "What are your names, boys?" he asked. "Where are you from?"

"I'm Billy and this is Chet," I said. "We're from upstate, sir. The Lehigh Valley."

The policeman leaned up against the patrol car and asked, "Are you here with a school?"

"St. Anthony's, sir. It's a Catholic school. Actually, it's our church's trip we're on."

The officer smiled, opened the car door and then paused. "Why are you out here? Where's your group?"

"I forgot my wallet on the bus," Chet said, pointing to a row of school buses parked conveniently nearby.

The policeman got back in his car. "Well, have a good time, boys. It's a nice day for it. Oh, and make sure you see the gorillas. My kids love them. It's a great zoo."

Chet and I didn't move a muscle as the patrol car pulled away. We just stood there for a while collecting our nerves, waving at the cop. Then we laughed, oh, how we laughed. We were proud of our little game we played on the policeman, and also very relieved.

The next problem we ran into was Chet's memory. His sense of direction wasn't too good. But after hours of circling, backtracking, ducking police cars and running from suspicious looking strangers, he began to recognize the neighborhoods. It was dark when we finally reached the park just across the street from his mother's house. Our timing was a little off to say the least. His mother was home. We found an overgrown area of thick bushes and shrubs in the park and settled in for the night.

There we were in the dark, exhausted and hungry, but bragging about our accomplishments until we finally fell asleep. I just knew that what we did would get someone's attention, hopefully Della's.

We awoke at first light and looked around. Our view of the house was good, so we saw when Chet's mom left for work. As soon as she was out of sight, we crawled from our hiding place and casually strolled around to the rear of the house, opened a kitchen window and tumbled in. The cereal, toast and orange juice hit the spot. But when Chet went off looking for some money, I heard the loud, muffled sound of voices. His mother had returned home on a hunch, knowing we'd show up sooner or later. She told us that the school had notified her when we hadn't turned up for dinner hour roll call the night before. She went on to explain how concerned everyone was, and it was good we were both safe. We sat together in the living room, telling her how we ran away and why we didn't want to go back. I felt quite comfortable next to her and most assured at first that we weren't going back unless we could tell our story. How could anyone who loved children return us to that hell after they heard the truth?

"Chester, I love you, sweetheart, but I have to take you back," his mother said softly. She was a tall woman and stretched her graceful arms around both of us. "Billy, if you don't want to go back, I won't force you. But running away won't solve anything."

We were both so eager to plead our cases, we started talking at the same time. It was just so good to have someone else listen to our story. I'm sure Chet felt as I did, that if we could win her over maybe she'd become an ally. I really believed that the heartstrings approach might work if people could only hear what is was like to be continually ignored.

"You don't know what it's like, Mom, to always be laughed at and called names. We just got tired of it." He made a fist. "But we finally showed them."

"Were you fighting?" she asked.

"You should've seen it. They don't mess with us no more, huh, Billy?"

"Yeah, but nobody hardly talks to us either, except to make jokes. It's like we got a contagious disease or something."

110

"Does your mother know about these things?" Mrs. Pursell asked.

"Yes, ma'am. She has for years. But I don't think she cares."

I went on and on for a long time, telling her everything. She listened intently to every detail, shaking her head in disapproval; and just when we were sure we had her convinced that Girard was a bad place, she said, "Well, Chester, let's get you back to school. I'll try to talk to someone about all this."

I felt like all the air had been sucked out of our soaring balloon. I had thought that we finally had a grownup who understood. But I guess that's the down side of being a kid. Sometimes no one hears you, or wants to.

She looked at Chet. "I'm sorry, honey. I didn't realize it was like that. But you can't run away. You're both just boys."

"What choice did we have, Mom?"

Where is a kid my age going to go by himself? I thought. I didn't even know what part of town I was in or what direction would lead me toward home. Even if I could have made it to the Broad and Erie bus station, I wasn't sure I had enough money for a ticket home. "I'll go wherever Chet goes," I said, "but would you really talk to them and explain why we ran away?"

The school had a very strict code of discipline. For serious offenses, a boy received what was referred to as a V.O. It stood for very objectionable conduct. I had received one earlier that year for fighting. So with another one for running away, I had to be on the possible expulsion list. No doubt about it in my mind, I was definitely in serious trouble. Chet and I were placed on daily detention with no privileges, which meant no free time after classes either. Our weekends became one G.I. party after another, and we must have cleaned every inch of Banker Hall.

I felt no remorse for my actions, and I prayed that I had done enough to get myself expelled from Girard. I had kept my promise, and there wasn't anything I wouldn't do to call further attention to my plight, including another escape. The school's intent to teach me a lesson afforded me various opportunities to gather the bare necessities for another chance to go over the wall. I was determined. From the laundry, I stole clothes. Dining and Services contributed a half dozen hum muds, and while working at the Founder's Hall candy store I stole some money.

I simply didn't give a damn anymore, and during exams I sat there, never raising a pencil to paper. My homework assignments were left undone and I refused to participate in anything. With a month remaining before summer vacation, I had barely gone through the motions of being alive. My grades and overall attitude weren't priorities anymore. I was angry and I wanted out from behind those walls, no matter how.

The remaining days of the school term dragged slowly by in the spring of '57. The only fire burning within me was a determination to see that what I had started would end in the way I had prayed so long for. My mind continually rambled back and forth between happy endings and sad ones. I wrestled with the possible reality of not being freed from my walled-in nightmare.

One Saturday afternoon I walked alone from one end of the campus to the other. I thought of Miss Hart and Mr. Swagg's special kindnesses to me. They had tried so hard to make my life without Della acceptable and bring joy to a six-year-old's troubled heart. Continuing up the main road, I once again was king of soccer and marched in the Founder's Day parade. At the Junior School and Good Friends buildings, I reflected on those bygone times: The fight over my hat, which could have easily caused me to kill Butchie McGraff that day; Miss Klunk's midnight spankings and her perplexed state of mind in dealing with me, especially when I slept with another boy; Miss Linstrom and her legendary "punisher of evildoers"; Miss Henson and Wednesday evenings with Walt Disney; Mr. Nichman treating me to Pepsi Colas and new roller skates; and, of course, my starring role as Robinson Crusoe. I gazed across the street at the medieval structure of Lafayette Hall. My thoughts immediately focused on Mr. Hector, a good friend who had encouraged me to explore the creative side of myself. I also recalled Mr. Kugler and his legendary whistle. Big Joe Costello came to mind and the night we discussed my future

D.A. hairstyle. Good and bad, my thoughts collided as I paused by the infirmary where the ugliness of the disease remained a medical mystery but Nurse Hood looked as good as ever.

The Chapel was next in sight, and it beckoned me toward its huge bronze and glass doors. From within I could hear Professor Banks and the boys choir rehearsing for Sunday's services. The school chapel was a magnificent edifice of devotion, and its lofty interior marble walls and towering gold-leaf-trimmed columns rose above a theater of prayer that accommodated the entire student body. As I stood in the outer lobby reading The Lord's Prayer from where it was carved into the wall, a tumultuous crescendo from the immense pipe organ filled my senses with the heraldic baroque chords of Trumpets Voluntaire. The sudden power and majesty of the music stunned me from my thoughts and sent me outside, humbly reciting The Lord's Prayer. The next building was Banker Hall, where on that day the memories were all too fresh, so I continued up the road. If my expectations of leaving Girard were not to be fulfilled, could I survive the four remaining years? That question loomed larger than life in every memory of the school. As doubtful as I was then, I never really found the answer. I walked past Merchant, Mariner, Bordeaux and Allen Halls. Those were the buildings I hoped never to live in. On the Founder's Hall steps that day, Stephen Girard's spirit and my mortal soul looked over the sprawling circular flower gardens, through the main gate and out into the city. My private yellow brick road to the Land of Oz was before me.

Della had been summoned to the school that May, but I never saw her. There were no discussions with me over any matters, and for a brief time I wasn't even sure whether I'd be going home at all that summer.

June finally rolled around and surprisingly I was permitted to go home. My mind was cluttered with doubts and many unanswered questions. Why hadn't the school talked to me? Why wouldn't they let me see my mother when she came there? Would I return that fall? Was Chet coming back? Why hadn't Della written? What would they say at home? Was it over? Was it all finally over?

CHAPTER FOURTEEN
HOME SWEET HOME?

My last day on campus, I sneaked out of the building late in the evening and went to Founder's Hall. It was as though time itself had stood still, sending me adrift into another level of consciousness. Something felt odd about being there. With the darkness came an eerie silence and stillness, while I sat on the steps thinking about home and how I wished my father was alive. I had never wanted to be with him so badly or prayed so hard for a miracle as I did that night.

"Well, Pop," I said aloud, "one more lousy year gone. Sorry about running away, but somebody has to listen to me. Mom hasn't. She's never even written to me since I went over the wall, and they got me seeing a shrink. Some joke. I'm not crazy. I wish you were alive. You'd show them."

Everything around me took on a surreal presence with only the immediate foreground left in focus. Nothing mattered but those precious few peaceful moments that drew me into a transcendental-like dreamscape. I stared intently into the gardens and along the narrow walkway leading toward the gates. Then, ever so faintly at first, I heard what I thought sounded like people whispering above the distant notes of an enchanting melody. I was drawn as if by some celestial force. I walked down from the steps and saw myself standing in the garden. My eyes were still looking toward the huge metal gates when they unlocked and slowly began to creak open. Had my dreams and prayers that night created illusions magnified by the desires in my heart? The whispering voices were all around me. I strained to understand every word and concentrated on recognizing what I heard. The closer I walked toward the gate, the more audible the sounds became. They were all familiar voices of family and Brickyard people from out of my past, each one bringing to mind more pleasant thoughts from long ago, nearly forgotten memories. As I stood in front of the opened gates, a misty, shadowy silhouette of a man appeared in the shimmering light. He slowly approached the gate. As I got closer, the piano melody grew louder and ominously familiar. It was the tune, *Where Have You Been Billy Boy?*

It all seemed real enough, in a macabre sort of way. But was it a dream or merely a symbolic vision that marked a happening I had prayed for so long? In any event, it did exist in my mind. The faint glowing figure paused by the gate, and at first I wanted to run. The haunting music grew fainter, and the voices waned into the silence of the night. My curiosity overrode all logic and fears, as I saw the glowing apparition and myself. I called out, "Pop?!"

"Don't be afraid, Billy," he said. "I'm here with you. There's no need to be sad anymore. You're going home."

"Yeah," I heard myself shout. "For one lousy month."

"It's for good this time. Have faith, I'll always be with you."

I was alone by the closed gates when I heard my name called once more. It was my old friend, Carl, the lodgekeeper. "Billy, what are you doing out here this late?" he asked. "Who are you talking to?"

"Carl! Did you see him?"

"See who? Do you realize what time it is? You're gonna get in more trouble."

"That was my Pop. Really, it was. Look, the gate's even open."

Carl walked over to the closed gate and tugged on the chain. "It's locked. Just the way I left it. You better get on back to Banker Hall before Coach Boggs comes looking for you."

I rubbed my eyes. "I'm telling you, my father was standing right there. Didn't you hear the music, and people talking?"

"Sure, from that apartment building over there."

"You don't believe me. I saw him."

"Your mind's playing tricks on you. You probably saw a vagrant. They look for handouts." Carl removed his big red railroad hanky from his uniform pocket and wiped his glasses. "You want to go home so bad you're seeing and hearing things. But I understand. You've had a rough time of it lately and you're tired."

"I'm not coming back after vacation, Carl. I know it now. My Pop said so. They can't do anything to me anymore. I'll be free of this place, finally."

Carl put his hand on my shoulder and gave me one of his big, friendly smiles. "Okay, I believe you. Now go on with you before you get caught and they don't let you go home for vacation."

"I've prayed a long time for this, Carl."

"I know you have," he remarked with a sadness in his voice.

"Take care of yourself. I'll miss you." I reached out and hugged him. "Some Founder's Day I'll be back. I promise, and you won't recognize me because I'll have my hair again. You'll see. It'll happen."

"And I'll be waiting like always, Billy."

For years I never discussed what happened that night. Whatever it was stayed locked up inside me; and although I went through two years of psychotherapy in my thirties, those images and sounds that night have remained a mystery to me.

The bus pulled into the station late afternoon that warm June day. I stepped down onto the loading platform and immediately inhaled the atmosphere of home. Those homecomings were a mixed bag of emotions for me by that time. I used to anticipate my mother's familiar stiff hug, but as I got older it didn't matter anymore. I guess the resentment inside me had completely taken over my feelings toward her.

Della and I got into a cab and left for home. The ride through town in those days was great fun because it afforded my homesick eager eyes the opportunity to absorb the many familiar sights. Christmas was by far the best of times to visit. The circle in the center of town would be festively decorated with giant candles and thousands of twinkling colored lights. My eyes and ears always delighted in the countless store displays and ringing bells that added to the good feeling of "There's No Place Like Home For The Holidays." But even in the month of June, that same ride was very much a homesick boy's delight, especially that year after all

I'd been through.

Much discussion had already taken place between Della, Jim and the school regarding my return to Girard in the fall. The trouble that I stirred up had effectively created the attention and concern I wanted so badly. After all those years, people were finally taking notice of how unhappy I had been.

I still kept to myself, much to Jim's disapproval, and avoided the neighborhood kids. Hour after hour I'd create imaginary worlds, either up in my room or down in the yard. There'd be times I was a great fireballing lefty pitcher throwing inning after hitless inning against the garage wall. Other days I'd just draw or hide by a bush in the yard, removing my cap to let the sunlight and fresh air caress my then practically bald scalp. I felt safe inside my private world, far from the threats of being exposed to strangers who didn't know me or the disease I had. I had a constant fear that somebody might see my ugliness and would taunt me, just like the boys at Girard. I even stayed away from Sam's shoe shop for the same reasons.

One afternoon while I was sitting in the yard, the tall hedges began to rustle. The voices of two boys startled me, and I crouched lower, looking to see where they were.

"I'm telling you, Wayne, he hides in that corner over there." One of them poked at the hedges.

"Where?" the other voice said. "I don't see anybody."

The first boy sounded agitated. "I'm telling you, the kid hides in there every day. I think he's some kind of a weirdo. I've seen him. He sits there for hours sometimes."

I knelt further under the bushes and didn't move for fear of being discovered. Visions of Girard played back in my head.

"Hey, Wayne, go around to the other side," the one boy called out. "Maybe you'll see him. Go ahead, no one's looking. I'm telling you the kid is in there. I'll stand guard out here."

My heart pounded, and I got as low as possible in the shrubs. I had a clear view of the entire yard, so I saw the tall, scrawny boy appear from the other side. He had a crewcut and one heck of a protruding nose, sort of like Captain Hook's.

"Frankie, you're nuts. I don't see anybody," he yelled.

"There's nobody in here."

Wayne was so close to me that I could have untied his sneakers. I feverishly looked around for the hidden opening in the thick hedges that only I knew existed.

"He's got to be in there, stupid. I know it." Frankie shoved a stick through the hedges just above me. "Look under the bushes."

The yard was big, but not big enough, and the tall hedges weren't a wall. I was frightened of being discovered, which would've meant new terrors and torments for me, but now at home.

"Frankie! I see him! He's right here under my nose." Wayne started to spread the bushes apart.

Wayne's nose was so big anything could have been under it. But I wasn't about to be sniffed out by him.

"Good going, Wayne. Grab him!" Frankie shouted. "Hold him for me. I wanna see this weird kid."

I dove for the nearby hole in the hedge just as Wayne reached out. "Come here, kid," Wayne called after me. "We're not gonna hurt you. We just wanna talk to you."

I squirmed through the tiny opening in the hedges. My baseball cap snagged on something, and I popped out the other side without it. There was no time to look for it, and I took off up the street toward the church playground, feeling totally naked without anything on my head.

Wayne and Frankie were close on my heels, and I ran scared into the dirt playground with the boys calling after me. It was happening again, but at home, and thoughts of running into the street in front of a car crossed my mind.

"Hey, kid, c'mon, stop. We're not gonna hurt you. We just wanna talk. Don't be afraid. We're nice guys. C'mon, let's be friends."

Shame and fright were what motivated my strides that day. I rounded the church corner and headed for the back of our house from the opposite end of the block. The secret of my ugliness was no more, and I felt as though a thousand eyes gawked at me.

The boys were gaining ground, and I could hear their comments. "Look at the scaredy-cat, Wayne. He's got no hair. I told you there was something strange about him. C'mon, let's catch him. I want a closer look."

"Maybe we should let him go, Frankie. It might be catchy."

"No way," Frankie said. "Let's get him."

"Hey, baldy, stop running. What happened to your hair?"

When I reached the back steps to our yard, all I wanted to do was run faster. I tripped up the steps and stumbled into the yard, scrambling toward the front porch and safety. I couldn't get inside fast enough, away from the neighborhood's prying eyes.

I flung the front door open just as Wayne clutched my shirt. Somehow I fought free and made it to the hallway stairs that led up to our apartment. Clambering up two and three steps at a time, I grasped the railing as Wayne grabbed at my feet.

Frankie stood on the bottom landing encouraging Wayne on, while still taunting me. "Come on down, kid. We'll get you sooner or later. We only want to know your name and why you look so funny. What in the hell happened to your hair?"

"I can't help the way I look!" I shouted, banging on the door. "Leave me alone! I wasn't bothering you! You guys don't belong in here! You better leave before my mother comes out!"

Della was a welcomed sight when she opened the door. She looked at me and then over the balcony at the two boys. "What's going on out here? Who are you two boys and what are you doing in this building?"

"We weren't gonna hurt him, lady," Frankie said. "We just wanted to meet the new kid on the block."

"They chased me, Mom!" I stood behind her. "The one with the big nose walked right into the yard."

She glared at the boys and spoke sternly. "You'd better get out of here before I call the police."

"C'mon, lady, we didn't touch him," Frankie said. "Why does he look like that? Does he have a disease?"

Della gritted her teeth and pounded on the railing. "Leave

the building, you two! I'm not going to tell you again. And don't bother my son." She wasn't to be messed with when angered. It was so good to finally see her defend me after all those years.

"Okay, lady, we're going. But you can't protect him all the time. We'll tell everybody. If what he's got is catchy, you'll be in trouble, not us."

Someone with alopecia areata in those days was a rare sight, and not a pretty one. Imagine a practically hairless scalp with random patches of hair, and one eyebrow half gone. Being totally bald as I am now isn't as bad to look at. Besides, nowadays it's in, but it wasn't then.

Frankie pointed at me. "We'll see you outside, baldy," he said. "You can't hide behind your mommy forever."

Some welcome home. And Jim made it even worse. After the Frankie and Wayne incident, I didn't want to go anywhere, which didn't suit him at all. "Get out of the house," he yelled one day. "You're always underfoot. Do something constructive with yourself. Make friends with other kids." He was a menacing figure of a man standing there looking down his nose at me. "Get a newspaper route. Earn your own spending money. Join a baseball team. Get involved in something."

"You don't understand," I said.

"What's there to understand? You're a mama's boy."

"I'm afraid of being made fun of."

"Stand up to them, sissy boy. You're not hanging around this house all summer."

I hated being called a mama's boy or sissy. But it's what probably gave me the guts to do what I had to do. It turned out to be one time in our relationship that Jim was right. I not only got myself a newspaper route, I also met my first new friend.

Johnny Siddons became a good buddy right from the start. He immediately got me a tryout with the baseball team he played on. I don't know where my courage came from to show up at the ball field that Saturday morning, but Sid's being there sure helped. The practice field behind the old high school building was called the "Dust Bowl" in those days. The infield playing surface had no grass anywhere, and when the wind blew you played in clouds of swirling dust. As bad luck would have it that day, the winds were strong and gusting. My biggest concern was keeping my hat from blowing off as I showed my stuff. I had so wanted to be at my best, but the elements made it tougher.

Sid warmed up with me before I took the field. "Hey, kid, grab a bat," Coach Fladd said. "Get in there. Let's see what you got."

I selected a bat, tugged hard on my baseball cap and stepped into the batter's box. The wind picked up, sending a cloud of dust across the infield. Backing out of the batter's box, I rubbed my eyes and pulled down on the cap even harder to make it snug. I was really nervous and took several practice swings.

"C'mon, boy," the coach said. "Get in there. We don't have all day."

I kept fidgeting with my cap but moved up to the plate. The wind blew hard as the first pitch whizzed by. Once more I backed out of the box and readjusted my cap.

"Hey, kid, take your hat off if the wind bothers you," the coach shouted. "I got a whole team waiting here. Now, get in there and swing at the ball."

I contemplated running off the field and not stopping until I got home. But out of sheer determination I stepped back up to the plate. My heart pounded through my shirt, and I dug in for the next pitch. The wind miraculously went still, and for the next several minutes the other kids watched the new boy crack one solid hit after another. I ran out the last line drive and slid into second base. With a sigh of relief and a tremendous sense of accomplishment, I proudly strode back to the bench to retrieve my glove.

"Okay, kid, get over to first base," Coach Fladd said. "Let's see if your glove is as good as your bat."

I tugged on my hat as the wind picked up again, sending clouds of dust swirling around me. Crack ... crack ... crack, one after another the grounders hopped to the right, left and in front of me. I fielded every ball cleanly and made the plays where they were called. The final ball was a high pop-fly over my head, down the right field foul line. As I turned to run it down, a strong gust of wind blew another cloud of dust, along with my cap, toward the infield. Time seemed to stand still as I circled under the ball, knowing full well that my head was exposed for all to see.

I felt like I was watching a replay of myself in slow motion. There were quick freeze-frames of open-mouthed kids staring in wonder at the new boy, who must have gotten a bad haircut. But when the ball finally came down, my glove was there to meet it. Nobody said a word as I jogged toward the infield to retrieve my cap. Sid met me halfway and handed it to me. "Great catch!" he said.

Well, I made the team and for the first time in many years hadn't been called a name or laughed at because of my odd appearance. What a satisfying feeling that was, finally being accepted for who I was, not ignored or mocked because of what I looked like.

The summer flew by and discussions continued about my return to Girard that fall. It was obvious to me that Jim had been the sole reason that I remained away at school. Della was deeply caught up in a struggle between love for her son and keeping peace at home. Then one day Mrs. Hill and Dr. Zarello from the school visited us. They tried hard to convince me, along with Della, that the best decision would be my return to Girard.

Miss Hill spoke first. "As Billy's legal guardian, we must insist that he return to the school come September. There are certain procedures we must adhere to from the school's point of view."

It made me laugh to myself that she was being so formal, because I really didn't care what anybody had to say that day. I knew what I wanted, and one way or the other it would come to pass.

Dr. Zarello seemed quite nervous about the whole thing.

"All of this has been such a travesty. We've shirked our responsibilities over this. But I've personally spoken with the teachers and housemasters your son will have this year. And rest assured things will be a lot different. Besides, the boys are getting older now and..."

"Why didn't you do this before?" I asked.

Jim sat forward in his chair. "Just listen and be quiet," he said, peering over his glasses at me.

"How come we were never told until he ran away about what was going on with the other boys?" my mother asked.

"I've been telling you for years, Mom. You just never listened or cared." I wasn't about to be silent that day, even if it did annoy Jim. It was my life being discussed, and I didn't much care what he said or did to me afterwards.

"We're sorry for his insolence." Jim nodded to Miss Hill and Dr. Zarello. "That's all the more reason why I feel he should go back to the school. His mother and I have a hard time controlling him at home."

"I wouldn't say he's uncontrollable, Jim. He's obviously very unhappy."

I almost applauded her and thought of giving Della three cheers. "I didn't want to cause any trouble or run away. But I don't want to be there anymore. This is the first that anybody's ever listened to me. So I'm telling you, if you make me go back I will go over the wall again, and then I don't know what I'll do."

Jim squirmed in his chair. "What about his hair problem?"

"We're going to send him to specialists this fall," Miss Hill said, "and as his legal guardian we will naturally absorb the costs. It's extremely rare what he has. And because of it I think he also needs to continue the professional counseling we started. He's a very angry young man. Understandably so mind you."

"That's all the more reason, Della, I think he should stay at the school. We can't afford specialists let alone a psychologist."

I felt like screaming at all of them. "I've been losing my hair for six years. How come all of a sudden I'm going to special doctors?"

"That's enough," Jim said in a gruff tone of voice.

"If he isn't happy at Girard, Jim, does any of it matter? I feel bad because I'm the one who put him there."

"Mom, I wish just once I could get you to live it like I've had to. Get my letters and read them to Miss Hill and Dr. Zarello. Show them some of my drawings too."

"Now you're being disrespectful." Jim made a threatening move toward me, which got me up quickly. "Go to your room!"

That's when I made my last desperate plea. "You can send me back, but I won't stay there. If you could only talk to Chet or maybe one of the other boys who would be honest, you'd understand. Please, Mom, don't send me back." I left the room not knowing if what I had said had made any difference. But one thing I did know for sure, and that was that their damn walls would never hold me; they weren't high enough. I so wanted to take her to Girard, just the two of us, and make her realize what it was like.

Not long after the great summit meeting, the words I had waited to hear for seven years were finally spoken. "Billy, you're staying home," Della said. How beautiful it was to hear her say that. I was finally free of all the torment that had made my days a living hell and the lonely nights filled with tears and prayers: no more onslaughts of abuse; no more mocking laughter; no more isolation because the disease was a "plague" to be feared; no more would I have to yearn for someone to hold and comfort me. My dream had finally come true, and once more in our lives Della and Billy would be together again, although Jim added a negative dimension from my perspective.

It didn't take me long to become comfortable with my surroundings and new friends. Aside from Wayne and Frankie, those days were a breath of fresh air. But even their ignorance ceased, after a bunch of older boys took them aside one day. Everything happened so fast that I feared those great moments were but a dream. It was difficult for me to believe that everyone had readily accepted me, because it was so contrary to the life I had lived for seven years. I loved every one of those neighborhood kids; and, even though I don't see them anymore, I always will.

Late August arrived, and soon the carefree days of summer met the disciplined school days of fall. That September would be totally different from all the previous ones I had remembered since I was six years old. Della and I discussed at great length which high school would be best for me to attend. There were two possibilities, and it wasn't an easy decision. The majority of friends I made that summer were public school students who had been together since their grade school days. But on the other hand, a brand new Catholic high school was opening out in the township countryside. What swayed me most about the new school was that many of its students would be starting new friendships also, just like me. Thus, Della notified our parish that I would be attending Notre Dame High School. When I learned that Johnny Siddons was also going there, I knew I had made the right choice.

I spent the final days that summer often in quiet moments of mental preparation for my big school debut. It wasn't easy to face that new beginning in my life. I drove myself nuts with worry. What to wear? Would my new dress hat look right? Should I go out to meet the bus early and talk with the others or wait until the last moment and sneak on board? No, I didn't handle it well, and the closer that day came the worse I was. For a time I even wished I was going back to Girard, where at least they all knew me. It was a mental boxing match with myself, but I was determined to go through with it. I just wanted to be accepted as a normal person, nothing more, nothing less.

ADOLESCENCE:
A TIME TO BUILD DREAMS

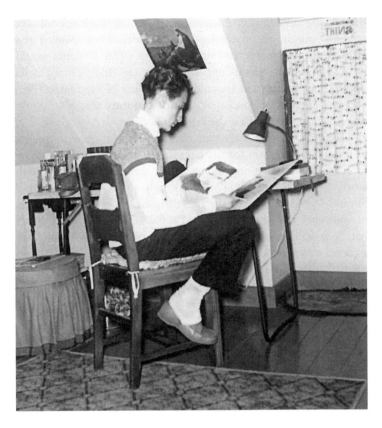

Ever the consummate artist. Today I paint with words in telling our story.

CHAPTER FIFTEEN
A NEW DAY

I prayed for school to be canceled that first day in September of '57. But no such luck. The bus could have picked me up at four o'clock that morning, because I hadn't slept all night. It was a typical start to a day at our house, without pleasantries, goodbye kisses, or any such family nicety. I had hoped that Della would've at least stayed to see me off. "Have a good day, Billy. Do your best," was about the extent of the good wishes. Oh, and Jim said, "Don't take any guff from anybody."

My preparation for the scariest day of my life was nerve wracking. I rehearsed over and over every move, gesture and word and repositioned my hat on my head in front of the mirror a hundred times. My Aunt Dot came from across the hall and was almost as jittery as I was, but her being there meant a lot to me. She made those anxious moments a bit easier to cope with, or I might have run off for parts unknown.

"I don't think I can do this, Aunt Dot." I kept retying my necktie. "Maybe I should go to public school instead. At least I know some of those kids, and they don't wear ties." Whether you want to call it stage fright, having butterflies, dry heaves or the willies, I had it all. I vomited once or twice too.

"You'll be okay," she said and brushed some lint off my jacket. "Johnny Siddons will be with you. He's such a sweet boy. Just the other day he told your mother not to worry about you. Anybody who makes fun of you will have to deal with him, he said. You're lucky to have such a good friend."

Aunt Dot was my favorite and the prettiest of all Della's sisters. She was always made up and dressed nice. Smelled good too. We had become good buddies that long summer at home. Uncle Nick didn't much approve of my being around a lot, and come to think of it, neither did the strange man who occasionally stopped by to see my aunt when my uncle was at work. But that was okay, because as I started to make friends I was never around, especially when Jim was home.

"Would you like me to walk you over to the bus stop?" she asked.

I looked at her smiling face, kissed her on the cheek and put my arms around her. "I have to do this myself. But thanks anyway, Aunt Dot. I love you." I wished my mom had been there. She could've been late for work just that one time.

"I'll watch you from the window, okay?" my aunt said and buttoned the top button of my sport jacket. "You look handsome."

I scurried across the street holding on to my hat. Sid stood there with the other kids, waving me on just as the school bus arrived. I was so nervous that as I turned to acknowledge my aunt up in the window, I stepped on my own foot and fell down in the doorway. So much for inconspicuous beginnings. I said "Good morning" to the bus driver and retreated to the rear of the bus, close behind Sid. The bus lurched forward, dropping us into our seats, and I landed on Sid's lap.

"Nice hat," Sid said, shoving me off him. "But it's on crooked. You look stupid."

I straightened it and looked at my reflection in the window. "How's that?"

He laughed. "Adorable. But don't ever sit on my lap. I like girls...with hair."

Many years later when I went to pay my last respects to Sid, that first day at school came to mind. As I bowed my head over him and looked at the unrecognizable shell of a man that cancer had ravaged, the memories brought us back together once more. His friendship had been most special, and still is in my heart.

Johnny wasn't a lady killer, but he was smooth and always knew the right things to say. Some of the kids called him "The Sid." The first time we met at the newspaper company, I had dropped my stack of newspapers, and they were blowing all over the street, along with my Cleveland Indians baseball cap. When he approached me, he said, "I thought you were some old bald guy." He stared at my head and handed the cap to me.

"What happened, you fall asleep in the barber chair?" When we finished picking up the newspapers, he said, "The hat has gotta go." The next time I saw him, he handed me a Yankees' hat. When I told him I was from Philadelphia, he replied, "That's a shame, but everybody has to be from somewhere."

Notre Dame High School was way out in the country between the towns of Easton and Bethlehem, Pennsylvania. The bus ride seemed to go on forever, but we finally arrived with what appeared to be a million other kids who were all waiting for the doors to open. Sid and I milled around checking out the new school, which nestled on a tract of farmland next to a golf course and a pasture full of cows.

A loud bang broke the morning calm as the large metal doors to the gymnasium swung open. Everyone's eyes instantly focused on the top of the steps. There stood the grandest Franciscan friar in the land, with his hands on his hips, sleeves rolled up and feet wide apart.

"All right, my precious ones," he said in a thunderous voice, "may I have your undivided attention! Welcome to Notre Dame High School." He paused for a moment then bellowed, "I am Father Matthew. It's good to see all of your smiling faces on such a fine morning. Are we all happy to be back at school?" The good friar didn't wait for a reply. "Good, my children! Now, listen closely. This brand new facility for learning is Our Lady's school, and at all times you will respect her presence in it. The moment you enter these doors you will act as ladies and gentlemen. Do we understand one another?" With a friendly smile, he concluded, "Now, if you would all be so kind as to oblige me. I want two lines formed going into the gym, girls on the right and boys on the left. You ladies will sit where the good sisters are, and you gentlemen will sit where my fellow priests are. And, if you please, let's do this in an orderly manner and in silence. The boss, our good Father Thompson, has a headache this morning. We wouldn't want to upset him, now would we?"

The moment that I feared most was at hand. My instincts

told me to run. I wanted to in the worst way, but Sid stuck close by my side. As we approached the doors, I stopped and reluctantly removed my hat, but he gave me a gentle nudge. I was sure everyone was staring at me by the time we reached our seats. A baldheaded boy must have been a strange sight. But Sid patted my knee, and I nervously looked straight ahead.

Father Matthew started the school's first assembly with a prayer and the introduction of Notre Dame's faculty. They consisted of Franciscan friars, St. Joseph and Immaculate Heart sisters, plus a select group of laity. It was a somewhat comforting feeling to be there, especially among the good sisters. They reminded me of my days long ago with Sister Francis at St. Anthony's.

"Ladies and gentlemen," Father Matthew said loudly. "I give you Father Thompson, *your* principal ... and my boss."

A great man of grace and wisdom stood before us. His presence was awe-inspiring as he held students and faculty alike riveted to his every word that morning. I personally felt as though his message of new beginnings, new relationships and a time for new dreams was directed at me. Father Thompson's commanding but soft-spoken manner served him well that morning as he walked among us. His occasional glance my way was reassuring, and I felt special, as though he'd be watching over me. I sat there tentatively, worrying about what lay ahead as my hands perspired and my head filled with doubts. There were moments I wanted to get up and run, but that's when Father would look at me. *How did he know?* I wondered. We'd have our differences in time, but that day began a lifelong friendship between us. He eventually became the Bishop of South Carolina, and we still correspond with one another.

"I like him," I whispered to Sid.

"He seems a little scary to me. I'm not getting on his bad side. Did you hear what he said about haircuts?" Sid winked at me. "But you're okay. Yours is short enough."

I rolled my eyes at him. "No, I missed that part."

"Do you think he'll make me cut this off?" he asked, pulling on the little lock of hair dangling down his forehead.

"Girls like this. It's cool."

Father Thompson stopped at the end of our aisle, looked at us, nodded and moved on. I followed him with my eyes, and a warm feeling came over me for being in his school. There was a special charisma about the man. The fact he had quietly acknowledged my presence lifted my spirits, enabling me to continue on with the day. It was as if his heart had touched mine and calmed all my doubts and fears.

Sid and I were assigned to the same homeroom, another small miracle. It was hard for me to imagine getting through that day without him at my side. But just the same my old Girard instincts kept me on guard for something to go wrong at any moment. Where were the insults, I wondered, the laughter, threats, name calling, the pointing and mocking whispers? I touched my head several times to make sure that hair hadn't grown since I entered the school. Perhaps Our Lady had performed yet another miracle.

"Please take a seat, people," Mr. DeBellis said as he entered the room, "Boys in front and girls in back."

Mr. D, a former state wrestling champ, was a small but impressive man with the patience of a saint. He waited for everyone to get settled, then walked up and down the aisles introducing himself.

We all took to him immediately. His personal handshake, pat on the shoulder and friendly smile did it for me. "I like to get to know my students one on one, right off the bat," he said. "The quicker we all get over the first-day jitters, the sooner we can commence with the learning process, mine and yours. Isn't that right, Mr. ..." He looked directly at me.

"Lonardo," I said in a weak voice.

"What school are you from?" he asked.

"Girard, sir."

"The boys' school in Philadelphia?"

"Yes, sir." I was hoping he'd move on to someone else.

"Excellent school, most of us teachers are familiar with it. A friend of mine taught there once. Tough academics, one of the finest pre-college institutions in the country." He glanced around the classroom. "Quite a few of their young men go on to West Point or the Naval Academy. So it appears we have a celebrity student in our midst, from a quality school. Strict discipline there, and excellent athletics too. Welcome to Notre Dame, Mr. Lonardo. We're honored to have you, uh, your first name is ...?"

"William, sir."

"Thank you, William. I'm sure you'll do well here."

I felt kind of special the rest of that period. Nevertheless, I wondered for the longest time after that whether Mr. D had set me up that day. I guess it didn't much matter, because it helped make me a curiosity in a different sort of way. Except for one question about my hair from the boy in the front of me it was never brought up again. That still amazes me. A bald teenager had to be a strange sight to behold in those days, especially one with only a small patch of hair in the back, like an Indian's scalplock. Aside from Sid and Ray Ferry, another neighborhood friend I made early on, plus the boy who inquired about my alopecia areata, I was off to a new beginning in my life that showed great promise.

The bell rang, and Mr. D dismissed us. One by one we filed past him out the door, and as I went by he smiled. We proceeded from class to class, meeting teachers, other students, maintenance workers, cooks and office personnel. Not once was there an awkward glance at me, a curious stare or even a "what happened to you?" That entire day baffled me. I was prepared for the worst at any moment. It was all so pleasantly new, and I welcomed it, placing every minute into my personal "Hall of Fame of Golden Moments."

"Well, William, how was your first day?" Father Matthew asked, putting his arm on my shoulder as he walked alongside me to the school bus. He gave me a reassuring look. "It's going to be fine, just fine." What a dynamic priest he was. He could've been a Marine drill instructor just like Girard's Coach Boggs, but there was one big difference between them. Father Matthew had a way of letting you know he could be a friend too.

"Thank you, Father. I enjoyed the day." I felt so relieved,

and I didn't even have to climb a wall to win the day. "Everybody was nice to me."

The bus ride home was full of conversation as everyone shared their new exploits. The girls talked about the cute guys and the other girls, while the boys discussed the sharp-looking girls and some upper classman's hot set of wheels. The pros and cons of every Notre Dame faculty member were bantered back and forth. For the first time I felt a part of my own generation, and it made being alive finally have a purpose.

Those bus rides cultivated many new in-town friendships. Ray Ferry, with his neatly combed Vitalis D.A., was the original Fonzie. MaryAnn Bender, my first teenage crush (aside from Nurse Flood); Stevie Shive, star basketball player; Mike Betts, the guy who comically knew a lot about nothing important; and of course "The Sid", the best. There were many others who made those first days a far cry easier than I had ever imagined. What a contrast to where I had come from. It was hard for me to believe at first, but teenagers could be nice.

I talked to Della for hours that night. She smiled and listened intently to one story after another, and some three times. It must have been satisfying to hear her son express so much joy after so many years of sadness. I lay awake well into the night, reliving and savoring every precious moment of that day. It was a dream come true. "Thank you, Blessed Mother," I said. "Is there more?"

CHAPTER SIXTEEN
A DIFFERENT KIND OF WALL

For the very first time in my young life, I looked forward to school as well as making new friends. It was a great feeling just being an average teenager.

But it didn't take my stepfather long to upset things. His dislike of having me around was obvious. When the newness of my presence wore off, everything became old real fast for Jim. His dark, brooding personality soon gave way to anger and what would be the beginning of a new hell and other walls.

I sat stirring my tea after dinner one evening, talking with Della. They were the quality moments I had dreamt of for years. My mother and I were trying so hard to reconnect after all that had happened. It wasn't easy for us, because I had repressed so much hatred inside.

"How many times must you stir that damn tea?" Jim grumbled from the next room. His voice always sent chills up and down my back when something bothered him.

"What did he say, Mom?" I looked at Della. He watched me like a hawk, and it was becoming difficult not to annoy him.

Jim raised his voice louder. "You heard me the first time, boy. Stop stirring and drink it!"

Della shrugged her shoulders. "He's not bothering me. We're just talking."

Jim threw the newspaper down and stomped into the kitchen. He was a huge man, and his ugly moods made him appear even larger. Towering over the table, he removed his glasses and glared at me. "You sit there every damn night after supper doing that, and it annoys the hell out of me. Stop holding up your mother from doing the dishes. If you're done eating, go to your room...Move, boy, Now! She's had a long day." He took a couple of giant steps in my direction, which propelled me fearfully over the back of the chair.

I shoved the chair in his path. "Mom, I didn't do anything," I said and made for the stairs up to my room.

Jim followed close behind me, with Della on his heels screaming, "Leave him alone, Jim…please, he's been through enough." She somehow got in front of him on the steps and blocked his attempt to grab me. "Don't you touch him! Can't you see how afraid of you he is? We didn't bring him home for this."

I retreated behind my bed as Jim muscled his way forward. "He makes me nervous. I can't stand his damn stupid habits, the little sissy."

He pushed and shoved but Della kept in front of him shouting, "He's no sissy."

"He's always down in that yard or around the house. Why doesn't he go out with the other boys in the neighborhood? He plays baseball and goes to school."

"Everything is still new to him. He needs time." She clung onto his arm, but he tossed her aside and broke free. Just when I thought I was trapped, Della put an open field tackle on him. A football coach would have been proud of her, as she hit him low, and like a towering oak he toppled sideways. They sailed into a bookshelf with a jarring crash, scattering books, records and teenage junk everywhere.

The room went silent in anticipation of further bedlam. I even thought of going out the window. But surprisingly Jim collected his Irish pride, got up, glanced at me and helped Della to her feet. "You're a tough woman," he said with a grin and then stared in my direction. "And you, young man, are a mighty lucky boy. Damn lucky, sissy boy."

Goliath turned and quietly went back downstairs. "Billy, I'm sorry this happened," Della said. "He didn't mean it. Give him time. He's not used to having kids around."

"No wonder he's divorced, Mom," I said. "His poor daughter."

What on earth had I come home to, a madman? Jim had scared the hell out of me, which further added to my mistrust of him. I was a kid. What had I done? What was this man's problem? I came out from behind the bed and picked up one of my plastic hotrod models. It was smashed and so was my dream of a happy family.

There were times when Jim really tried to establish a father-son relationship, but often his attempts were awkward and came at the most unexpected moments. Two o'clock one Sunday morning he showed up drunk and wanted company. Weekends he usually exercised his rights to Irish Independence, and he'd stumble home with a snoot full of beer. I was in bed but clearly heard Jim banging around in the kitchen. He was quite the chef when sober, but his culinary genius couldn't have helped him that night. Between the clanging pots, cursing, thumping into chairs and comical overtures for Della to join him, it was funny, but also very sad, for all of us.

Della repeatedly refused to join him. She was never amused when Jim was in a drunken state. He turned his attention upstairs and called out to me, "Billy, are you awake? C'mon down for lobster. Pssst, they're the big ones. C'mon down, buddy."

His pitiful pleading finally got to me and in order to keep peace, I went downstairs. He was a sight for my sleepy eyes, swaying around the kitchen with his shirttail out and lobster bib on. "Your mother doesn't know what the hell she's missing. These are great lobsters...they're from Maine," Jim said as he haphazardly prepared the feast.

There's nothing quite like half-cooked lobster, frozen butter and stale crackers early in the morning with a drunk. The lobster party was a rare but comparatively pleasant moment with my stepfather. I spent all the years we lived together trying to please him. It was no different in some ways than being at Girard, except Jim was a hateful kid in a man's body.

Jim's excessive drinking served as stimuli for many violent outbursts in the house. Some weekends got so bad that Della and I would walk the streets late at night looking for someone's house to sleep at. God forbid one of the family should put us up without a fuss. One Saturday night upon returning home, we entered the downstairs hallway and found it strewn with all sorts of debris. In a fit of drunken rage, Jim had dumped what appeared to be the entire apartment out over the landing;

whatever fit through the door. Chairs, lamps, end tables, knickknacks, pillows, pictures, magazines and linen lay everywhere. The stairs were impassible, and we could still hear him rummaging through the apartment, cursing and slamming things. That was the first of many times Della decided it was no longer safe to be near Jim, especially when he was drunk. The next morning she called the house, and Dr. Jekyll answered the phone. It was like dealing with two different people. He'd apologize, promise never to do it again, and everything would be fine, until the next time. We'd return on Sundays, and it was like nothing had ever happened the night before. Jim would be on his very best behavior, which made him all the more unpredictable to live with. Della's patience lasted longer than most. But eventually their arguments grew more frightening, and I found myself the object of most of their confrontations.

803 Walnut Street felt like a personal purgatory of punishment for my interfering with Della and Jim's marriage. They had always appeared happy together before I moved home, so why couldn't it be the same with me there, I asked myself over and over. I didn't understand. They should be happy times. I had earned the right to a good home life like everyone else seemed to have. My questions, doubts and confusion persisted, but without any solutions. I tried so hard to be good and satisfy Jim's every whim. He wasn't a stupid man, so I encouraged conversations about all sorts of topics. But my efforts would only appease him for a while, and sooner or later there'd be an uprising over something. It got worse as time went on, and I stayed away from him as much as possible, which meant hanging out in my room or finding places to go weeknights and weekends. I'd often roam the streets alone until I knew he was asleep.

Our lives became a constant tug of war among the three of us. It was supposed to be my time again with my mother, and no one should interfere, I thought, not even her husband. At least that's the way I saw it then, but it wasn't happening. The wall Jim and I were putting between us grew higher, leaving Della to bridge either side on a tightrope.

That summer after my freshman year when Jim took

vacation, it really got bad. He harassed me if I slept too late or hung around the house longer than he could stand. "Get out of bed. Don't you have anything better to do?" he'd yell up the stairs. Or, "You still in the house? Where the hell are all your new buddies?" If I stayed home, either my music was too loud or I spent too much time in front of the television. "Read a book, maybe you'll learn something," Jim would bark. "Get a hobby, like stamp collecting." No matter what I did, it never was good enough. I knew he didn't want me around, and my hatred for him became explosive and directed at Della. Finally I decided to take matters into my own hands as I had done once before to get attention.

After baseball season ended that summer, I thought it would be best for me to spend some time in Trenton, New Jersey, with my Uncle Frank's family. I approached Della with the idea one day while we were home alone, because it gave me the opportunity to express my honest feelings about Jim. She was a woman obviously caught between two loves, but I didn't see it that way, nor did I care to. "Mom, I have to get away. Let me go to Uncle Frank's." My comments took her by surprise. "Jim doesn't want me here. Why did you marry him anyway? He hates kids."

"It was his idea to let you stay home all last summer," she responded. "Besides, we didn't take you out of Girard for you to live somewhere else."

"First of all, you guys had no choice, and secondly, I don't call this living. Girard was even better than this. At least I didn't have to live with a drunk."

It seemed logical to me that being away from our dysfunctional family for a while would be good for all of us. What she had said made no sense. I paced from room to room, my words becoming more heated. By the age of fifteen, I had an uncontrollable temper that would send me into a world of devils and violent hysteria. I was like a runaway freight train heading downhill when that happened. It always took running into something for me to be stopped. Once, in a fit of rage, I literally threw myself down two flights of stairs. My anger displayed pure lunacy at times, ending in bodily harm to myself or destruction to things. I wanted to be heard at anyone's expense, including my own. And if no one listened, I'd get their attention somehow.

Della remained firm in her conviction and I in mine. In a blind rage, I ripped the door to the upstairs off its hinges and retreated to my attic sanctuary. The only solution, as I saw it, was to frighten her. I firmly believed she'd understand my desperation if I caused a scene. I wanted to be free of Jim and that's all there was to it.

I came back downstairs with my prized Bowie knife strapped to my side. Della was sitting in the bedroom by the window, and I slowly approached her. "Mom, you better listen. It doesn't matter what you say. I'm not spending the rest of the summer here. Do you understand me? I want to be with my dad's family."

She kept looking out the window. "I've told you no, Billy, and that's final. You'll have to learn to get along with Jim. Give him a chance."

I drew the knife from its sheath, clenched the handle and repeated once more, "Mom, you're wrong. I am going to Uncle Frank's. And you can't stop me."

She turned toward me and caught site of the knife at my side. "Okay, tough guy, what's the knife for? Don't you dare threaten me. Scaring me won't change my mind. Now, put it away before you hurt yourself."

I had never threatened her with bodily harm before, but that day there was no remorse in my actions. It was as if all the years of anger and frustration had caught up with me. I reached down, grabbed Della's arm with one hand and pointed the knife at her throat with the other. "Mom, you just don't get it, do you?" I yelled in her face. "I am going!" I plunged the knife into the arm of the chair and stood over her. "If you force me to stay here the rest of summer, somebody will get hurt. And it doesn't matter to me who it is. I won't put up with Jim anymore. I'm a teenager, dammit, and I want to live like one. Your husband is nuts. If you love him more than me, you live with him."

Della pulled her arm free. "You're the one that's crazy! Look at you. You want to stab your own mother!" She jumped out of the chair, shoved me aside and ran into the living room, where she flung open the door. "He's crazy!" she yelled. "My son is going to kill me!" I could hear her cries through the walls as she pounded on my aunt's door. "Dorothy, let me in. Billy's lost his mind. He has a knife. Help me...He's crazy! Call the police!"

Fear, anger and hurt played emotional tag with me and I released every bit of it as I retreated up to my room. Hurling things in all directions, I screamed, "The hell with this damn house!" At Girard I didn't expect them to care about me. But this was supposed to be my home, and it had no love there either. "I hate you, Mom, and the asshole you married! He's not a father. He's sick. The son-of-a-bitch shouldn't be allowed near people. I hate all of you! I hate my life and I don't want to live anymore."

I held the knife at my throat and stood in the center of a totally destroyed room searching for the courage to die. The thought of death and the peace it could bring tantalized me. As I wavered between reality and insanity, a familiar voice called out to me. It may have saved me.

"Billy, it's Coach Charlie. Come on down. Let's talk."

I stared at myself in the mirror momentarily then dropped to my knees, grasping for the good things about life to cling to. Coach Charlie called out up the stairs again. "Billy, it's okay. Nobody is going to hurt you. C'mon, we just want to talk."

I hid the knife under my mattress and went downstairs. Waiting for me in the kitchen was the city's juvenile officer and a policeman, Charlie Mesa. Coach Mesa was also one of our baseball league's greatest friends. He was the kind of man who couldn't do enough for kids. He put his arm around me and motioned for me to sit down while introducing Mr. Bartin, the juvenile officer. "Well, sport, what happened here between you and your mother?" Mr. Mesa asked.

"First things first, Charlie." Mr. Bartin stepped forward.

"Tell me, young man, where's the knife?"

I was scared, but I told them, and Officer Mesa went to get it. "Well, son, I'm all ears," Mr. Bartin said. "Let's hear your story. Why did you threaten your mother? What was so terrible that made you pull a knife on her? Didn't you get your own way, or maybe you just wanted to show her how tough you are. C'mon, speak up. What's the matter...not so tough now are we?"

I didn't like Mr. Bartin at all. Neither did most of the kids. He was arrogant and pushy. *Big deal cop*, I thought. *He doesn't know me.* By the time Officer Mesa returned with the knife, the only words I managed to say were, "Sir, you just don't understand. I wasn't going to hurt her." The next thing I knew, Mr. Bartin ordered Officer Mesa to cuff me, and they led me out of the apartment.

My mother and aunt were waiting out in the hallway. "Where are you taking him?" Della asked. "Why is he handcuffed? Is that necessary?"

"It's standard procedure, ma'am," Mr. Bartin said. "Your son's crime is attempted assault with a deadly weapon, and cuffs are required by law. He'll be taken down to the police station and questioned before he's booked. I'm afraid he should have thought before he acted. This is a weapons charge...a felony."

Della cried hysterically down the stairs and onto the porch. "No! He's not a bad boy. What have I done? I didn't mean for this to happen. They're treating him like a common criminal. Dorothy, stop them. He wouldn't hurt me or anybody." Every word she said echoed in my heart, and I still shudder to think of the anger that made me capable of such violence.

All the curious neighbors stood by in whispering disbelief as the police took me away. Sam the shoemaker scratched his head in complete bewilderment, and I felt frightened and ashamed as he mouthed the words, "What happened?"

They booked me for 'attempted assault with a deadly weapon'. It wasn't exactly the attention I'd hoped for. The entire experience seemed like a bad dream. I had only wanted to frighten Della into letting me go away. I guess I thought that doing bad things always worked, because it had gotten me out of Girard.

Another police officer came into the interrogation room. "Billy, is Vince Roman related to you?" he asked.

Detective Lieutenant Roman was my cousin. He was an ex-marine, good-looking, very popular in town and my mother's favorite nephew. Vince was out on assignment and had requested that no formal charges be filed until he returned.

"Okay, Billy, we're taking you next door," Mr. Bartin said. "You're in serious trouble."

The adjoining building was the detention center for juvenile delinquents. I was locked up in a very drab room with bars on the door and one tiny window. The next few frightening hours I spent alone with my thoughts. What had I done? What was going to happen to me? Would I be sent away to a reform school or another boys' home? No! I screamed inside. My dramatic approach to problem solving had obviously failed. I had carried it too far this time. But just when I figured they must have thrown away the key, the cell door opened and in walked Cousin Vince. Was I ever glad to see him!

"What happened, Billy?" he asked.

I hugged him and in a tear-choked voice said, "I'm sorry. I wasn't going to hurt Mom. I just wanted to get away from Jim."

For the next hour I spilled my guts and told Vince everything that went on in our house. It didn't matter to me anymore if Jim would be angry. Vince listened intently, then talked about the proper ways of solving problems. "I'm afraid this is a lesson you had to learn the hard way," he said. "Never take on a problem in anger. Most times you'll be sorry for your actions and wind up with the wrong result anyway. Then you'll wonder why the problem explodes out of proportion and people get hurt. Calming down first will help you to better deal with anything. Too much is often said or done in anger, and that only creates trouble that could be avoided. We see it all the time."

Boy, was he ever right. Not only had my anger frightened Della, but I also faced criminal charges, which meant possible jail time. I had committed a felony against my own mother.

Assault with a deadly weapon and intent is what they called it.

Vince hugged me and said, "Well, cousin, let's see what we can do about this mess you've got yourself into."

It was early evening when we returned to the police station. I felt a little more at ease by that time with Vince at my side. We sat down in Mr. Bartin's office, and Della and Jim were brought in. I started to cry the second I saw them, out of fear as well as shame. Jim surprisingly had some compassion and shook my hand, but I knew it was all show. He always pretended to be nice around others. Both of them hardly said a word, and the decision was made to release me into my parents' custody, with Vince serving as probation officer for one year.

Life at home remained somewhat normal for a while, and Jim tried to do things right. Occasionally he'd even take me on his Saturday outings to several clubs and introduce me to his drinking buddies. He'd brag about me, saying that someday I'd play in the major leagues. That particular observation of his always amused me, because Jim never came to one single ballgame. As for my mother, she only saw me play once. Nevertheless, those comments made me feel somewhat special, which at the time was far more important to me. I'd do almost anything to get a little praise or feel accepted back then. There hadn't been much of that in my life to that point, especially from my mother. I guess she just didn't know how to say those things … not even "I love you."

Jim's years with Della and me were eventually cut short by his sudden illness, but not before he returned to his old ways. The battles were worse than before, and out of sheer desperation Della finally threw him out, only to take him back time and time again. Jim eventually suffered a mild stroke one night and was taken to the hospital. That would be just the beginning of his slow demise.

In the months ahead, several disabling strokes rendered him a vegetable. He had arteriosclerosis very bad. Little by little his body began to fail him. First part of his speech went, then all of it, and before the end, paralysis. For three months, Della watched her hulk of an Irishman slowly fade away to a mere trace of what he once had been. The last time I saw Jim was at Temple University Hospital, and I didn't recognize him. Those were tough days for my mother, as she helplessly stood by and watched her man die piece by piece. As usual, there was no support from our family, except from my cousin Vince, and her vigil at Jim's side was a lonely one. Jim Mahony's life ironically ended somewhat in the same fashion he had lived it, alone. Even throughout his illness and then his death, we never met his daughter. How tragic, it struck me, that families can be so heartless to one another. I see it more and more every day now and wonder, how can we expect there to be peace in the world when even families can't get along?

CHAPTER SEVENTEEN
SOUND BODY, TEENAGE MIND

The "Fabulous '50s" were by far the most fun-filled and exciting years of my youth, outside the house that is. My hair began to slowly grow back in, my heart soared, and the music of the times echoed the heartbeat of a new generation and a rebirth of life for me.

It was a great time to be a teenager and I was thankful to be a part of it outside Girard's walls. The U.S.A. was experiencing a post-war renaissance, a growing nuclear attitude, but a wholesome peace about itself. Our generation established a separate identity from grownups through rock 'n roll, fashions and cars. "Greasers" they called us. The D.A. (duck's ass), crew cut, beehive and ponytail were the hairstyles. We wore black leather jackets, chino pants, poodle skirts, white bucks, bobby socks and saddle shoes. There were souped-up muscle cars with fender skirts, continental kits, wide whitewalls and glass-pac mufflers that made them sound tough. Those were the days of standing on the street corner with the guys naming cars as they passed by or harmonizing to a current rock 'n roll song. It had been a readjustment period for me, but in time my past adolescent fears, doubts and pressures slowly faded. All through those fantastic years, not once was I ever called a name, abused or made the object of a practical joke.

Record hops, drive-in movies, football games, girls, drag races, running the strip, cornfield clearing parties, soda fountains, teenage mischief, playing baseball, school, sweetshops, my art, going steady and good ole Rock 'n Roll were a teenage smorgasbord for me, especially going to class with girls. I was falling in love almost every day, but always from a distance. Not having all my hair still was an uncomfortable barrier to deal with. I wanted to be normal looking.

The first school dance was an event that Ray Ferry and I prepared for literally weeks in advance. Neither of us were accomplished hoofers. Coming out of a boys' school, I didn't know any steps, and Ray wasn't much better. For about a week we watched *American Bandstand* and tried to commit to memory the kids' different moves. Then one evening we decided to go into Ray's basement for rehearsals. With an old 45 record player, some records, a transistor radio and a flashlight, we set out to become self-taught jitterbug stars. We danced with each other late into the night, even the slow numbers.

We were ready for action by the time of the record hop and spent most of that day deciding what to wear and practicing our moves in front of the mirror. I was nervous for the same reasons as Ray and the other guys—girls!—but even more so because there wasn't yet much hair on my head, at least not enough to comb and make me look cool.

We strutted into the gymnasium like two cocky studs. Our first school dance was run by the faculty and supervised by the good sisters. Needless to say this put a definite damper on our plans for female conquests. In each corner of the gym stood a nun, while Mother Superior patrolled the floor. If that wasn't enough vigilance, occasionally one of the priests looked in. No boy/girl mingling was permitted. The girls were on one side of the gym and boys on the other. The music began and the dancing was fast and furious, girl dancing with girl. During a slow song, only a few couples going steady went out on the floor. The rest of us hung out in groups, staring across the dance floor at each other. No one had the guts to make the first move.

In the midst of our rapidly deteriorating social event, Notre Dame's resident cheerleader made an appearance. "Awright, gentlemen, what's the problem? The ladies are waiting," Father Matthew barked. "All week you gawk at them. Now's your chance." He paced up and down our male ranks like a football coach on the sidelines, urging us into the fray.

My inhibitions finally broke down that night, and I found the courage to venture across the gym. The song was Tequila by the Champs, and the girl was Karen. She was the prettiest girl I had ever seen. My heart pumping and shoe cleats clicking on the floor, I nervously danced my very first jitterbug. Karen was a doll, and I asked her to dance many more times, but always in fear of being told "no." It was a definite downer to the male ego to be rejected. Nothing was worse than being refused in front of your buddies at a dance.

Karen and I eventually became regular partners at many record hops and, in time, steadies. She was my first true love, which made her even more special. Everything was perfect about her, and she accepted me for who I was, not what I looked like. I never thought it was possible for a girl to like me the way I looked. How beautiful she was, with her long brown wavy hair, olive complexion and big eyes. We were inseparable for a year or more, and her parents and brothers were the kind of family I always dreamt about being a part of. Their happy household filled a tremendous yearning for love inside me, and my friends became less important, as did Della.

Karen was my whole world during that time, and I wasn't about to let anyone or anything change that. For the first time since my father's death, it felt so good to be loved. The affection and caring consumed me totally in such a way that nothing else mattered. I had fallen helplessly and selfishly in love with being loved, but in the dark recesses of my thoughts lurked a resentment toward women and a new fear. Those times weren't as sexually promiscuous as today, but when our romantic moments reached passion, I found myself repulsed by the possibility of lovemaking and withdrew behind yet another kind of wall that I didn't understand. My reaction was so defensive, and I looked upon her as cheap. I so wanted to experience that kind of intimacy but couldn't. An unbearable pain in my groin would also accompany these desires, which at times would double me up, forcing the moment to end. The frustration of it all turned to anger, and my anger to periods of indifference and coldness toward her. That was the beginning of doubting my manhood, which brought on years of self-pleasure and fantasies about women. I'd allow them close, but never too close for them to satisfy their own love for me. My friends' boasting of female conquests would disgust me, yet I pretended to be the man I wasn't around them. My impotence would continue on well into my thirties. But as a teenager, being a virgin wasn't the worst thing, and I felt safe.

Karen and I were walking in the park near her house one day when my world fell apart. We hadn't been getting along like before. The arguments between us were more frequent, and my brooding and temper tantrums only made matters worse. She was on edge. I realized something was wrong but couldn't stop myself from smothering her or being a childish fool, especially if she was inattentive to me.

"Billy, we have to talk." She stopped under a tree but looked the other way. "I'm sorry, I don't want to hurt you. But it's just not the same between us."

I pretended not to hear her. "Is your dad bringing you to my baseball game tomorrow?" I asked. "You haven't been coming lately. How come?"

"I can't do this anymore," she said.

"You mean not come to my games?"

"I mean going steady."

My body tensed. "You're kidding, right?" I grabbed hold of her arm tightly, forcing her to turn around. "Look at me. You don't mean that."

"I'm afraid I do, Billy. I'm sorry."

"But why? You can't. What did I do?" That was a bigtime hurt I felt in my heart. I shook and my knees grew weak. I wasn't prepared for that kind of rejection. The thought of her abandoning me seemed impossible. We were a couple madly in love.

"It's best we break up," she said. "I can't handle your moods anymore. You don't even let me breathe."

I tightened my grasp and took hold of her other arm. "Look at me and say that." I shook her. "I'll change. I love you."

"I'm transferring to another school in the fall," she said, staring at me as tears filled her eyes, while disappointment filled my heart.

This couldn't be happening, not to me. I had spent too many years in an unloving hell, and now that I found what I believed was eternal happiness, it was over? It wasn't fair. I didn't deserve this. I looked at Karen in desperation. "Can I have another chance?" I asked. "I'll do whatever you want."

"It's too late, Billy." She pulled away. "I can't be the way you want me to be. I have no life. You're always around. And your jealous tantrums are just too much. You have to grow up. You're too childish. You even scare me sometimes."

I followed close behind her like a wounded puppy. "But I love you, Karen. Please don't do this to me." That old feeling of abandonment overwhelmed me. My life wouldn't be the same without her. She had given me what I lacked in my own home and I couldn't understand how she could be that cold. We had been close for so long. I kicked a trash can out into the street and ran up to her. "Stop! I can change. You'll see."

"It's over." She turned part way around. "Accept it, Billy. We can be friends, but I don't want to go with you anymore."

I clearly remember falling to my knees and taking hold of her hand. "Please don't leave me, Karen. What am I gonna do without you? I need you. I'll kill myself. You and your family are the only ones who ever loved me." I had been a total jerk that day and even writing about it now reminds me of how self-centered I was then.

"Stand up," she said, helping me to my feet. "See how childish you are? It's not the end of the world. You'll meet another girl. But you have to grow up. Go on home and spend some time with your friends...and your mother. We can't be your family. You have your own."

It was lonely without Karen for a long time after that. She never did return to Notre Dame in the fall, and that's when I really took notice of the bitterness toward women that was festering inside me. My most important loves, Della and Karen, had deserted me when I needed them most.

The months passed and our little school dance went through a big transformation. *Notre Dame Bandstand* became the biggest record hop in the northeast. The school's fame attracted teenagers from New Jersey and even *American Bandstand's* dancers from Philly. The weekend dance soon became the big social event. If you weren't at Notre Dame on a Saturday night, you were nowhere, man!

The "Bandstand" brought the top teen idols. Throughout the late '50s, many stars performed on the school stage. It was just one more fabulous highlight of my high school days. Notre Dame's arrangement with a local radio station included the hiring of a few students to assist backstage. I was one of the lucky ones, and my duties were to see to the comfort of guests and operate the curtains. In the late '50s, record companies paid for promotional appearances, which made it possible to attract the big names. What great times we had! I served pizza and coke to Paul Anka, played poker with Jan and Dean, talked about the old Philly neighborhoods with Fabian and Bobby Rydell, presented to Duane Eddy and Frankie Avalon charcoal portraits I had drawn, joined in the backstage harmonizing with Dion and the Belmonts, talked about Italian food with Annette Funicello, listened to jokes by the Coasters, and even got a personal twist lesson from Chubby Checker! Some dance crazes even got their baptism at our school. The area teenagers were introduced not only to the latest music and dance steps, but to clothing styles, the current teenage gossip and jargon too: crazy, cool, groovy! Although Girard had become a distant bad memory by then, I often thought about what I might have missed, yet there was still an emptiness inside me. I immersed myself in living life as fully as I could outside our home. There wasn't anything I wouldn't do to get people to like me. It seemed as though I had to be a part of everything and everyone. Being alone was intolerable.

We had gathering places where kids could be themselves in their own world. If it wasn't *Notre Dame Bandstand*, there was the Ritz, Stewart's Rootbeer Stand, the V-7 Drive-in, the Dolly Madison Sweetshop and William's Cup. We would even go across the river into New Jersey and hang out at Joe's Steak Shop or the Key City Diner (last of the area's Silver Diners). There was always a place to be ourselves. I loved standing on street corners shooting the breeze with the guys, or playing pinball at the Dolly Madison, then hitching rides to William's Cup. Everywhere we went there were always other teenagers hanging out, and the police didn't chase us. The '50s and early '60s were far different from today. Drugs weren't a concern in our small town, and street violence didn't exist. Innocent times they were.

The neighborhood people sat on their porches or even on sidewalks in the summertime, talking back and forth. In the evenings when everyone would be outside, you could walk down the street and pause for a conversation at practically any house along the way. The teenagers in my five block area were very tight. There were about eight who hung out together, and I became one of them. They helped me forget Karen and deal with what I didn't have at home. The Easton High bunch were the kids that I got in most mischief with. Thank God they weren't delinquents, because I probably would've followed them to jail.

We never were bored or lacked something to do. There were the cutthroat pinochle games at Jack's, tackle football on the courthouse lawn, fast pitch with a tennis ball in St. Anthony's school yard or animal-rules basketball in the neighborhood youth center.

Our escapades were legendary around the neighborhood, but we weren't destructive teenagers, just mischievous ones. My scrapbook of memorable highlights featured weekend party crashing at college fraternities, ghost hunts at the haunted house on Library Hill, sneaking into drive-in movies with guys crammed into car trunks, late night swimming parties, drag racing on the main street of town, boxing matches in a neighborhood garage, throwing cats off of Firestone Tire's roof (one floor) or night block chase. I never knew that life could be that much fun.

It was a good feeling to run with the guys for different reasons than what I always ran from at Girard. It was all just in the doing of nutty things and sometimes being chased by the police or other grownups for doing them. I wasn't about to miss any of it, although at times my stepfather saw to it that I did.

As a 5-foot, 9-inch lefty first baseman with speed to burn and a quick bat, I really felt a part of something good and couldn't get enough of it. At Notre Dame, it took me until the end of my junior year to break into the starting lineup, and as a Legion ballplayer it meant more friendships as well as new experiences.

One summer during the Legion Season, our all-star team made it to the state finals. We were good and I had my best season ever. The team swept through the districts and the regionals. The state championships were held in Uniontown, Pennsylvania, that year, near Pittsburgh. Early one morning we all piled into a caravan of cars and, along with the coaches, set out for baseball immortality. We arrived five hours later, checked into our living quarters and drove out to the practice field. Young athletes always check out an opponent's physical size first, and those farm boys were huge. It was also the first time we had ever seen teenage ballplayers chewing tobacco. We psyched ourselves right out of the championship then and there.

The team returned to the boarding house after dinner and settled in for early lights out, but after the pillow fights every room was a total shambles by daybreak. We certainly weren't ready to play baseball the next day. The team committed six errors and lost by nine runs. The only consolation for the ten hours of driving and two days without sleep was a record hop held for all the teams. It amazed me how fast our dejected players suddenly found new life. I, on the other hand, wasn't too excited. The dance meant taking my hat off, and I couldn't gather the courage to do it, especially around strangers. I didn't even want to go, but I did, and stood in the dance hall shadows most of the time.

Hats had remained the most important part of my attire. They disguised me from the ignorant gawkers and their potential verbal abuse. My experiences at Girard had instilled in me a lot of insecurity and fear, and I was never comfortable being anywhere around strangers without a hat. It was like standing naked in a crowd for all to see my ugliness. The very thought of it panicked me, especially around the opposite sex.

The dance was a good time and my teammates tried to get me to join in. Coach Fladd knew how uneasy I was and stayed by my side. He'd point out some of the more attractive girls, hoping to entice me out onto the floor. But, with hat in hand, I wouldn't budge and admired them from afar.

One girl in particular caught my interest. She was a nice looking country girl with a bright wholesomeness about her. Our eyes met several times, but I looked off in another direction, hoping not to be noticed. As the night wore on, it happened more and more, and it made me feel uneasy. The glances we gave one another were the warm, curious kind that you can feel deep inside. I wanted to meet her but my fears held me back, and much to Coach Fladd's obvious disappointment I excused myself and went out the door.

I thought of Karen as I strolled around the grounds outside the ballpark pavilion, and how this girl might compare with her. It was a beautiful moonlit night. The park was peaceful, and as the summer breeze blew I tugged on my hat and walked into the nearby wooded area.

"Billy," a voice called from behind me.

I turned and there stood the girl from the dance.

"I'm sorry if I startled you," she said. "I just wanted to meet you, but you left the dance."

I smiled awkwardly. There was always that backwardness in me when it came to girls. They were intriguing, but then the fear of getting close made me uncomfortable. Even when the guys would just talk about them, especially in amorous ways, the uneasy feeling was there and I'd retreat inside. Lovemaking frightened me. That wall was insurmountable and I didn't know why.

"I saw you play today." She picked up a fallen tree branch and took a baseball swing with it. "You're pretty good. I play baseball too, or softball that is. Same thing."

The moonlight broke through the trees, casting a glow about her. I remained speechless, looking for somewhere to hide behind. A flower-scented gust of wind lightly tossed her flowing blonde tresses in the warm night air. She walked up to me and touched my arm softly. "My name is Debra. Don't be afraid," she said.

"How did you know my name?" I asked.

She looked up at my hat and then reached for it. "From the game, silly. Everyone was calling you Billy."

I backed away, trying to think of some excuse to leave her. That was not a comfortable situation, and I didn't want it to continue at first.

"I'm sorry," she said and withdrew her hand. "What happened to your hair? Were you in an accident or a fire?"

I had never been approached by a stranger quite like that before. Especially a pretty one. "It's a long story," I replied.

"C'mon now. Don't be bashful." She sat down on a big rock and motioned for me to sit beside her. "We've got plenty of time to talk. Please, I'm really interested. Now c'mon, smile. Talk to me."

It took me a while of stuttering. I was nervous, but I told Debra my complete story. When I finished, she looked at me teary eyed, reached up and cocked the baseball cap on the back of my head. "I'm so sorry," she said. "That horrible school must have been a nightmare for you. I can't imagine nobody caring, especially your mother. My folks would never have done anything like that. Your mom couldn't have had any heart to just turn her back on you."

"Well, I live at home now," I said. "I'm trying to deal with it and forgive her. But we still don't have much of a relationship. I feel like a boarder, not a son."

"So, it's not going well between you?" she asked.

"I've been home for a couple of years now, and we're still not very close. I have a stepfather too, and he doesn't help. He hates kids and makes me feel like I don't belong there. Like I'm in the way or something. I don't know whether I'm still mad at my mom or just jealous that she loves him more than me. I stay away from them as much as possible. I've been thinking of running away." As I unraveled from my gut, it occurred to me that nothing had really changed from my Girard days. I still wanted to run from my life to some nowhere place where it didn't matter who or what I was … or what I looked like.

"Do you have a girlfriend?" Debra asked.

"I did."

"What happened to her?"

"She dumped me. I guess I don't know how to act around girls. I just feel different and uneasy. Who knows? That whole thing was so confusing."

She took my hand in hers and smiled. "I'm not normally this forward. But c'mon, let's go dance. Nobody will make fun of you, not if you're with me. I won't let them."

I kept my hat on, but we danced until the last song, enjoying our moments together. When it finally came time to say goodbye, with a gentle kiss and warm embrace she said, "Billy, you're special. Remember it's what's inside of a person that makes them who they are, not what they look like. I know I'll never forget you, and maybe now and then you can think of me, okay?"

I never have forgotten Debra. She was really special. During my loneliest moments in the coming years, I wished we could've remained friends somehow. It had been one of those brief encounters in life that, for a long time after, I wondered about what might've been.

The days weren't always smooth sailing, especially at home, but my friends helped make it easier. I tried so hard to live every day to its fullest, but there was something emotionally missing deep inside me. Even the hopes of my hair growing completely back couldn't change that fact. Having a girlfriend no longer mattered either, as I began to fear loving and ever being loved.

My hair loss became a crusade for my mother. She so wanted to find a cure, and after I had cut my pictures out of the yearbooks, her determination became more evident. I even drew hair on one portrait. Della experimented with every supposed cure she heard about. Whatever the expense, her efforts to rid me of the disease possessed her. She took me to a traveling specialist who claimed to have a secret remedy. Only by purchasing his specially formulated hair follicle stimulant, conditioner and shampoo was the secret known. It was called money. Della bought a case of liquid lies. Another miracle cure forced us to go out of town once a week for private treatments with a country barber. He placed some sort of electrified metal rod in my hand and, with sparks flying, massaged my head. The process supposedly prepared the scalp for some home brewed hair regenerating solution, known to me simply as firewater! Once the liquid touched my skin, following a Frankenstein-like electrocution, the burning immediately beamed me into another dimension of agony. The outcome was sheer pain, not hair growth.

The human pincushion treatment was next. A local dermatologist was experimenting with the drug cortisone. I visited his office twice monthly to receive a series of injections directly into the scalp. One morning, following a previous day's treatment of approximately eleven needles, I awoke to the horror of seeing "Elephant Man" in the mirror. The entire one side of my head, including the forehead and cheek area, had swollen tremendously during the night. Fortunately, it was only a temporary condition, and so were my visits to the mad scientist.

Wherever there was hope, my mother took me. Several times we even pilgrimaged to certain Catholic shrines in search of healing. One trip we stood in line for hours just to be able to wipe the saint's statue with a handkerchief. Kneeling in solemn prayer, Della passed the cloth over my head in hopes of a miracle. She was a mother bent on finding a cure for a disease she felt responsible for causing.

The in-and-out hair loss finally ceased altogether midway through my high school years, and the mother of all wondrous miracles happened. Glorious baby fuzz suddenly appeared almost everywhere on my head. Even the one small patch that hadn't fallen out started to take on a healthy luster, and the hair roots were no longer black. They were healthy and white, a sign of being born anew. I reveled in the growth of hair, good friendships and good times, but if only I could've learned forgiveness and forgotten the dark years of my childhood. Those past times haunted me as much as living with Jim had in the present, before he died.

CHAPTER EIGHTEEN
THE GRADUATE TO WHAT?

Senior year arrived and I felt that exhilaration of finally reaching the twelfth grade. I was on top of the world, but those months were also a time of questions. What was I going to do after graduation? Where would I go, and was I prepared for what lay ahead?

That fall was not one of my better starts to a school term. For four years I had an ongoing personality clash with a certain teacher who also was one of my baseball coaches. We never seemed to be on the same wavelength. It was frustrating, and there was no compromise between us. I even tried to maintain a low profile, not drawing any negative attention to myself. But unfortunately there were more times than not that our personalities collided and my temper showed itself.

Class had just begun one day when Mr. Yavorski was called into the hallway by one of our priests. My classmates in political science that year consisted mainly of the senior jocks and no girls. Henry, the star running back on our football team, was telling off-color jokes. He had the entire class in an uproar as he told one story after another. My high-pitched cackle stood out, and I was delirious with laughter, doubling up in my seat from Henry's rapid fire monologue.

The door flung open. "You, Loudmouth, get out of my classroom!" Mr. Yavorski called out. "I'm sick and tired of your disturbances. Get your books and leave. Now!"

I was taken back by his singling me out. "Why do you always pick on me?" I asked. "Everybody else was laughing."

"Because you're the loudest," he said. "Now, get out of my sight." It was true in some respects that I attracted attention to myself. I guess sometimes I just tried a little too hard to be a part of the "in" crowd. That was very important to me, because I had always felt the outsider before. But I never meant to be obnoxious.

I gathered my books and walked to the back of the room,

banging into every chair as I went. *What is this man's problem?* I wondered as I slammed the door against the wall and stormed out into the hall, where I was greeted by Father George.

"What seems to be the problem, son?" Father asked, standing in my way. "Slow down."

"I'm tired of him picking on me all the time," I answered loudly. "He's always on my case, and I've had enough."

My remarks echoed down the hall, as I rudely walked off in the other direction, toward the principal's office. I marched in and slammed my books down on the counter, demanding to know if Father Thompson was in.

"Yes, he is," the secretary responded, "but..."

Father Thompson looked up over his glasses as I barged into his room. "What can I do for you today, Billy?"

I ranted and raved about the injustice I felt the coach had done to me and ended in a huff. "I demand something be done. It's not fair. I won't put up with it anymore. He hates me!" When it came to someone singling me out for anything, my mindset was still back in time the way it had been at Girard. I would go on the defensive in a heartbeat.

The meeting was brief and concluded with Father Thompson's solemn promise to personally get to the bottom of my personality differences with Mr. Yavorski. The rest of the day I anxiously anticipated our final confrontation. There weren't going to be anymore teacher-student injustices as far as I was concerned. That was one more side of me that had gotten way out of control...me, me, me. The old hatred for authority had raised its ugly head.

I was summoned to report to the principal's office with all books at the end of the day. My fate was instantly made clear. With Coach Yavorski looking on, Father Thompson informed me that my attitude wasn't appreciated and would not be tolerated. The punishment for such conduct was a school suspension from class and all activities. I was not to return to Notre Dame until Della could accompany me.

"Only when you return with your mother, and not before, will I deal with the situation," Father said. There was little doubt how angry he was with me. I could feel his eyes penetrating through mine and rummaging around inside my self-centered mind. It was like he was looking for what made me tick so he could fix it.

"But that's unfair. We were all laughing." I scowled at Mr. Yavorwski. "You know that's true, Mr. Yavorski. You treat me the same way on the ball field too."

Father Thompson stood up. "I told you, Billy, we will discuss it after your suspension, and with your mother present. And just for the record, don't ever come charging into my office again. Who do you think you are coming in here like this? There are proper ways of settling matters, and what you did was not one of them. I'm sure Mr. Yavorski has his reasons for what he did."

"Yes he does, Father. He doesn't like me."

Mr. Yavorski never said a word, simply shook his head in disgust and looked out the window as if he didn't care.

I hated him and wanted to say so. He reminded me of the unfairness I had dealt with at Girard. I simply viewed him as one more adult who didn't give a damn. Ironically, he too was a redhead with freckles, and I saw Butchie McGraff all over again.

I thought my complaint against Mr. Yavorski was legitimate, but I sure learned the hard way that I wasn't in charge. When Della found out, it wasn't long before her tirades were joined by Jim's. Not since my trouble with the police had she had so much to say to me. My mother and I didn't often communicate, only if absolutely necessary. Mother-son chats about life in general rarely happened. In any event, I felt she overreacted and should have taken my side.

"Your temper is going to get you in big trouble one day," Della said. "I don't know where that anger of yours comes from. Certainly not me. Now you've embarrassed me at this school. Since I took you out of Girard you've gotten worse. You're still selfish, opinionated and think everything has to be your way. What scares me more is that now that your hair's growing you're getting too cocky. What will you be like when it's all grown in?"

I listened to her ramblings without uttering a word. She was dead wrong as far as I was concerned and so was the school. They didn't understand, that's all. I was being picked on for no reason, and nobody wanted to hear my side of it. Some things never change, I thought.

"You know, Billy," she went on, "your hair problem still doesn't grant you special treatment. I've noticed that about you, and when something doesn't go your way, everyone else must pay."

"What would you know?" I said. "The only time you talk to me is when I've done something wrong. You don't bother with me otherwise. I might as well not be here."

"You're never home."

"What for? We're not a family. You don't participate in anything I do. You're no better than Jim. I thought we'd get closer when I came home from Girard."

Della got up from the kitchen table, slammed her chair in and struck her familiar arms-folded, teeth-clenched pose. "What's that supposed to mean?" She gave me what I called her Mount Rushmore stone-faced look. Even the lines on her face were chiseled in a frown, because I rarely saw her smile.

"You weren't even there for me my first day of school four years ago," I said. "That was important to me. I was nervous and scared that day."

She glared at me. "You're still thinking about four years ago? We had to go to work. Besides, your aunt was here. Are you always going to drag the past behind you all your life?"

All the things she wasn't as a mother raced through my mind. "You've never seen me play one ballgame," I said and got in her face. "And when I was going with Karen, you didn't want to know her family. As for my friends, I have to sneak them in here so that Jim isn't bothered. I can't even make a phone call without him watching me. That isn't being a family, and it's not what I came home for."

"Maybe we should have left you at Girard." She walked out of the room.

"You would have rather done that, wouldn't you?" I yelled

160

after her. "But I gave you no choice."

We exchanged some mighty nasty words that day. It was then I fully realized how high the wall was between us. She had her way of looking at things and I mine. We were two exact opposites carrying a lot of baggage from the past. But I was the teenager. She was supposed to comfort and counsel me. From that moment on, when we argued, nothing was held back and we said many things that hurt. Della thought she did her best, and I always felt she owed me big time for her mistakes.

When we returned to school, Della just sat there in the principal's office not saying a word on my behalf. I accepted the punishment but added it to my list of reasons for despising my mother.

A senior class privilege granted every year at Notre Dame was to have a "theme dance." Produced by the twelfth grade, it was for the sole enjoyment of seniors and juniors. It didn't take our class of creative impresarios long to come up with an idea. A "Beatnik" theme was perfect for teenagers looking to make a statement of independence. They were the counterculture in our days. Society's rebels, and I loved it.

The class yearbook described the dance as a novelty Beatnik Bounce, complete with poetry, art, bongos, coffee and costumes. The photograph caption read, "The dance will be remembered by the seniors as one of the most unique and hilarious events of our school days." And it certainly was.

A good amount of preparation went into the Beatnik Bounce. We searched for props weeks in advance, selected music, planned costumes, wrote poetry and, in my case, grew a goatee. Yes, I had hair to grow. When the big day arrived, Maynard G. Crebbs, the resident beatnik of TV's "Dobie Gillis" fame, had nothing on me. The tufted beard on my chin was a growth to be proud of. When I walked into my homeroom the day of the dance I was ecstatic to have gone all those weeks without being asked to shave. The dance had given me an opportunity to make my hair statement. But my bearded pride was soon cut short...like, to the skin, man.

Sister Amelia, our regular homeroom teacher, was out sick. In her place sat the much feared Sister Mary Michael, Prefect of Studies. She was the one person I had diligently avoided. As the class stood up for morning prayers, I folded my hands purposefully over my chin. We no sooner said "Amen" than Sister loudly voiced the eleventh commandment: "Facial hair is not permitted on school grounds. Put your hands down, Billy. Prayers are over. Young man, what is that on your chin?" She tugged on it. "This is a school infraction."

"It's only hair, Sister." I thought I'd get away with it, because I had been Billy, the boy who had no hair, but there would be no exceptions allowed.

With her hand still affixed to my chin, Sister yanked me out into the hall. She ordered me to stand there and went back into the classroom. Within moments, she returned with my buddy, Donnie, in tow. "Gentlemen, follow me." Sister Mary Michael marched us into Father Thompson's office and paraded our chins in front of him. It was obvious that he saw more humor than harm in our goatees, but to appease Sister he ordered us home to shave. Upon our return we reported to the office for inspection and one more lecture about good grooming. Although it had upset me to shave, I was darn proud of that infraction. Growing hair had actually gotten me in trouble. It also excited the rebel in me. I was still looking for ways of standing out among my peers and challenging authority.

Donnie and I were the talk of the dance that night. We were heroes, and the evening was a gas. The dance was heavily supervised by faculty, and the good sisters' floor patrol most certainly got an eyeful. The Beatnik generation had come to Notre Dame High School. Our dancing was classified as naughty, smoking in the building was foolhardy and the poetry just a bit risqué for a Catholic school. We had definitely raised the eyebrows and ire of the faculty, and for the first time I had grown facial hair.

At an impromptu class meeting held the very next morning, we were read the riot act by Father Thompson. His oration was thunderous, spellbinding, moving and punctuated with priestly expletives. Even the good sisters were afforded the opportunity to speak their minds. Father's summation was brutal. "Your class's punishment will serve as a reminder to all classes," he said. "Such scandalous behavior will not be tolerated!" The loss of our Senior Prom was the torch for all Notre Dame students to set their behavioral standards by. Not until almost two weeks prior to the prom did Father Thompson give in. He even stopped me in the hall that morning to say, "It was a nice goatee." To this day he and I occasionally have a good laugh over that incident, but the Bishop still reminds me about the lesson learned. "There are right and wrong ways of calling attention to yourself," he'd say. "Breaking rules usually will bring about the wrong consequence." How often in my young life I learned that the hard way, just to be noticed.

My attitude did change, especially toward girls, with the growth of my hair. I went from being reserved around them to having a rather haughty opinion of myself, a ladies man, if you would. The sad part was, unconsciously I was already striking back at them for how I had been rejected by my mother, and possibly Karen too. Those I would let get the closest to me paid the dearest. There was this really sweet underclassman I had promised since the beginning of the school year to take to the prom. She was a good friend who had always stuck by me, especially during my down times. But one day when another girl caught my roving eye, I dumped her without hesitation. Two weeks after the prom, my date dumped me. That same girl went on to marry one of my good friends years later. I guess there is justice.

My hair continued to grow, and I tempted fate once again. The D.A. hairstyle was forbidden in Catholic schools. So that spring one of my visits to the barber shop was ordered by Sister Mary Michael. But what a thrill it was to sit in a barber's chair and, for the first time in my life, say, "Just a trim, please." I actually had hair to cut, hair to comb, hair to style, hair to shampoo, hair for the wind to blow, hair for a girl to caress, hair for a nun to pull, hair that a hat needn't cover, hair that was wavy and dark brown ... hair, hair, wonderful hair! I finally looked as normal as the other guys. When I was three years old, Della had saved the clippings from my very first haircut and put them in a clear plastic bag. Many times over the years I'd stare at that bag and tearfully dream of my very own crowning glory. How fantastic it was to finally have those days behind me. The only sadness was the disappointment that my home life had not been what I hoped for. Socially, those times were magical and had given a lonely, unwanted, ugly duckling one of the things I wanted so much, acceptance from my peers. But moving on was an entirely different story.

The Beatnik Bounce. We were the grooviest cats, or at least we thought we were.

CHAPTER NINETEEN
HEALING OLD WOUNDS?

Girard was always in the back of my mind. It was a bad dream I couldn't shake, scars that wouldn't heal and forgiveness I needed to find. A burning desire to return to the place of my childhood fears had become an obsession by my seventeenth birthday, and I knew I had to confront the past one more time with Della. I felt compelled to walk through those walled-in memories again in search of an end to my haunting nightmares once and for all. Maybe my real reasons to go back were to exact some form of sick punishment on my mother or to gloat over my past enemies.

Founder's Day at Girard was a day of celebration and perfect for what I hoped would be a triumphant visit. As we left the bus station that morning, Della's reluctance to go was apparent. She had been against making the trip, insisting that no purpose could be served by going back. Her fear was that it would only open old wounds, not heal them. Our debates on the subject often turned to heated arguments, but I stuck to my convictions. "It's a cleansing," I said. "A purification of something ugly. It's the only way I feel I can flush those years out of me. It's important to face those kids once more. I just can't bury it away. I have to deal with it now. Then maybe I can get on with my life."

"But you've been home for four years."

"Is that what you call it, Mom? I've felt more at home in other people's houses, or even in school. This hasn't been a home. It's just a place where we eat and sleep." I knew that hurt her every time I said it. "Maybe if you see the worst of what it's like to be without a home or family you'll understand. You don't care any more about me here than when I was away. The only difference is, I'm closer. True, my hair problem probably made it tougher for me, but then again that all started on a lie, didn't it? Nothing beats family...nothing. That's what I want you to see."

Della didn't want to be forced to confront her own demons. "Why must I go through this with you? You don't need me there. They weren't pleasant times for me either, and I really don't care to relive them. They're in the past and that's where they should stay." Back and forth our arguments went on for weeks, but I held fast to my beliefs and Della eventually gave in.

The moment we took our seats on the bus that Saturday, my internal clock began ticking off the minutes to arrival. I had carefully thought out every detail of our trip and rehearsed everything I wanted to say, how and where I wanted to say it. It was important that everything I planned fit in. Traveling along the familiar stretch of Route 611 churned up the memories, and with them came the hate and disdain for those days when I had to return to Girard. My heart saddened with every landmark along the highway. By the time we reached the outskirts of Philadelphia, we were both immersed in the reliving of those dreaded bus rides. We remembered familiar sights along the way, especially the many places where the bus drivers had pulled over countless times to let me vomit. The two-hour ride that day did have one pleasant thought. Unlike before, I'd be on the bus for the return trip home.

The bus pulled into the Broad and Erie Station about 9:00 AM. That part of town had been my last bastion of freedom and peace, where in years past we'd spend some final moments together before leaving for the school. Of course, even that had stopped towards the end, with Jim's insistence that I was big enough to travel without her. It was still a bustling neighborhood with many restaurants and shops lining its wide avenues. But what had changed the most was the presence of garbage in the streets and drunks on the corners.

That same location also resurrected another memory. Just one block from the station was Germantown Avenue, which led north to the Brickyard and my home as an infant. My emotions raced with melancholy and sentiment. On that very spot, a disenchanted boy and his mother had prepared themselves many times for the heartbreak of separation. Our sad ritual that had played out over the years left its mark on me, and I didn't want to linger there.

The subway ride to Girard Avenue was also laden with memories. As the cars screeched and swayed through the tunnel and the underground stations flashed by, every lonely feeling from those days welled up inside me. Each block drew me closer to a place I had hated. Every step was indelibly etched on my heart, soul and mind.

At Girard Avenue, we left the subway and boarded a trolley on the final leg of our journey, which brought us to Girard's main gate. My nervous anticipation grew until the cold granite buildings loomed up ahead and I could see the wall extending in either direction. It was a view of hell itself for me, and the old feelings churned in my stomach once again like they always had.

The front gates were wide open, welcoming the thousands of Founder's Day visitors. I recalled the anxieties I felt every time we had walked through those gates. We paused by the circular flower gardens, glanced around and remembered. I looked up at the gates where so many times I had wept as a child. Their towering austere presence had punctuated the beginning and end time of my seven years at Girard. They brought to mind that first night when I fled up the main road in pursuit of my mother. And also the evening when I thought I saw my father beckon to me. The haunting notes from *Where Have You Been Billy Boy* played back in my memory.

"Look at this place, Mom. It hasn't changed in four years," I said. Everything was exactly as I remembered it. I didn't want to find anything different. My purpose for being back there was twofold: first to somehow find inside me the strength to forgive all of it, the place and the people. But even more than that, I wanted her to feel my pain during those times from within the very walls she had imprisoned me. It was a cruel thing to do, but I believed that I needed her to know everything behind them before I could hope to move on.

The crowds filed through the gates as the day's magnificence brightened my expectations. I was anxious to tour the campus with Della and nudged her from her own thoughts. There were many parts of the sprawling fifty-acre school Della had never seen. Those I was determined to show her. By day's end I wanted her to have seen and heard my Girard story, not just what the school had wanted her to know, or not to know.

As I directed her toward the lodge building, my head buzzed with heightened obsession. The reckoning with the past had begun, mine and Della's. I took a deep breath and fought off the feeling of being swept up by something beyond my control.

"Mom, I'd like to see Carl," I said. "I hope he's still here. He was the first friend I made in this place. You know, that night after you left me at Westend, I got away from Miss Hart and ran like hell up the main road. I came around that circle full speed yelling for you. When I got to the main gate, I thought I saw you getting on the trolley. But I guess you never heard me. How come? Christ, I screamed loud enough."

"We were probably gone by then. Mr. Swagg drove us right over to the trolley stop."

"Did you ever look back?"

"What do you think?"

"I still don't understand what you did or why."

"What's there to understand? I've told you many times. I had no choice. But I did get you out of here, didn't I?"

"Yeah, seven years later. But you never told me the truth from the beginning. So it's got nothing to do with choices. Maybe if I would've known you were gonna desert me, I might've handled it better."

I can still see her planting her feet and glaring at me. "Desert you!"

"What do you call it?" I asked.

"I call it giving my son a better chance, that's what. A decent life for a little boy, something I couldn't give you."

"A decent life!" I stepped forward close to her face. "Since when is not having a mother, or any parent, a good thing?! It's even worse when you do have them and they don't seem to want you or even care."

"Is that what this is all about?" She walked over to the iron fence alongside the lodge and grabbed one of the bars. "Did you bring me here to punish me? These bars and that wall were my prison too. I really believed this was a good place for you. How was I to know what would happen with your hair?"

"I want you to feel what I felt."

"I can't hurt any more than I've already hurt myself. I'll take it to my grave."

She looked so forlorn peering across Girard Avenue watching the trolley cars come and go, but I had no pity for her as she stood there trembling.

"It's always about you, isn't it, Mom? At least you knew what your plans were back then," I said in a cold, deliberate voice. "I sure as hell didn't."

Her voice broke and she choked back tears. "How can you be so selfish? When I walked out of House D that night, I left my whole world behind me. You! That's not easy for any mother to do. Maybe if you'd stop worrying about yourself long enough, that might occur to you. I cried all the way up that same road, just like you did. I cried through those gates, on the trolley, all the way home and for a long time after that. No, I'm sorry, Billy. You weren't the only one who was upset."

"There was one big difference between us back then, Mom." I grabbed her at arm's length, stared into her eyes and faced her toward the wall. "That damn wall. You were out there, and I was locked in here without even knowing why." At that moment I felt the anger surge inside me once again.

"You were hard to handle, stubborn too. If I had told you the truth ahead of time, I would've never got you here."

"You delivered me to hell. What did you think would happen to a kid abandoned in a place full of strangers, without any warning?"

"Excuse me, may I be of some help?" an old familiar voice from behind us said. I glanced over my shoulder, and there stood Carl the lodgekeeper. I had wanted to see Carl again, but his sudden presence embarrassed me. "Sorry to interrupt," he said.

I hoped he hadn't recognized me just then, and I took Della by the arm and walked away. I felt terribly guilty for what he might have seen. I wanted so much to speak with him too. It hadn't made for a good beginning to Founder's Day, but I knew a confrontation between my mother and me was inevitable once we were inside those walls. "C'mon, we're wasting time, Mother," I said. "Let's go meet Stephen."

"Stephen who?" she asked as I hurried her along. "I thought you wanted to see your friend, the lodgeman."

"I do. But not right now." That wasn't how I had hoped to meet Carl after all those years. I wanted him to see me as the good kid who had done well for himself with his full head of hair, not the vengeful boy I apparently became. It was a point I felt I had to prove to everyone that day. Look at me, the conqueror. See, I'm all better now and I did it away from here, just like I said I would.

Our first stop was Founder's Hall and Stephen Girard's tomb. Walking up the steps with Della at my side, I was hell bent on retribution. We passed through the fifty-foot high Doric column portico and entered the mausoleum portion of the building. The immense chamber was some forty feet high, lined in marble, with a black and white tiled floor. Positioned along the far wall on a raised platform was the burial vault. In front of the stone sarcophagus stood a life-size statue of Stephen Girard, accompanied on either side by the U.S. and state flags. The solemnness of that austere room was regal in its setting. But I always felt that the statue of Venus De Milo might have been more fitting, because she no longer had arms to hug with.

No one else was in the chamber when we approached Girard's tomb, which was a good thing. If there was a way I could've locked the door, I would've. "Say hi to Stephen Girard, Mom, founding father," I said, slightly bowing toward the statue with all my arrogance. "Eighteenth century businessman and philanthropist. He was a poor Frenchman who made it big time in the colonies. From cabin boy to a banker, he's considered one of the great financial success stories of his time.

Amazing, isn't it? Only in America, your basic rags to riches story." I paused to make sure she was paying attention. "Hell of a guy old Stephen, starting a school for orphaned or fatherless boys. I guess I fell in the latter category. I was no orphan, but I sure felt like one."

"This isn't necessary." Della shook her head and started for the door. "I said I would come here for your sake. Don't make this harder than it already is."

"Whoa, where are you going, Mom?" I said and took her by the arm. "There's more. You're gonna get a complete education here today."

Della tried to free herself from my grasp. "Let go of me. I know what you're trying to do, and I don't care to be any part of it. Neither one of us needs it."

"Wrong, Mother! I think we do. Let's be respectful here to this great man. His school did wonders for your son." I pulled her toward the statue. "Did you ever listen to the school song? 'Hail Girard. Acclaim her manhood'. Hell of an opening lyric for a school anthem, sure helped me a lot. I was robbed of my childhood here, Mother, and maybe my manhood too. I was so messed up I thought I loved another boy. Now don't get me wrong, I'm not blaming Mr. Girard. He had good intentions. But you all overlooked one thing. Nobody can replace your father or your mother. You can't recreate home, especially behind walls."

"How did the other boys handle it?" She kept trying to free herself from me, but I wouldn't let go.

"Seven years, Mom, and most of that time nobody listened to me."

"I've heard enough!" she shouted as I forced her even closer.

All of Girard's cast of characters should have been present that day as I poured out my soul to Della. "It's a damn shame. Old Stephen really cared about kids. That's the reason he wanted this school built in the first place. There's even a lyric in the anthem's second verse that refers to children of the great republic. I guess that made him like an early day Father

Flanagan of Boys' Town, or a Milton Hershey. They cared about homeless and orphaned kids. But I've had one problem with all of it...What the hell was *I* doing here? I had a home and a parent!" I practically shoved her over the rail in front of the tomb. "Oh, I'm sorry, Mom. Forgive me. I'll rephrase that. Officially, I guess I wasn't homeless or an orphan until you dumped me here."

"Don't you dare talk to me like that!" she said and raised her hand as if to strike me. "For the last time. I had no choice. My family wouldn't help me. You were a mischievous little boy. I never knew where you'd roam off to or what trouble you'd cause. What was I supposed to do? Let you run wild? I did care. That's why you were here."

I grinned and held on to her hand. "That's pretty sad. You ignored me for seven years. A loving parent wouldn't have done what you did. You took the easy road. You got rid of your inconvenience, me, your only son! Ironic as hell, isn't it? An innocent haircut cost me my home and my hair."

"Let go of me. I don't want to hear any more of this." She tried to pull herself free, but I was enjoying my power over her.

"You have to listen." The adrenaline rushed through me, and I relished watching her squirm. "Do you think you can do that? Just this once?" I wanted to dump all my hurt on her.

She pulled free and smacked me across the face. "I warned you."

"All I've ever wanted from you was your love. Is it too much to ask for a mother to love her son? Even now you don't understand what I'm feeling. Why is it so hard for you to say, it's all right, everything will be fine. I love you. Or maybe even give me a kiss. I've been home four years and I can count the hugs on one hand. You're so pitiful. Jim too. Neither of you knows how to be a parent. All it takes is heart and to show you care. Maybe I *should've* stabbed you when you wouldn't let me go to Uncle Frank's last year."

Della stood there quietly, shaking. "You were wild that day. I thought you were going to kill me for sure. Look at you now."

"How does it feel, Mom," I responded, "to hear the truth?"

I had finally said all the things that had eaten at me for so many years. Our lives had been a struggle after my father's death, but I also wanted her to know how she failed me as a mother. Yes, I had thought about killing her. Jim too. I'd lie in bed some nights for hours fantasizing how to do it. Once I even sneaked downstairs while they slept. Seeing her side by side with him turned my stomach. Oh, how I hated them both at that time.

An eerie silence filled the chamber. The only sound was the echo of Della's soft whimpers. I stood in front of Stephen Girard's statue looking at the two images before me. One was carved of stone, and the other had a stone for a heart. Girard was the sculpted white angel of mercy who cared for children, and Della was the mother who hadn't. A ray of sunlight filtered in from the partially opened doorway, casting a warmth where there was none before. I looked at Della and suddenly felt sorry for her.

She clasped her hands together as if in prayer and turned toward me. Her voice broke softly through the silence. "Billy, what is it you want from me? Your hating me the way you always have only makes this harder. I know I'm not the hugging or kissing kind of mother. People are different. That's just not how I am. But I guess that's not enough for you." She rested up against the railing of the tomb and pleaded, "Please, this isn't doing us any good. Let go of the past. Get on with your life. C'mon, why don't we leave now. Forget what happened here. You have so much to look forward to. Why can't you forgive?"

I took the handkerchief she was holding and gently wiped her eyes. "Mom," I said, "I need to do this. Being here with you today means a lot to me. Maybe we both can find some peace and forgiving. I just can't erase all those years I spent here. It's not that simple. God only knows I've tried. No matter where I'm at or what I'm doing, the memories never leave me. There's so much about this place that needs forgiveness. I have to feel it all just once more. Maybe then I can flush it out of my system.

Having you here is important. I need for you to know what happened here. None of this will matter unless we do it together. Do you understand?"

She looked up at Stephen Girard and then at me. "If that's what you want, I'll do it. Just let's not fight anymore."

I led her toward the large bronze doors. "For seven years it was like being in hell, and I finally had to do bad things to get your attention. Now you'll see how much I needed you. Then we'll go home, together this time."

We walked outside and down the Founder's Hall steps. The sun's brilliance bathed us in a promising light, while a pleasant breeze tried to cleanse the air of the foulness in my senses. I knew it wasn't right what I was doing. "Let's go down to the Westend, Mom. Remember House D and Miss Hart?" I groped for better ways to get us through all of what was inside of me, but it wasn't easy. "You should've told me the truth from the beginning, Mom. Honestly I didn't know I was going to be left here by myself."

"Do you think you would've handled it better if your hair problem never happened?"

"Who knows...but maybe if you would've been honest with me from the beginning, or tried harder as a..." I put my arm around her shoulder and gave her a reassuring hug as we walked down the main road. "It's just not right turning kids over to total strangers. Nobody can replace a family. Of course, it's different if they got nobody. If I ever have kids, I'll never leave them."

We didn't say another word for a while. It was a festive day at Girard, and all around us people were celebrating Founder's Day. The school was decked out in all its steel and garnet banners. Music from The Chapel's huge pipe organ flooded the grounds with elegant crescendos, the aroma of hum mud gingerbread from the bakery ovens filled the air, and the tolling of "Big Ben" marked the hour. All the familiar sights and sounds enhanced my memories and it certainly wasn't a homecoming for me, nor was I a stranger there.

At Westend, Della and I walked through the main portico

174

and onto the immense playground. As a "newbie" my first night there, I had fled across it in desperate pursuit of my mother. The scene played itself back as if it had just happened.

"Mom, I was fast as hell. You should have seen me," I said, pointing toward House D. "I was a blur coming out of that door over there. Nobody would have caught me that night. I streaked across this playground like somebody possessed. I can still hear Miss Hart yelling after me. I'll tell you, if the main gate would've been open, I was out of here, right on that trolley with you, heading back home."

Della looked over the playground as if imagining me running across it, but she said nothing. I took her hand and we walked over to House D. "C'mon, Mom, let's go inside and look around. Maybe Miss Hart is here."

The inside of House D was pretty much as I had remembered it, except for the smallness of everything. The furnishings hadn't changed, even down to the rows of tiny wooden desks, which were in the same identical positions as before.

"Wow. The place looks the same," I said as I squeezed into a chair at one of the desks. The memories flooded my mind. Most of them made me sad, but then there was Miss Hart, whose caring had kept me sane. I wanted so to see her smiling face once again, to feel the softness of her gentle touch and hear the kindness in her every word. She was the one person who gave a little boy the reason to have hope day after day. From out of the darkest nights, she was my sun in the morning.

Della got my attention real quick. "You don't think she's no longer governess here?"

"Don't say that, Mom." I got to my feet and called out. "Does anybody know where Miss Hart is?" I just had to see her.

"I'm Miss Cavanaugh," an elderly woman said, coming down the steps. She was the epitome of the stereotyped craggy-looking old school marm. "What can I do for you, young man?" she said and walked up to me, peering over bifocals.

I didn't care for her the minute I saw her. "This is my mother, Della, and I'm Billy." I offered my hand. "I was a new boy in House D back in the fifties. We stopped to see Miss Hart."

Miss Cavanaugh turned around to scold a boy across the room for being too loud then looked back at me. "Miss Hart? I'm afraid you're a couple of years too late. She's gone. Got married and moved away." Her piercing eyes continued to dart about the room, never once looking directly at me.

I withdrew my hand. "That's a shame. She was a good governess."

"Miss Hart was too easy with the boys, coddled them too much." She adjusted her bifocals, leered at me and then at Della. "She had a lot of unruly boys in her care. Since I've been governess here that has not been the case. Now, if you'll excuse me, the boys have chores to do."

"Sure, she probably frightened them to death," I whispered to Della. "What an old witch." I wanted to throw something at her. *Where do they find such horrible people?* I asked myself. "We had the best governess when I was here," I said.

"You really liked Miss Hart, didn't you?"

"What wasn't to like about her? She cared. And if you had a problem, she'd listen. We talked a lot."

"How come that didn't help you?"

"She wasn't you, Mom, and this wasn't home, big difference."

The Founder's Day celebration was in full swing. There were kids and adults involved in all sorts of activities out on the large playground. The mood was festive as boys whizzed by on roller skates, while others jumped rope, played hopscotch, had foot races or rode the swings, seesaws and slides. A soccer ball sailed over our heads and a softball bounded by.

"My first escape attempt," I said as we walked through Westend's portico, and I pointed toward Dr. Freedman's house. I recalled that day with Kevin and Benny helping me, and how I ran to the rear gate, only to catch a glimpse of the outside world as the giant green doors closed in on me.

Della listened intently but barely smiled as I told her all about Dr. Freedman and his dog Luther. "Where were you going if you got out?" She stepped aside as a group of boys darted between the portico columns, playing tag. "You were only eight years old."

"Home," I said.

"Did you really want to run away back then?"

"I sure did," I answered.

"How come I never heard about it?"

"Because nothing happened, that's why." I stuck my tongue out at her. "You probably would've squealed on me anyway if you knew, and they would've watched me closer after that. Heaven forbid if your son would have gotten loose."

Next to Westend back then was an immense grass-covered playing field with the varsity baseball diamond in the far corner. Kevin, Benny and I had played there as little boys, sometimes pretending to be big-time ballplayers. The outfield that day was filled with visitors, faculty, alumni and students assembling for the Founder's Day parade.

"C'mon, Mom," I called to Della, who seemed absorbed by all the activity. "Let's go onto the field. Maybe when the battalion marches out I'll see some of my former classmates."

What a sight that was. Bands were tuning up, costumed participants readied themselves and final touches were being completed on floats. Della stared in awe of the growing spectacle that she had never seen before. From the enormous armory building came the bugle sounds of "call to muster." In anticipation of seeing the "gray line" after all those years, I moved further onto the field. The armory's main doors swung open, and from within came the muffled drum cadence signaling the battalion's march. Out into the brilliant sunlight the color guard strode smartly, followed by the Steel & Garnet band and then the battalion, which consisted of five companies. I reviewed the memory of that awesome sight as it covered me with goosebumps. The company flags unfurled and the young troops stepped out. I had thoroughly enjoyed being a cadet as a Girard student. To me it was a thrill to be a young soldier, and I was a good one.

Down the semicircular ramp they marched, onto the

playing field. Column after column of boys stepped out dressed in their West-Point-styled gray uniforms with white gloves, Eisenhower hats and rifles at right shoulder arms. They formed on the field while the band struck up a Sousa march and company captains barked out drill commands. I smiled as the chills went up and down my spine. For that one brief moment, I was a hummer once again. I stared at the battalion with its assembled ranks of cadets and smelled the sweet grass they stood on. The Cadet Major barked his commands. "Battalion...Order arms! Battalion...Parade...Rest!" In unison, 600 rifles smartly came to the ground. What a splendid sight they were to behold. I wondered how it might have been had I stayed at school. The battalion was the one thing that had made me feel a part of something special.

I wanted to get closer and tugged on Della's arm. "You go ahead," she said. "I'll wait here."

I pulled her along anyway. "Don't they look sharp? Remember how you used to like to look at the pictures of them? Here's your chance to see our Gray Line up close. They're better than the Valley Forge Military School guys."

She stopped. "Our Gray Line? Do I detect some Girard pride?"

"I enjoyed the battalion, Mom," I replied and automatically stood at attention. "It made me feel like I belonged to something in this place. Besides, I always looked forward to Founders Day since I was a new boy here when I was the soccer king. It was my one happy time."

I moved closer to the cadets and scanned their faces, hoping to recognize someone. I longed to see a familiar face, and it didn't matter if it was from out of a bad memory. Just to be recognized by anyone was important to me. I so needed to make a connection between then and now.

"Do you see any boys you know?" Della asked.

I stopped alongside one of the companies. An exceptionally tall cadet had caught my attention. I shaded my eyes, straining to see him in the glaring sunlight.

"Battalion, Halt!" the Cadet Major shouted. "Left shoulder,

Arms! Battalion, Dress right, Dress. Front! Battalion, Orderrr, Arms! Paraaade, Rest! Battalion, At ease! As you were, men."

Della seemed disinterested and restless. "What are you going to do if you find somebody?" she said. "You can't talk to them if they're in the parade."

I ignored her and kept looking. What would I say, I wondered, if I found any of the boys? Hey, check out my hair? What would they say? Would they even remember me? Would there be ill feelings after all these years, or guilt on their part? Could they face me? I wanted that day to be so perfect. But looking at my watch, I knew there just wasn't enough time.

My mind wrestled with the doubts and questions, but I remained focused on the large Cadet Captain anyway. There was something warmly familiar about him, and I studied his every move. He was impressive in full uniform as he reviewed his troops. Decked out with sword and scabbard, the officer had a swagger to his step as he walked up and down the company ranks. There was an air of leadership and pride about him. It couldn't be Chester Pursell I thought, the same awkward kid I had gone over the wall with. But the more I watched him, the more excited I became.

"Chet!" I called out. "Chet Pursell!"

The tall cadet stopped midstride and looked in my direction. He acknowledged me with a slight wave, obviously not knowing who I was, and returned to his inspections.

Della poked me in the back. "You can't bother him now," she said.

"They're at parade rest." I stepped a short way out onto the field and called Chet's name again. That time the cadet turned around and glanced at me, but he still didn't know who I was and shrugged his shoulders.

"It's me, Billy...Billy Lonardo! Don't you recognize me, you overgrown..." When I looked closer at the cadet, my heart sank. It wasn't Chet. I wanted it to be him so bad that I continued to stare, not noticing another cadet approach me.

"Billy? It is you. You got hair. I don't believe it. I didn't recognize you until you shouted your name." He stepped in front of me to get my attention. "It's me, Brian Lehroy. Man, are you a sight for sore eyes. You look terrific."

I was so taken aback to see Brian that I didn't know what to say at first. "Oh, yeah…uh, hey Brian," I stuttered. "Sorry, I didn't see you coming. I thought that captain over there was Chet Pursell."

He touched my hair, which made me very nervous, just as the bugle sounded. "Uh-oh. I gotta get back on the field. How long you staying? Let's meet somewhere later. What d'ya say?"

"Uh, well…Mom and I have a lot of places to go to yet." My memory of Brian and me and Miss Klunk was making me hesitate. "Okay, why not. How about by the equipment shed near the wall on Lafayette playground. That's where Chet and I went over the wall, ya know. Say about six o'clock?"

"Sure, I'll be there, Billy," he said and returned to his troop.

It's funny how there are certain things that happen in life we sometimes don't want to deal with. I hadn't planned on meeting up with Brian that day, and even though I agreed to see him I wasn't looking forward to it.

"You weren't really excited about seeing him," Della said. "How come?"

That was one memory I wasn't prepared to deal with at the time. "You wouldn't understand, Mom. Maybe someday we'll…"

"Battalion, Attention!" rang out the Cadet Major's command. "Dress right, Dress! Right shoulder, Arms!" The Steel and Garnet's drum line began its rhythmic march cadence, and the final command echoed across the field. "Battalion! Forward, March!" Thus, the Founder's Day parade began, led by the corps of cadets. I searched their ranks for Chet but didn't see him. What a spectacle it was. Following them was a large contingent of alumni, who along the parade route handed out hum muds, the school's famous gingerbread cakes. After the alumni came the first of several marching bands. Ironically, just as when I was the Soccer King at Westend, that same band was the Reilly Raider Senior Drum and Bugle Corps I had marched behind in the parade. Out onto the main road and toward

Founder's Hall the long column of Girard celebrants went, the Steel and Garnet Band leading the cadets, old and young alumni, visiting marching bands, school athletes, graduating class floats, Philly mummers strutting to string band music, the mayor of Philadelphia, and lastly the symbol of Girard youth sports, the little Soccer King. That memory put a lump in my throat. I recalled how proud I had felt marching up the main road. It made me wish all my thoughts of those times could have been as pleasant as that long ago Founder's Day.

We walked alongside the parade, up the main road. Della hadn't said much, but I started to ramble on to her about the memories. "This is about where Chet and I faced down a group of boys. You had to be there to appreciate it, Mom. It was beautiful. They cornered us in front of the armory."

"Why were they after you?" Della asked. "What did you do to them?"

I threw my arms up in frustration. "What a dumb question," I said. "They didn't need a reason. When you're a kid and there's something different or odd about you, that ain't cool. You just don't fit in. What happened that day is a good example of what I've been trying to tell you."

I always had difficulty getting my mother to understand kids. She simply couldn't comprehend what made young people think or react the way they do. It was frustrating. Not only was there the obvious generation gap between us, but Della only ever saw things her way no matter what it was.

"Now listen to me," I continued. "Even before Chet and I became friends, nobody bothered with him. First of all he was real tall and stood out like a sore thumb. Second, he was awkward as hell, which made it even more fun for the other guys to joke about him. Talk about two left feet. He couldn't get out of his own way. One time we had a fire drill, and after we all made it outside nobody could find him. When we went back into the building, there he was stuck to his locker. Somehow he got his shirt jammed in the door and when it shut the thing locked. Being the big guy he was and the scariest didn't help him either. So he kept to himself most of the time.

181

Kids don't bother with loners. That's what made him an outcast, a weirdo, just like me."

Della stood there expressionless. "Well, that's not very nice," she said.

"Any of this sinking in, Mom?" I tapped her forehead. "Then, after I got to be his buddy, his fate was really doomed. Don't forget I was the school's walking disease. Associating with me was forbidden. Taboo!"

"How come nobody ever put a stop to all that nonsense?" Della asked. "If I would have known, it wouldn't have continued."

"It was all in my letters." I walked in front of her. "I wrote enough of them. Did you think I was making it all up?"

"Aren't the mummers costumes colorful?" she said and maneuvered around me. "I haven't seen a string band since your father was alive."

I caught up to her. "You're not going to avoid this anymore, Mom. That's why we're here, remember?"

"I guess I thought you were exaggerating in your letters. Kids do that. Besides, you wrote so many of them. They filled an entire barrel."

"How come you never checked out the stuff I was telling you?" I asked. It was the one question that plagued me more than any.

"There was nothing I could do anyway." She gazed blankly at the parade. "The school was your legal guardian, not me."

"But you were still my mother."

"I know, and I'm sorry."

"For what? Being my mother?"

"No. For not being a better one. Maybe I just didn't want to believe it was that bad. Besides, everyone told me the school wouldn't let things like that happen."

"You mean you believed that whatever I told you or wrote were lies?"

"I didn't know what to think." She turned away and walked over to a nearby bench. I followed her and we sat down.

"Well, for what it's worth, Mom," I said, sliding close to her, "Chet and I were the victors that day."

"Did you get into a lot of fights?" she asked, appearing as if it was just idle conversation.

I wondered why I was even trying to make sense to her after all those years. "Yeah, enough of them, Mom. I was wild when they made me mad. One time I got a hold of a guy right over there in that playground. He was a bully." I pointed to the large sandpile in the Junior School playground. "What a fight that was. We were a bloody mess. I was so angry I wanted to kill him. If it wasn't for Mr. Nichman pulling us apart, it could have been worse."

Della sat there quietly lost in her own thoughts, staring blankly at the crowds of people. I nudged her. "C'mon, Mom, let's go in the Junior School Building and look around. I'd like to see Section 1 again. I hope the Bulldog is still here."

"The Bulldog?" she asked.

"Miss Klunk," I said. "My Section 1 governess. Remember, I used to tell you why I called her that. She really looked like a bulldog, jowls and all."

"That's disrespectful." She shook her head. "Miss Klunk wasn't a bad looking woman, maybe a little short and round-shouldered."

I laughed and nudged her again. "She did bark sometimes. Really. It went with her personality."

Melancholy swept over me as we entered my old homeroom. I spotted the desk I had right away. My initials were still carved on the back side, and it struck me odd that everything I had seen so far hadn't changed. It was as if time had stood still.

An elderly white-haired woman approached us. "Excuse me, folks," she said. "May I help you? My name is Mrs. Potts."

Another relic, I thought. *The school must have gone to a used people lot to find this one.* "Yes, ma'am," I said. "I'm Billy and this is my mother, Della. This used to be my homeroom about nine years ago. Where's Miss Klunk? She was my governess when I lived here."

Mrs. Potts stuttered slightly with a pronounced lisp, spitting out certain words. "I'm sorry, Miss Klunk is no longer

183

with us. She retired a few years ago."

Miss Klunk was another person I had really wanted to see that day, especially with Della. Oh, I had it all figured out all right. She was number three on my list. I was curious to see how she'd react to me with my hair grown in. The lady never knew how to take me, especially after that night when my hair came out in her hands. It seemed funny to me that she began to habitually comb her hair after that incident. But our parting hadn't been all that bad, considering how confused she always seemed to be. My condition did that to a lot of people over the years.

We thanked Mrs. Potts for her hospitality and left Section 1. I took Della down into the Junior School basement catacombs, which consisted of washrooms, recreation areas, storage rooms and a maze of corridors. It was where Chet and I had hid that day when we went over the wall. The dark nooks and crannies made it an ideal place to conceal ourselves. Everything was the same there too, even the Junior School theater where I had performed as Robinson Crusoe. Back upstairs on the main floor, we passed the large dining halls. I told story after story as we walked along. Some of the tales were lurid; some were typical boyhood mischief; but most were about how I had lived constantly on edge, not knowing when the abuse would come. "It was in all my letters, Mom," I said. "Every bit of it."

"I know, you told me that." She went by each place as if she had horse blinders on. There wasn't anything that seemed to interest her as I had wanted it to.

We climbed the stairs off the main hallway and went up past the second floor to the third. "What made it even harder being here," I went on as I opened the door to the Section 1 dormitory, "is that it seemed there wasn't any way to escape it, Mom. That's a hell of a feeling when you can't get away from something that you hate or fear."

Della silently walked into the largest bedroom she ever saw. Wall to wall white metal single beds were neatly arranged in three rows, each one with a wooden chair by its side. Nothing had changed there either.

"How many beds are in here?" she asked.

"Thirty-five," I replied, "and it doesn't look like they've moved any of them since I slept here." I went to the row of beds by the windows and directly to the fourth one. Kneeling down beside it, I felt underneath and passed my hand along the supporting metal rails. "Hey, Mom! Look, here's my old bed. The gum I stuck between the rails is still here."

Della roamed from bed to bed, gently touching each one, occasionally straightening a pillow or tucking in a corner.

My thoughts drifted back to a time when as a ten-year-old I had stared out those windows, wondering if my mother was watching the same stars at night. I had prayed she could hear my prayers and talk to me in my dreams. In that very bed I had imagined the world outside, each night returning home to play on familiar streets then closing my tired eyes in hopes the sandman would soon come. I reflected on the pain of those memories as Della strolled about the dorm, still silent. I watched her every move and wondered what effect all of this was having on her and hoped that for the first time she understood how it must have been for me in this faraway place. Was she punishing herself with every thought or merely numb to the growing reality of it all? There was such sadness on her face.

"I didn't realize all this," she said and slumped down on my old bed. "This is a lot of boys sleeping in one room."

If there was ever a first fleeting moment of truth in our lives, it was that one. I sensed that maybe there was some remorse in her after all. Throughout all those years, there never had been a closer moment for Della and me, but sadly neither of us embraced it, or each other.

"C'mon, let's get out of here, Mom," I said. "The place still depresses me. I'll show you one of the shower rooms. Talk about no privacy...and we stood there naked." I took her hand and we walked out.

She stared back at the dormitory as the door slowly closed. "It's certainly not as cozy as our one little room was. We didn't have much then, but they weren't bad times were they?"

The bright sun and festivities picked up our spirits

somewhat, but I think we were both in a mental daze. "It's almost four o'clock," I said. "Let's go over to the Good Friends building. I want to see if Miss Henson and Miss Linstrom are still there."

Della nodded and walked at my side as though she was being led from one hell to another.

"You know, I never really understood why they named this building Good Friends." I opened the main door. "This place was far from friendly. Most of the real bad stuff began here. These kids are about eleven or twelve years old, preteens, ugly time for kids. And heaven help you if you're different in any way. They can be rough at that age." I shuddered, recalling all the torments that had happened there. Child abuse in the first degree, and I don't mean just from the boys.

Homerooms at Girard were quite different from a regular school's. They were like oversized living rooms. Each boy had his own desk with drawers for personal things. The rooms were as homey as they could make them, considering an average of thirty boys spent a lot of time there. Miss Henson's Section 15 had its bookshelves, plants, paintings on the walls, a sitting area with a couch and end chairs, a big Philco radio, throw rugs, plus an adjoining cloak room for coats and junk. The only television set was in the TV room on the first floor, and it would be turned on only for special programs, like Walt Disney on Wednesday nights. Sometimes sixty kids or more jockeyed for a good seat on the floor. Often that would be the only television show we would get to see during the school weekdays.

As we entered Miss Henson's homeroom, I recalled the lonely hours I had spent at my desk writing home. My letters had become incessant at Good Friends. Each one more pleading than the last, they were often smeared with tears. It wasn't always the abuse but rather my longing to not be in that place at all, ever since I was a "newbie."

"Hey, Mom," I said. "Whatever did happen to all the letters I wrote you? Especially the ones from here, they were real tearjerkers."

Della hesitantly looked around and sat down. "I was afraid

you'd ask me that. There were a lot, you know. They filled that big barrel up in the attic."

I sat next to her on the couch. "And?" There wasn't a thing I was about to let go unanswered. Not anymore. Not if I wanted to leave any of those years behind and try to move on.

"I threw them all away," she said. "I needed the storage space, and I didn't see any reason to keep them."

That stung me, but I decided to let it go. "Yeah, it's probably better that way. Reading them again wouldn't change anything now."

We were the only ones in the room, and I was eager to see Miss Henson. I went behind the governess' desk and casually snooped through some papers. I remembered Miss Henson sitting there years ago watching over her flock of boys. She had been the nicest of all the Good Friends governesses. As long as you behaved and did what was expected, Miss Henson was fair, although her forms of discipline could be grueling. She'd make you stand at attention for hours in front of a wall with your nose touching! Or walk the playground perimeter in all sorts of weather. I soaked in the memories, especially those of when she'd sit with me as I wrote my letters home. Miss Henson had known how difficult it was for me and occasionally would offer a suggestion to help make the days bearable. I could still see in her eyes the concern she felt for me. I wanted to see her once more, to be able to thank her.

Just about that time we heard boys yelling and running in the hallway, followed by a collision.

"Whoa there—oomph!—boys," a man exclaimed. "No running in the halls."

"We're sorry, sir," a boy's voice said. "I didn't see you coming around the corner. They were chasing me."

Della and I went out into the hallway and found the man had corralled several boys and was helping one of them up. I did a double take. It was good old Mr. Nichman. "Are you okay, sir?" I asked.

"Yes, I'm fine. No harm done." He straightened up and adjusted the glasses on his nose, while the boys stood there shaking in their boots.

"Mr. Nichman," I said excitedly. "It's you."

"Sure is. Sixty years now." He glanced at me and then turned his attention to the boys. "Well, gentlemen, you can go on now. But slowly." There was a twinkle in his eye. The same kind look I remembered of him when I was a boy. His belly shook as he laughed.

"Mr. Nichman, I'm Billy, and this is my mother, Della." I took her by the arm to move her closer to him. She had never met Mr. Nichman before.

"I've heard a lot about you, Mr. Nichman." She shook his hand.

"All good I hope."

"I told her how you used to buy me Pepsies," I said and rambled on. "And you gave me a pair of roller skates. Do you remember a real bad fight you broke up in the sandbox? I mean a real bloody one, over a baseball cap."

"Boys will be boys, I guess. It's tough enough for these youngsters growing up without family and living close like this day in and day out. You can't be with them all the time."

Mr. Nichman stopped and stared at me. He looked at Della and then back at me. "Yes, now I remember. You're Billy Lonardo. My goodness." He shook my hand vigorously. "I never thought I'd see you again. Not after all these years. Let's have a good look at you. Your hair grew. No wonder I didn't recognize you. God bless you, boy. It's so good to see you. You look wonderful."

I savored his exuberance as he nearly shook my hand off. "Where's Miss Henson?" I asked. "I haven't seen her."

"She left us about two years ago. She took an administrative position upstate with the Milton Hershey Children's Home. We really miss her. She was an excellent governess. The kids adored her."

"How about Miss Linstrom? Is she still here?"

Mr. Nichman shook his head slowly and pursed his lips. "Nope, early retirement. Confidentially, I think the job wore her down. She was getting a little too strict with the boys."

"I'll say she was," I commented and patted my rear end.

Della showed me her watch. "Don't forget your friend Brian."

I had noticed throughout the conversation that she seemed withdrawn and somewhat uncomfortable. It was obvious she was anxious to move on. As for me, I could've kept right on talking. That's what I came there for.

"Well, I guess we should be going, sir," I said. "There's a lot we want to do and see yet."

"Well, I've certainly enjoyed our little visit, Billy." He walked outside with us and turned to Della. "I'm glad you came to see us. It does one good sometimes to relive old memories."

"I hope so for his sake," she responded. "It hasn't been easy. He's got a lot of anger bottled up inside him."

The kind look on Mr. Nichman's face lifted my spirits somewhat. "This was a good thing you did today." He pulled us close to him. "I mean the both of you coming here."

"It's been hard for me to forget what happened here, Mr. Nichman." I looked toward the wall. "I see that wall all the time." Even that day it still bothered me somewhat.

"Keep working on it," he said. "Good things will come your way. But Billy, live for tomorrows, not what happened yesterday. If you can do that, the walls will come down. All of them." He shook our hands and went back into the building.

Those moments spent with Mr. Nichman were precious. He always had had a good observation to share or some sound advice to give about life. Of course, years ago it didn't much matter to me who said what about anything, no matter how logical it may have been. If you couldn't help me, I didn't much care what you had to say. But that day I saw clearly how genuine a person he was, not just the man who bought me sodas or gave me roller skates. When I thought hard about it, I began to recall our little private talks, sometimes in his room, and the words of encouragement he always gave me. It had to be difficult for anyone in his position to not be able to change the wrong around me with the boys. As for the school overlooking the situation, I guess that was just the system of things back then.

CHAPTER TWENTY
A TIME TO WALK AWAY

Most of that Founder's Day had gone by without any resolve between myself and the boys I once lived with for seven years. The visit to Girard wasn't panning out as I had hoped. I so wanted Chet, Kevin, Benny and especially Butchie McGraff to see me with hair. Even meeting up with Big Joe Costello again would've been satisfying.

Della and I arrived at the wall just before six o'clock. Seeing that spot again by the old equipment shack got to me, as the memories flooded by. "Mom," I said. "This is where Chet and I went over the wall. Once we shimmied up the rainspout, the rest was easy. What a neat feeling that was when we took off up the street. The wall seemed so high back then. I shook the spout. "But it didn't stop us. We were outta here and that's all that mattered. I still think about it."

"Billy, isn't that your friend coming toward us?" Della redirected my attention to the other side of the vast playground.

"Yep, that's him all right." As I watched Brian coming closer, my emotions were mixed. Although he was a Junior School classmate whom I had befriended, after that year we got caught in bed together I distanced myself from him. Our friendship in Section 1 began innocently enough as my rejection by the other boys started to worsen. Those days were very difficult to get through, but he stuck by me, even during the lonely nights. At ten years of age we had had a strange attachment to one another that seemingly felt like more than just being pals. In my eventual failed relationships with women over the coming years, I'd always think back to him and me, which made me question my manhood. It wasn't until I turned thirty-six that I'd finally make love to a woman and father a daughter. What a monumental triumph that was, putting to rest many of my doubts about who and what I was.

"I never thought I'd see you again." Brian held out his arms to me.

I hesitated and shook his hand. "Yeah," I somewhat

nervously agreed. "After all these years."

He looked at my hair. "You know, I think I liked you better bald. I can't kid you now." He acknowledged Della with a nod. "Hello again, ma'am."

"Brian, tell her how everybody made fun of me. She never believed me when I was here." I was hoping he'd be helpful.

"It doesn't matter now. You have hair. Forget it." He playfully messed up my hair. "That was a long time ago. This is a day to celebrate."

"Inside these walls? You gotta be joking." It was apparent that he didn't want to talk about the past, but I certainly wasn't ready to let go of it.

"What better place? The wall shouldn't mean a damn thing to you anymore." He took his hand in mine and walked with me toward the wall. "There's nothing here for you to run away from. No more walls to climb."

"Maybe not, not here anyway, but how about inside me?" Oh, how I had wished Chet could've been there that moment. "When the Battalion was forming on the parade grounds this morning I didn't see Chet Pursell anywhere. Is he still at Girard?"

"No. He left the hum a couple of years ago. Nobody knew why either. I'm sorry. You two were good buddies like you and me were once back..." He looked away from me, and I could see the emotion in his eyes.

The school's Big Ben tolled the hour, and I shook my fist at the wall. "I beat you, you damn wall," I said. "Chet and me both did."

"Yeah, that was something." Brian turned toward Della. "They surprised all of us that day when they went over. But I can't say as I blamed them, especially your son. We weren't friends then like we had been before, and I really felt bad for him."

My plan for that day with Della needed more time. There were people I still wanted to see, places to stop and past moments to share with her. But seeing Brian Lehroy again at least gave me some closure. I really had wanted to talk to my former classmates, especially Butchie McGraff and of course Chet, the best friend there ever was. "You know, the school tried to keep Chet and me apart after we were caught. I guess they were afraid we'd try it again. If I had come back that fall, with or without Chet, I swore I'd burn the whole damn place to the ground."

The crowds were dwindling as the day's festivities began to draw to a close. We started back up the main road with Della in the middle, passing by the old buildings and the memories one by one. Westend, The Mechanical School, The Armory, Good Friends, The Junior School, Lafayette Hall with Mr. Hector, The Infirmary, and my last place of residence, Banker Hall. Good old Banker Hall, the place where I had reached the limits of my tolerance and fled.

Della picked up the pace, while Brian and I walked behind her talking on and on. I was trying to get all I could into that day, knowing my time there was growing short. I hadn't even seen any of the other classmates yet, and boy how I wanted to.

"Let's go to Allen Hall with Brian, Mom." I ran up to her. "I might not get another chance to talk to Kevin and Benny. Graduation is in a month, and who knows if I'll ever see them again." I would have stood in front of the entire class that day, just to show them how I looked with hair.

There were so many nameless faces I recalled that I had wanted to see, even though my reasons might not have been the best, because I wanted to gloat and watch their reactions toward me. *Which ones would squirm,* I pondered, *and how many of them would have the guts to say they were sorry like Louis Stewart had?* But in the end, Brian was right. It didn't much matter anymore.

"You can come back down some other time, without me. This was too long a day for me. Way too long." Della looked weary as she stared at The Chapel. "I always wanted to go inside there."

"Please, Mom," I insisted. "It's important to me. Let me just see a couple of the guys." I glanced at Brian for his support, but he was watching Della, who at that point appeared rather withdrawn.

"Kevin left the school a couple of years ago, Billy," he said. "He never came back after Christmas vacation. I meant to tell you."

"What about Benny, and Louis Stewart?" I asked.

"When Kevin didn't come back, Benny kind of withdrew from everybody. I didn't even see him around today except when the battalion was on the parade grounds. As for Louis, his mother took him out of Girard also about three years ago."

Della walked over to The Chapel's main entrance, paused and glanced back at me. "I'm going inside for a moment. Maybe Brian can get Benny to write to you, or you can call him."

That wasn't good enough as far as I was concerned. "I really hoped to at least see some of the guys today, Mom, especially now with my hair." I had wanted them to know that what happened between them and me was forgotten. "Boy, except for Brian here, I didn't get to see anybody that I wanted to. It's not fair."

Della slipped into The Chapel's vestibule. When we caught up to her, she was standing before the gold engraved Lord's Prayer on the granite wall, just like I had stopped to read years ago. "Why is it called The Chapel?" she asked. "It's so big, like a cathedral."

"Wait until you see the inside. The pipe organ is one of the largest in the world."

"The building seats about two thousand people," Brian said. "That includes our student body, and guests in the balcony."

It was early evening, and a few sightseers milled about as a recording of the Girard Boys' Choir played softly in the background. Della stared silently at The Lord's Prayer a while longer and then opened one of The Chapel's large wooden doors. We watched her slowly walk down the center aisle to a pew and sit down.

"Let's sit here." Brian motioned toward a pew several rows back. "Maybe she wants to be alone. This had to be a tough day for your mother. You once told me she ignored what went on here years ago. You can bet the school told her nothing. They weren't obligated to share any information once they became our guardians. But I'm glad I stayed here, because I sure didn't want to live with any foster parents."

"Yeah, I was surprised when I found out they never even sent report cards home."

"Go easy on her."

"I never looked at it that way," I said. "Even when Miss Hill and Dr. Zarello came to the house that summer, I felt like my life was being toyed with. Mom stuck up for me a little bit, but of course my stepfather put his two cents in. It was obvious he didn't want me home. But I let them know I'd run away again."

"What was it like between you and them after that?" Brian asked.

"I tried to forget everything about this place but couldn't. You kidding me? I had nightmares. Still do. I can't shake the anger inside me. I even pulled a knife on my mom a few years ago. But that had a lot to do with Jim. I hate him. Big time. All I wanted to do was stay with my father's people in Trenton for the summer, but my mom wouldn't hear of it. So I flipped out and she called the cops. They had me scared shitless. But things didn't change."

"Wow, he must be real bad. How was school up there?"

"Hell of a lot better than Girard. The kids were super to me. I made a lot of friends. It's a damn shame my home life hasn't been as good. We're not a family. I still feel like an outsider, just like I did here but in a different way. My stepfather is a scary man, especially when he's drunk. I'll never understand why she married him."

"Maybe for you, to bring you home."

I had often thought of that, for all the good it had done. "Sometimes it's worse than when I was here. I always feel like I'm in the way, Brian...and not wanted."

"It sounds to me like maybe your mom is caught in the middle. And then if you add all the past stuff, like losing your hair and everything."

The Chapel obviously impressed Della, because she kept glancing all around. I wondered if any of what happened throughout the day had had an effect on her. She was a difficult person to read. Nobody ever quite knew what was going on in her mind. It was extremely rare for my mother to share a thought, offer an opinion or discuss much of anything. Our conversations throughout that day were the most we had ever communicated with each other. It was frustrating for me not to have a parent to turn to for advice, or even just to be a sounding board. That sort of thing never came easy for my mother, nor did ever saying, "I love you." But I would learn later on that was the kind of home life she had grown up in.

I thought about Chet and me climbing over the wall four years ago. It had only freed me from the ignorance of innocent children, not that of an adult. My mother and I had a different wall between us, but ironically it too was made of stone. And who knew then if it was surmountable. "Can you believe it?" I said to Brian. "After all these years, here I am in The Chapel with her praying."

Della stood next to the pew. "C'mon, Billy, let's go now, it's getting late. We should eat something before we meet the bus."

"I'm not hungry, Mom," I said.

"Well, I am." She walked up the aisle.

It was dusk when we got outside, and the old fashioned street lamps were just lighting. The people remaining on campus were all headed toward the main gate. I went out into the center of the road and watched the lights come on all the way down to Westend. How beautiful it looked, yet the sight of it didn't match the memories in my heart. The day had gone too fast, and what I had planned with my former classmates wasn't going to happen.

"Are you coming?" Della was already up the road.

"We'd better get moving," Brian said. "She seems in a hurry and upset about something."

We caught up to her, but she looked straight ahead without uttering a word.

"What's wrong?" I tugged on her jacket sleeve to make her stop. "Please, Mom, there's some time left to talk to a few of the guys."

"You had all day to do that." She continued walking.

"Besides, you found Brian, and that will have to do, as far as I'm concerned. He can say hi to everyone for you."

"You still don't really care, do you?" I felt the anger swelling inside me again, but I didn't want to lose it in front of Brian. To come all that way and not see any of the other guys frustrated me.

Although we were in sight of the gate, Allen Hall was where I wanted to go. *The hell with Della*, crossed my mind. What was she going to do, leave without me? I wanted to scream at her, but I didn't. Brian knew what was on my mind and put his arm around me as we all walked toward the gate together. The spotlights came on, bathing Founder's Hall, the circular flower gardens and the main gate in a flood of brilliant light. I reflected on how deceiving that warm picture was. But then again I guess that was the only way I permitted myself to see it. I recalled the night of the Billy Boy melody, the whispering voices and the misty image that I thought was my father beckoning to me. Wanting something as badly as I did that night, maybe I did dream it, but it seemed real enough at the time.

Della stopped and stared out across the circular gardens, looking up at Founders Hall. "You know, it does look different at night when everything's lit up. It is a beautiful school."

I remembered how the newness of Girard had appeared to me all those years ago, when I innocently believed that my mother and I were beginning a new adventure together. "Yeah, Mom, but it didn't look so good after you left me here. And even now it still doesn't."

"That's the memory you must let go of, Billy. Every bit of it." Her face was expressionless. "Look what it's doing to you, and us."

"You have to do the same, Mom." It was difficult for me to hold the words back. "You're still pretending none of this ever happened. Maybe I'll be able to let it go when I feel you understand the consequences of what you did."

She stood her ground and gave me that defiant, cold look that I had grown all too familiar with. "I can't make it better for you. Nobody can. Only you have the power to do that. I came here and did what you asked. And I sure don't need to relive it over and over."

Brian handed me a slip of paper. "Excuse me," he said, "my phone number's on there, Billy. Call me sometime. I have to get going. I got finals to study for." Then he turned to Della. "It was hard for him here, ma'am, but I believe he might've made it with a little support from the school and the rest of us. Nobody listened or tried to understand how lonely he must have felt. No, nobody can change the past, but denying our mistakes only keeps things from getting resolved."

I stood there not knowing what to say, but I was thankful for Brian's words. At least Della had finally heard it from someone who was there with me. I wanted to hug him, but unfortunately, I still had my reservations.

Brian stared straight into my eyes. "Your mom isn't hurting you anymore, you are. What good was all this today if you keep letting the anger eat at you? You'll have to try to let it go."

"I understand, man. Thanks."

"Where have you people been all this time?" Carl, the lodgekeeper, joined us in front of the gate. "I was beginning to think you left before I got a chance to say hello."

"Hi, Carl," I said. "Hey, you must've seen us this morning?" I said.

"Sure did. The moment you two came through the gate. These eyes may be old, but they still work. Just because you grew some hair doesn't mean you look different to me. You're the same little boy I held in my arms back in '51. How could I ever forget your frightened face the night you came charging up the main road and threw yourself into that gate?"

"You're lucky it was closed. How come you didn't say something when you approached us this morning?"

"I didn't want to bother you just then." He acknowledged Brian with a nod but gave me a stern look. "Did you and your mother have a nice day?"

"Let's just say it was an experience for the both of us," Della interjected.

I couldn't have asked for a better conclusion to that day.

There he stood, the keeper of what was my private school of misery. Carl was the first to reach out to me at Girard when I needed someone. Just knowing he was at the gate made the wall appear less ominous at times. When I needed a good thought to hold onto, it was him I often thought of.

Della gazed at her watch nervously. "We really should be moving on."

Brian put his hand out to me. "Yeah, me too. I got to get back to Allen Hall. Let's keep in touch, okay? You know, after graduation I'll be living in Reading, Pennsylvania. Not too far from where you live in the Lehigh Valley."

"Well, uh, you take care of yourself." I didn't know quite what to say at that moment, but I knew there would come a day we'd talk.

Brian patted me on the back and smiled. He glanced cordially at Della and then back at me. "See ya, Billy...I hope. Nice to have met you, ma'am."

I watched Brian until he was out of sight. I've had a lot of friends over the years, but few like him. After that day I never saw or heard from him again, until about two years ago when he phoned me out of the blue. We've spoken a few times since on the phone, but for now I felt it best to leave our past lie where it was.

Carl walked my mother and me toward the gate. "Yep, I guess it's time to lock up the old place." You know, Della, I've seen a lot of boys in my time pass through these gates. But none I ever felt as close to as your son. Billy, just you remember it's people that make things right or wrong, not places. And when we keep holding onto what has hurt us, then we're hurting ourselves, and sometimes those around us. Doesn't make much sense to do that, does it?"

"I guess not. But it's easier said than done. Take care, Carl. I'll come back again, I promise," I said, not knowing whether I ever would.

Eventually I did return to Girard with my stepson many years later, but Carl had passed on by then, and I could only share his memory with Michael. The fond recollection of the old gatekeeper will always warm my heart. When my daughter Nikole visited there with me not too long ago, she stood at the front gate and spat on the ground. She had a hatred for the school, having grown up hearing all the stories. There's a lot of my sensitivity inside her that in time I'd eventually rid myself of. Hopefully she will also learn to forgive my mother. Nikole went on to major in child psychology and today is a caseworker for troubled children. I couldn't be more proud of her and pleased with what she's chosen to do in life. There are so many children who need someone to care.

Della walked across the street, and I waved a final goodbye to Carl. I glanced up at the walls that were my towering intimidation for so many years. Their confining coldness still had a grip on me, and there seemingly was no release from it. Why did I feel so incomplete, confused and angry for so long?

"The trolley's coming," Della called out from across the street. "Time to move on, Billy."

I turned toward Founder's Hall one last time. Yes, she was right. It was time to move on, and I hoped one day I could. The faint notes of *Where Have You Been Billy Boy* played ever so softly in my heart, and the image of my father drifted closer in my mind. For a brief moment I thought I saw him working among the flowers in the circular garden. He tipped his hat at me, and in my imagination I heard him say, "Be strong now, my son. There are no more walls for you here. Never tire of striving for truth, and believe in yourself. Life can be forgiving if you learn to forgive and love the person you are." The questions were too numerous, and the answers remained so few at the end of that Founder's Day. Della and I sat side by side on the bus trip home, and yet we were still so far apart.

I'll never know if the visions of my father were real or the mind's desperate desire to fill empty dreams and the loving hopes of a little boy. But I do know that when children reach out for what nurtures their innocent hearts or teaches inquiring minds and disciplines the wrong of their ways, someone caring must always be there for them.

CHAPTER TWENTY-ONE
PAINFUL LOST LOVES

Doubting my manhood never gave me peace of mind for years to come as I sought to find my way in life, no different from any other young man aspiring to fulfill his dreams. Haunted by old memories of Girard brought on by the return of my hair loss, I drifted back into a world I thought I would never experience again. It was a horror show to once more see my crowning glory leave me naked and incensed over its hideous onslaught. There were days and nights that taking my life seemed to be the only answer. As the hair fell from my head strand by strand, clump by clump, it caused the madness in me to often fester into sheer rage. I saw my dissenters at Girard and blamed each one of them for the torment that had returned. My nightmares were filled with the hatred of it all, and the picture I once drew of myself standing on the wall repeatedly came to life. I ran along the top of it in my dreams many nights, desperately searching for a friendly face to comfort me.

Genine and I had first met at my old high school's Saturday night dance. Those had been my cocky days when I finally could comb through a full head of hair, slick back the sides '50s style and pull a few curly locks over my forehead like a rock 'n roll star. I was cool and knew it, strutting like a peacock, especially around Genine. She came from a very strict Catholic family who frowned upon premarital sex or foreplay, which saved me from having to prove my lovemaking prowess, or lack thereof. It made it easy for me to carry on with my manly charade as the thoughts of a long-ago nocturnal tryst with Brian Lehroy resurfaced.

In time Genine and I were married and moved to the city where I attended the Philadelphia College of Art. I wouldn't realize until many years later that it had been a marriage not of love and devotion on my part, but rather one of companionship. Living alone, especially back in Philly, wasn't something I had handled very well. Being by myself then, and now, I digressed back to those lonely boyhood times at Girard. The remnants of our youth are always there to some degree. It's just how we choose to live with the memories. Most times I deal with the past the best I know how, but those empty moments can still rattle me.

Neither one of us were employed when we first set up housekeeping, living off our wedding money for several months. When Genine eventually found night shift work as a keypunch operator, our husband-and-wife existence became even more infrequent. We were more like brother and sister than a married couple. It was rare when we went to bed together and our weekends were usually spent back home visiting the folks. Heaven forbid we'd dare think of making love sleeping near her parents or my mother. All this did was prolong the inevitable sadness between us, for I doubted my capability to function as a sexual man. Even the mere thought of it was painful.

It was during those days that I started to notice extra hair on my comb or towel after I dried off following a shower. I managed to keep it to myself until one Saturday night at Della's when I caught her curiously staring at my head during dinner.

"What the hell are you looking at, Mom?!" I exploded. I knew what she was staring at and it lit the fuse in me. "Yes, my hair is falling out again. The damn thing is coming back!" I pounded my fist on the table and stood up. "I can't deal with this. Why is it happening again, Mom?"

"I don't know, Billy," she replied with tears welling in her eyes.

"It's not that noticeable, honey," Genine commented. "You're sitting right near the wall lamp, that's how come she saw it."

I charged into the bathroom and slammed the door so hard the wall shook. For a brief moment I stood quietly in the dark gathering myself before turning the light on. With my eyes closed I stood in front of the mirror, paused, and then opened them. It was hell revisited as I tugged lightly on my hair and the strands began to easily fall all around me. I couldn't stop. Clump after clump slowly laid parts of my scalp bare, and their roots were as black as my heart felt.

"Billy, what are you doing in there?" Della asked, knocking on the bathroom door. "Come on out. Don't do this to yourself."

"I'm not, Mom. It's doing it to me. Why? I can't go through this. I'd rather be dead than see myself bald like before. Please, God, no." I yelled at the top of my lungs. "No, don't let this happen to me again!"

When I opened the door, my mother entered, grabbing a brush and comb. "Really, Billy, it's not that bad. Look. See, you can cover it up." She frantically combed and brushed my hair every which way, causing more of it to fall out. It made me think of Miss Hart many years ago at Girard when she too would try to hide the bald patches.

"Stop, Mom! You're making it worse!" I took the brush out of her hand and threw it at the mirror, cracking the glass. "Look at me! The freak has returned! Damn this all to hell anyway. See what Girard did to me, Mom? The nightmare won't go away."

Genine stood in the doorway wanting to help in some way. She reached out to comfort the both of us, but I shoved her aside and went into the living room. "I won't go through this again," I shouted, glaring at myself in the large picture mirror. "You ugly son-of-a-bitch. They did this to you. All of the bastards in that hell hole." My mind raced on remembering everything and everyone that I felt had ever hurt me at Girard. I had myself convinced that it was all the school's fault from when Della deserted me there. "I should've burned the goddamn place down…and maybe killed Butchie McGraff that day on Girard's main road."

"Why would you want to do that, Billy?" Genine asked, timidly walking into the room. "What did anyone have to do with your hair falling out?"

"You don't understand. How could you? You weren't there. They never let me alone. Besides, I shouldn't have been there in the first place." I picked up my jacket. "Come on, get your things. We'll stay at your parents tonight. I don't want to be in this house right now. Living here wasn't any better."

We said goodbye to Della, who had gone into her bedroom and sat by the window. I should never have left her that night feeling the way she obviously did, but it was all about me back then and I just didn't give a damn.

"Slow down, Billy." Genine tapped my arm. "You're driving too fast. Get a hold of yourself. You're scaring me."

I was like a crazed fool that night with thoughts of ending my life and hers. Everything seemed so wrong, including being alive and married. As we crossed the Hill-to-Hill Bridge in the town of Bethlehem, I lost it and steered the car off the road up onto the pedestrian walkway heading straight for the bridge's concrete side barrier. At the last second I slammed on the brakes, bringing the car to a sliding stop.

Genine screamed. "What are you doing, trying to kill us! I don't want to die, and neither do you."

I collected myself, backed the car onto the road and continued on without uttering a word. There were other times after that incident when suicide tempted me while driving, but I never did that again with Genine at my side. No, unfortunately, I frightened her in other ways, like the time I locked us in our bedroom and insanely fully intended to harm her.

It had been a pleasant enough evening at our apartment, and after dinner I went into the living room to watch some television before working on my presentation portfolio for semester finals. Genine finished the dishes and went to take a shower. I was engrossed in a movie and hadn't paid much attention to what she was doing until I heard her call me.

"Billy, look. Do you like this nightgown on me? Is it sexy?"

I glanced up and there she stood in the archway looking seductively at me. The short black negligee was very low cut and sheer. "Yeah, it looks good on you," I replied and went back to watching the movie.

"C'mon, honey, let's go to bed. I want us to make love. Please." She sounded alluring, like I had never heard her before. It would've been difficult for any man to refuse her advances.

What followed is extremely hard for me to describe, but it

will show how twisted a young man I was. I did want to please her and make things right between us, but the ever-present fear of being unable to make love crept into my consciousness. It would be the first time in my life that I had to face my sick reality, and yet I didn't know why. What was I to say? Sorry, dear, I have a headache? *You're a married man* were the words that came to mind. *This is expected of you.*

We lay side by side for a while kissing and fondling one another. Genine was an attractive young woman and, if not for love's sake, any healthy man would've wanted her, but a growing discomfort in my groin began to render my desires useless. I recalled one other time during my high school days with my first love that the oncoming of such pain befell me. "I'm sorry, Genine, but I can't do this," I moaned and crawled out of bed, hardly able to stand up at first.

"We've been married over a year and you haven't made love to me. Why, Billy? I need to feel your love inside me."

"Maybe I don't have any love to give you, or anyone else. Something's wrong and I can't explain it. It's not you. It's me." Once I knew that I wouldn't have to perform, the pain subsided. How odd, I felt, as I stood there holding myself. It made no sense, and for years it never would. Until this writing I never mentioned to her the pain I experienced. It made me feel so ashamed that I couldn't be the man to satisfy her desires.

"Is that all you can say? Why did you marry me?"

"I thought I loved you. Really, Genine, I did."

She got out of bed and came up to me. "You thought you did? What does that mean? Aren't I good enough? I love you…and I want children some day."

"So do I."

"You have a strange way of showing it. You ignore me most of the time when we're alone. How do you think that makes me feel? Maybe you should see a doctor or a psychiatrist."

As honest as her words were then, they angered me and I lost all self-control and decency. I slammed the bedroom door shut and shoved her backwards into the corner. "Maybe it's you.

You don't excite me. Who knows, if we would've made out before we got married things might've been different. You and your damn Catholic holier-than-thou parents...and now I'm expected to be your sex machine. Well I can't do that. I'm not a light switch that you can turn on and off at your whim. No, Genine, it'll never happen. Do you hear me. Never!" I raised my hand to strike her, but something held me back and the rage ceased. It had been a frightening moment for both of us, because I really did want to hurt her. There was even drool dripping from my mouth as I stammered and was short of breath. My tantrums could be volatile.

She cowered in the corner, sobbing and trembling out of fear. "I can't live like this, Billy. You scare me."

Two years later at my mother's house, Genine had come with her attorney to get what personal belongings and wedding gifts that were there. The last words I heard her say were to my mother. "Somebody should've smacked your son a long time ago. He's got real problems."

In time I moved back home from Philadelphia because I couldn't make a go of living alone. By then I was practically bald and had lost most of the hair over my entire body. Della eventually put up the money for a full hairpiece, and I began working in the area as an Art Director for a publishing company. I became friends with a nice young teenage girl who lived down the street next to my cousin's house. Felicia fascinated me with her gentle nature and the attentive way she'd listen to all my woes. In time we became more than just good friends, and I grew close to her family, visiting them often, which didn't please Della at all. "Their daughter's a kid," Mom would say. "You're too old for her." We'd argue, but to me it was comforting to have someone who honestly cared about me. More important, I didn't feel threatened about having sex with Felicia because she was underage. Yes, there I was once more, hiding from the truth behind the walls I built around me.

The years marched on, and before I knew it Felicia and I were engaged to be married, much to Della's disapproval. I wasn't sure whether or not it was because of my marrying a teenage girl or that I would be moving out. In any event, our Lutheran ceremony was a beautiful candlelight service with over five hundred friends and family in attendance who later that evening danced the night away to a live band that sounded like the group Chicago. It was one fantastic affair, and early the next morning my young eighteen-year-old bride and I set out for the Pocono Mountains and Sunset Lodge that was owned by my Uncle Frank. No secluded hideaway was better suited for a honeymoon, but as we drove there I wondered if I'd be able to fulfill the loving expectations of another wife. I was twenty-six years of age by then and yet still had never made love to a woman. But this time would be different because I honestly believed I was in love with Felicia.

Sunset Lodge was a romantic log cabin set deep in the woods near a babbling brook. Upon our arrival, I immediately started a fire in the large fireplace and went about preparing lunch for the both of us. It was late spring and the cool, fresh mountain breezes gently blew as we ate outside on the patio. Later we went for a walk in the woods and returned with freshly-picked wild flowers. Yes, romance was in the air, as they say, and I was ready to finally put my sexual demons to rest forever. Felicia and I had had our moments of innocent foreplay before, but she was never made aware of my impotency. Those secrets I kept from everyone as I continued living the lie.

We lay for a while on the couch by the fireplace that evening after dinner. Listening to music and watching the dancing flames, we talked about our plans for the future. The mood couldn't have been more serene and arousing, especially when Felicia went to the bedroom and returned after preparing herself for our night of long anticipated romance. I remember how seductive she looked standing there in front of the fireside light, beckoning to me. For a brief instant I thought of Genine and how I had disappointed her years before, but I couldn't let that happen again. No, I was going to be every bit of a man that Felicia deserved and desired.

"Come to bed, Billy," she whispered tantalizingly and took

hold of my hand. As we walked toward the bedroom arm and arm, suddenly a discomfort in my groin made its ugly presence known. It was familiar to me because I had felt it before, but why always when the thoughts of making love were on my mind? It was a mystery to me and as we reached the bedroom I grasped for the bedpost to keep myself from doubling up with pain.

"Billy, what's wrong?" Felicia asked, taking hold of my arm. "You don't look right to me."

I can still remember how it had hurt when I sat down on the edge of the bed. "I really don't know what this is. But I feel sick to my stomach and got a hell of a pain in my groin. I've had this before."

"Do you get it often? I don't recall you ever mentioning it to me."

At first I didn't want her to know anything about it. "It's probably from when I got hit down there with a baseball in high school. That was the worst pain I ever felt. I wound up in the hospital for two weeks. They were even thinking of removing the one testicle. You should've seen how swollen it got."

"Has it ever bothered you before when you've made love … or were about to?"

That was the toughest question I had ever been asked in my life up to that time. After a moment or two, I looked at Felicia and the words just blurted out. "Uh, yes," I stammered. "Once with a girl I dated in high school and then with Genine."

"You mean when you were married?"

"About a year or so after we were living together."

"Not on your wedding night?"

"I'm afraid not, Felicia. But I really don't think I loved her from the beginning. Besides, she was shy about the sex thing. That's the way her parents raised her. We should've never married."

Felicia moved across the bed and affectionately put her arms around me. "I love you, Billy. Is there anything I can do?"

"I love you too," I replied, but inside I recall asking myself whether I really did. Felicia had never looked so good to me as she did that night. I wanted to take her in my arms and love her. "I'm really sorry this happened. Maybe the pain will go away in a while. I really want us to make love."

"Well, let's not worry about that right now. We have our whole lives ahead of us." She helped me lie down. "When we get back home, maybe you should see a doctor. I'll go with you."

Sadly, we never did make love that night or any other time throughout our seven-year marriage. In the few attempts there were early on, the same impotent thing always happened. The most shameful wrong that I committed back then was in never seeking any physical or mental help. For years I kept promising myself as well as Felicia that I'd work it out somehow. Her tender loving care of me was loyal and faithful right up to the end of our marriage. I had hurt her deeply and caused a good woman much heartache. All she ever wanted was my love and to have a child. Instead, I would fantasize about actually making love and then torture myself over the reasons why I couldn't. Often as I searched for the truth there'd be the image of those two boys lying in bed at Girard, me and Brian. The doubts of my manhood would become the highest wall in my life I'd ever climb, along with finally accepting that being bald was nothing to be ashamed of.

After the loss of Felicia, I found myself in a constant state of confusion, not knowing who I was and traveling along lonely roads that led me in never-ending circles. I longed for whatever brought me happiness, even if for only a temporary stay of sanity. There were several women along the way, but the longer I continued to fail as a virile man the more my depression turned to drinking. Those were the darkest years in my adult existence when all of the anger smoldering inside me became my personal Dante's Inferno. The more I tried to fit into society the more out-of-place I felt. But I was a great pretender and had everyone fooled except for two people, my mother and me.

A HOPE FOR TRUE LOVE FOREVER AND A DAY

Into all of our lives during troubled times a light eventually does shine. And for once in mine, it wasn't another train barreling out of control toward me in the tunnel. Kathy's glowing persona was unlike any woman I had ever known before. There was a radiance about her that when she smiled, so did the light in her eyes. Ironically, she was in the hair business and we knew each other in passing through one of my close friends who owned the beauty shop where she worked. One night at my favorite watering hole she entered into my life, thanks to her cousin and a radio disk jockey friend who had decided to play cupid on our behalf. Kathy also was coming out of a divorce. Cupid's arrows found their mark in both our hearts, and we began what would be eighteen years of the most happily fulfilling lifetime moments I would ever know. From the start, Kathy seemed to be aware of the good, the bad and the emotionally ugly sides of me. She was remarkable in every way, particularly the night all the bells chimed in loving harmony and together we'd resurrect the man in me. It had once been told to me that it would take a very special woman for me to fall truly in love because I had no concept of what love was. I hadn't spoken of my impotency, and yet somehow she knew. We had had our sexually playful moments like all new lovers do, but I continued my manly charade. I would use the excuse of not violating the sanctity of her home with her seven-year-old son sleeping just upstairs. Then there came that surprise weekend when Della decided to visit her sister. Before leaving, she let it be known to me that maybe Kathy and I could spend some time alone together. I guess it was a mother's way of finally expressing her approval of the new lady in my life.

What a beautiful winter's evening it was at our secluded mountain home. I was nervous and stoked the fire in the family room fireplace, prepared a gourmet dinner of Veal Picatta served with wine, lit candles and had the music playing. Little did I know that what was in store for me would change forever the little boy who had never found his way into manhood. In my mind I was simply looking forward to a private weekend with the woman I so adored. Throughout the night Kathy would nurture me with loving care and gentleness as we explored our passions like I had never imagined before. When the morning came and the sun arose, once more my entire being was aroused and filled with her love. There had been no fear of failure, no anxiety and, most of all, no pain.

It was the greatest of new days for me. I wanted to share my happiness with the world and embrace the feeling of being a part of someone other than just myself. A month later as we wrapped Christmas gifts together, I spoke the words that I had never before believed in my heart. "I love you, Kathy," I said, in a shy way.

She glanced at me with her big smiling eyes and replied. "How can you say that? We've only been seeing each other for a little while."

"There wasn't any pain."

"What does that mean?" she asked.

"I've never been able to make love to a woman because of it." I went on to explain all that I had been through. For the first time I talked freely about the impotency I had lived with and kept a hidden part of my life. I even mentioned my doubts and fears of being a homosexual, but couldn't get myself to speak of Brian at Girard.

When I finished, Kathy sort of chuckled. "Well, it's obvious that you're not a gay man. But I did sense that you had never made it with a woman before. You were so innocent, not even realizing that you had done it. That's why we made love again. I wanted you to know for sure."

It would be a while before Kathy expressed her feelings of love for me, but I've never forgotten our special moments together that winter weekend when life itself became worth living. I couldn't wait for the dawning of all our tomorrows.

We were eventually married in July of 1981 and I officially became part of my very own family, with a boy I affectionately called son and three years later the birth of a daughter. I promised myself then that I would always be a caring father to them like my father whom I never really got to know, except in dreams. Most of our eighteen years together were a wish come true for me, the family man. Sadly though, there isn't much to be said for what in time would tear our family apart. But as I write these words, I can honestly say that what we allowed ourselves to lose should never have happened. Like far too many families nowadays, we became one more statistic in society's epidemic of broken homes.

We only live but for a mere spec of time in history, and each of our experiences are seemingly as vast as the stars above us. It's how we move on from adversity and look ahead to the coming of new days that make or break us. My learning process had been labored, but we never know what lies just up ahead, do we? So allow your wounds to heal, gather strength and wisdom from the past errors of your ways, be kind of heart, never dwell too long in yesterdays, and stand tall and loving amongst the crowd. Teach these things to your children and you'll be a hero in a world where there are few heroes. Where I find myself today, all around me is a new, wonderful family that I call my friends. Yes, I would certainly welcome the closeness of what I once shared. But like the countless photographs in a family album of memories, I will always hold them dear to me, remembering those days as a husband and father, and it was all good.

CHAPTER TWENTY-TWO
THE SUN DID COME OUT TOMORROW

The years filed by, and once again I felt out of step with life, this time also dragging love affairs behind me. The hair loss had fully returned, but wearing wigs gave me some consolation. Yet I remained convinced that I would move on and overcome the traumatic loss of family life, no matter how deep the wounds were. The dark shadows wherever I walked cast their coldness down on those who had loved me. The encircling walls for a time seemed an insurmountable fortress from within and without. Love was an emotion I had experienced, but now feared I might never know again. My anger returned, and I became helpless once more to the inner turmoil and ugliness that was me. The forgiveness I thought I had given my mother was no longer there, and I unleashed the savage fury pent up inside me against her.

Doctor Landry was a man of small stature, with a psychiatrist's ego as big and all-encompassing as his brilliance. Sigmund Freud was his hero and mental combat his way. My many sessions with him would eventually reveal to me all the complexities about myself that I didn't realize let alone understand. His professional manner was direct, spellbinding and often mentally punishing, but the night I stood vigil outside Della's hospital room, he was comforting. That was my time of dancing with devils, nourished by alcohol.

"What have I done to my mother?" I asked, peering in at Della. "Look at her. She doesn't even want to see me."

Doctor Landry's piercing and inquisitive stare from under his bushy eyebrows went right through me. "I'm afraid she's turned herself off to you and possibly to living. She's a very sad and broken woman. What happened?" he asked. "What brought her to this?"

"Me," I said and turned away, fighting back the tears.

"How come she's holding a crucifix in her hand?" He went to her bedside and tugged on it. "We can't get it away from her."

"I came home drunk tonight, and we got into an argument about God."

"What about God?"

"Oh, I questioned his existence."

"That's all?" The doctor's eyes seemed to search deep into my soul. "There's got to be more to it than that. Look at the mental state she's in."

"It was stupid what I did. I lost control and ripped the crucifix off her bedroom wall."

"Go on," he prodded me.

"I threw it down the hallway and screamed at her, 'Where in the hell is your God?!'" My lips quivered as tears streamed down my cheek. "'Where in the hell is he? Why won't he help me?' I kept repeating in her face."

Doctor Landry shook his head, sighed heavily, and motioned me away from the room. "I'll try to talk to her."

It was midnight when he finally approached me in the waiting room. "Here," he said and handed me the crucifix. "Take this home and put it back on your mother's wall."

I remember trying to shove my way around him, but he put his arm out and blocked me. "Can't I talk to her?" I asked.

"Not now." He held my arm firmly. "I'm sorry, she doesn't want to see you. It's going to take a while, but I think she'll be all right. She's had a nervous breakdown and needs plenty of rest and quiet. I'll let you know when it's best to visit her. Meanwhile, you have to keep up with your sessions and stop canceling them. This can't continue between you and your mother. It will kill her. She's a strong woman but blames herself for so much of what happened to you. You need to find forgiveness somehow inside of you. It's difficult for her seeing you unhappy and acting like a madman. Your baldness alone is more than enough guilt she's placed on herself."

Della returned home in a month, and Doctor Landry continued to counsel me, slowly unraveling my twisted state of mind. We delved deep into my childhood, where all the shadows of those early times were first cast from the walls around me. Every open wound, beginning with my father's death, through abandonment, peer rejection and abuse were explored. He laid my life open before me like a surgeon would diseased flesh. We'd often painfully relive those days of my youth by first dissecting them and then diagnosing their meaningful influence on my life. The hair loss had served as a catalyst to everything else, as I became a smoldering ember before the firestorm to come. In time it became clear to me how the unloving and neglected childhood I lived had rendered me so helpless to myself and others. Doctor Landry would probe those parts of my psyche and with ease be able to touch the nerves that had been laid bare. He was not gentle at times, and I would even strike back at him. The emotions he wanted to surface for reasons of my understanding them most often would, and I'd leave his office on those days physically drained and mentally spent. I had never looked at myself in the way he was showing me, because I never did like the image in my mind's eye, nor the one I saw in the glass. For most of my adolescent years on into adulthood, I had never looked directly at myself in the mirror in a well-lit room. The image repulsed me.

"See yourself clearly in the present for what you are, but don't dwell on the past reasons that made you so," Doctor Landry said one day. "Understand them and then move on."

"But why was making love so hard for me?" I asked. "I had been married twice before Kathy and couldn't satisfy either of my previous wives sexually. When I attempted to, the pain in my groin was unbearable. What was wrong with me?"

"The women you had let close to you, you also punished. You were still a boy in that respect who was not in love and didn't even know what it was. Revenge upon your mother was still controlling you. As long as you looked for her in others, your heart could not find true love in them, and then you made them pay for it dearly, especially if they were in love with you."

Until Kathy, it was the biggest mystery of my life. "But why?" I asked. "Why hadn't I been able to perform? I never rejected it intentionally." At that time I was in my thirties and desperately wanted to be in love and have a family. Family was always the most important thing to me in my life and still is.

"A son can't make love to his own mother," Doctor Landry said. "It's not the natural order of life. No matter how we may feel toward them, most men hold their mothers in high esteem, or on a pedestal, as if they were saints. Your relationship was far more complex, and it took a very special woman for you to fall truly in love with. One that you didn't see as your mother, to punish." His words hit me hard, as if he had struck me with them.

That session ended in a most peculiar way that day. The doctor introduced me to his mother. She rested on a shelf in a bronze urn behind his desk. Good old Doctor Landry.

I had certainly been a network of jumbled contradictions stemming from my childhood. I could feel for the needs of strangers, yet I had despised and mistrusted the innocent women with whom I had shared my bed.

"Your wives married a confused little boy who wanted so badly to be a loving husband and father but didn't know how. Unfortunately, you were the sum total of an empty childhood like so many I treat today, but in your case let's be thankful for the inner strength you possessed." He lowered his head slightly, removed his glasses and peered at me through those bushy eyebrows of his. "At least I'm not counseling you in a prison cell. It's a wonder with all the anger that was stored up inside you, that you never committed acts of violence against women…especially now, after losing the love you had searched for all your life."

I've always found that amazing myself. There had been no instant cures or miracles, but what I learned from Doctor Landry helped me to better understand my life and how the little boy in me began to mature. Those were the days of my laying to rest all the old demons. I finally began to surmount the forgiving walls that had confined me, or that I had once hidden behind, and opened myself up to the light of angels, especially the one who had come into my life for a time, whom I truly loved and then lost. When Kathy and I parted after our eighteen years of being together as lovers and parents, for a time I digressed back into hell and, sadly, did drag my mother along with me.

Then, one Christmas about seven years ago, Della and I were having dinner. We had been living together and struggling to keep the house we had bought with Kathy. It was just the two of us and our little dog, Molli. We spoke about the irony of our lives and all that had happened. She wasn't a talkative person normally but rambled on quite freely that night about her life.

"I'm almost ninety," she went on to say, petting Molli. "I've begged for God to take me many times, and I've grown so weary of struggling. And after seeing your marriage break up and you so unhappy, I feel helpless. I know how much she meant to you, because you never loved anyone else like her."

I was glad Della was there with me. We had fought through so many adversities over the years. My heart went out to this little but mighty woman as I listened intently to her.

"You know, Mom," I said, "it's fate that we're here together now in the twilight years of your life. We've earned some good times together. This is giving me and you the opportunity to make it completely right between us."

"I never thought I'd see you brokenhearted again," she said. "You've had more than your share of sadness in your life."

Yes, it seems like ages ago that I had met and fallen in love with a wonderful woman, who had a son. I recalled how those days filled me to the brim with such happiness. We were young and so in love. It was glorious to finally feel, with every part of me, what love meant. Kathy was truly that special woman Doctor Landry had talked about. My being a loving husband and dad, not only to her boy, Michael, but also to our own daughter, were the greatest of times. I'll always remember the joy of my life when our Nikole came into the world. "It's a girl!" I shouted. That moment was captured in my heart, and on a photograph I took as she appeared from her mother's womb. It was a Caesarian birth, but she was healthy and made our world complete. I looked at her little round face resting on her mother's tummy, and once again I was a king in my own parade. There is no greater experience in life, and when I gaze at the poster I made from that picture, I happily shout all over again as if it were yesterday.

I *had* fallen in love with love, plus all the good things that can warm a heart about family life. But unfortunately, like myself and so many of us, Kathy had also lived with hurt from out of her childhood. At the age of nine, as she sat on her father's lap, he suffered a coronary and died. It's said that such a trauma causing a young child's broken heart can innocently create inside of a person their own self-blame for what happened. Thus, my wife and I came from extreme backgrounds, she the gentler and myself the tougher. I believe a man and woman are the family's foundation, but she lived through the children in a very overprotective way. We couldn't seem to find a middle ground. The walls that eventually came between us we permitted to grow so high that we lost sight of each other from the other side, along with what we once had.

Della squeezed Molli gently and put her down. "You should hold her," she said. "She'll give you some sugar. It's unfair what happened to all of you. I thought for sure this time your life had finally turned for the good, especially when your daughter was born. You must feel abandoned again."

I guess in a way I had felt deserted, but I wasn't going to let it beat me. "It'll be okay, Mom." I reached across the table and touched her hand. "This time you are here for me. You know, I never told you before, there was one positive thing I did get from you."

"What?" Della asked.

"The stubbornness to survive. Girard gave me that too. It was a hell of a way to learn it, but I've drawn a lot of strength from those days. They were hard times. So here we are again, without a family, but inside me I know I gave it my best. I loved my wife and children with all my heart. They were the most important things I ever had. But I'll be all right. I have to be."

It took a lot for Della to cry, and as her eyes welled with tears, she watched Molli play with her stuffed animal. "Look at her," she said. "She's such a happy dog."

Molli picked up her toy and brought it to me. She got up on her hind legs, laid it in my lap and looked up at me with her big eyes. "You know something, Mom." I rubbed the toy against Molli's nose. "We humans can learn a lot from dogs. They seem to know our moods, especially when we're sad. But no matter what, they're faithful. They're always there to love you unconditionally."

Before Mother Della later passed on, she gave me the greatest gift ever from her. I was at the hospital the evening before she died. Suffering with pneumonia at her age, she was very ill, yet sharp as always. Three times during our final visit together, she turned toward me and said, "I love you, Billy."

A year passed and one night about three o'clock in the morning I awoke out of a dream. It was the first time I had dreamt about my mother since her death. I sat up and noticed that Molli was standing next to me on the foot of the bed peering down the hall toward Della's old room.

"Billy," came the voice, seemingly from that direction, like Della had often called to me. Molli's tail began to wag as she continued looking down the hall. Once again I heard my name. I got up and turned the hallway light on. If it wouldn't have been for the dog's reaction, I would've thought that it was only a dream, or maybe the wind outside. Upon checking my mother's room, I returned and got back into bed, as Molli still looked down the hall. I told her Della wasn't there and lay back down, closing my eyes.

"Billy, I'm sorry," were the last words I heard Della say. To this day I still wonder about that night. Had she come back one last time to ask for my forgiveness? She had carried in her heart all her life the pain of what had happened between us so long ago, never forgiving herself for what she had done. As I wrote these words, I glanced at her photograph on the dining room wall and said, "Mom, it's okay. I forgave you a long time ago. I love you, and we'll be together again."

IN MEMORY OF A GRAND LADY

"I love you, son." My mother rarely spoke those words although I knew she loved me. Hearing them uttered that final day of her life proved to be so special, as on the following morn she drew her last breath. Della had valiantly fought the after effects of pneumonia, which eventually robbed her of the dignity with which she lived life. From the anticipation of her return home to the repeated heartbreaking medical setbacks, I was extremely proud of Della and how she endured through it all. The strength and will she possessed didn't surprise those who knew her. "Little, but mighty," was my description of this ninety-three-year-old phenomenal woman, who had reached the top of one more wall ... her last.

I imagined her standing tall, with arms typically folded, first glancing to one side and then the other. She smiled down toward me and gave a casual nod to the world she had known. We waved to each other, sharing that final earthly moment. It wasn't an end, but rather a beginning of something new and wonderful for a mother and son, who knew in their hearts that they'd never be separated throughout eternity.

Mother Della. She never forgave herself for what had happened.

219

CHAPTER TWENTY-THREE
AN EPILOGUE TO ALL PILGRIMS

John Bunyon's book, *Pilgrim's Progress*, is about how adversity, obstacles and choices are very much a part of life's way. Bunyon's story is a religious allegory in which people and places represent vices and virtues. Christian, the hero, sets out from the City of Destruction to go to the Celestial City (heaven). He's laden with burdens and along the way meets many people. Some try to harm him, such as Apollyon and Giant Despair, and others, like Interpreter and Faithful, help him. Christian finally crosses a river and reaches the Celestial City after many adventures. I've read the book several times and it has served me well. Like the story *WALLS*, it's intended for all ages.

You can be the hero or heroin of your own *Pilgrim's Progress*. We all carry a backpack full of burdens just like Christian, and most often they're from childhood. Adversity and obstacles can either deter an individual or spur them on to succeed, to conquer the odds and tear down the walls. Setbacks can be used for self-pity, excuses or as an ally from which to gain strength and wisdom. Some folks take their pain and turn it on others, while settling for untruths to explain away failures.

My youth left me with many deep wounds. Today I have broken down the walls from the psychological aftermath of those early years, but the challenges it presented me with as a boy also instilled positives in me as a man. My father's death when I was four, the loss of my hair and the loneliness at Girard were all mere catalysts. They gave me an undaunted courage to surmount odds, and they taught me humility and to care about those less fortunate than myself. I've learned that all life has meaning and serves a purpose. The roads may twist and bend, sometimes ending nowhere or up against towering walls, but continue on. The Celestial City is somewhere up ahead.

Most of all, remember that those who are different from you in any way also need love, understanding and the same respect you desire. They will probably need even more. Don't cast them aside, for they too have a heart just like you.

Finally, if we can all remember that what we are is in part because of where we've been, maybe our children will be the better for it. Love them, be there for them and teach them well. *They are tomorrow.* And always remember that the only person any of us can change is ourselves.

MY DIFFERENCE
REFERENCE TO ALOPECIA AREATA

Alopecia areata (AA) is a disease which occurs in 1.7% of the population (Safavi et al, 1995), often with devastating effects to patients and their families. In the United States alone, over five million people and 115 million worldwide, most of them children, will be affected at some point in their lives by this autoimmune disease, making it almost as common as psoriasis. For those with the disease, there is no escape from its devastation. Using a direct quote from an NAAF publication, you can clearly imagine one young woman's hurt: "When I'm not wearing my wig, my dad cannot look at me without pain in his eyes." Taking another quote from an 11-year-old who suffered with both insulin-dependent diabetes and alopecia areata, we learn how her disease tolerance clarifies the balding horror. Given a choice of the two, she'd keep her diabetes, because, "I can see my alopecia areata every day in the mirror."

The relationship between alopecia areata and other medical conditions is likely correlational rather than casual (Shapiro, 1996). Its course is unpredictable with periods of remission and exacerbation and yet it is not possible to predict when hair will fall out or begin to grow.

1. Alopecia areata occurs more frequently in atopic families and where family members have asthma, atopic eczema, or autoimmune diseases. Alopecia areata has been associated with thyroid disease, type 1 diabetes, pernicious anemia, systemic lupus erythematosus, vitiligo, Addison's disease, and rheumatoid arthritis.

2. Atopic patients seem more likely to have a form of alopecia areata which is resistant to treatment.

3. Eight percent of alopecia areata patients have thyroid disease as compared with 2% in non-alopecia areata patients.

4. Vitiligo occurs four times more often in alopecia areata patients than in non-alopecia areata persons (Shapiro, 1996).

Alopecia areata is psychologically devastating and can

wreak havoc on parents, siblings, spouses, friends and even employers, as it does on those with the disease. Parents helplessly watching the disease affect their children are sometimes traumatized by its hideous onslaught; even friends can be estranged because of their ignorance; and employers can also react unfavorably due to its appearance. Yes, alopecia areata is an unpredictable and psychologically challenging disease.

Alopecia areata has been scientifically proven to be an autoimmune skin disease, although the direct cause or causes have yet to be defined. Following an epidemiological study of 499 patients, the notion that alopecia areata is infrequently precipitated by psychologically stressful events has been widely held by both dermatologists and patients. The study simultaneously assessed the magnitude of psychological stress preceding the onset of alopecia areata using the Social Readjustment Rating Scale (Holmes-Rahe); the prevalence of psychiatric disorders after the onset of the alopecia utilizing the Diagnostic and Statistical Method of Mental Disorders (DMS-III); and the prevalence of autoimmune and atopic disorders in this group of alopecia areata patients. The conclusions drawn were that in a majority of the patients the onset of alopecia areata was not associated with preceding stressful life events, but the after-effects can be, and are in many cases, very devastating.

What happened to me still happens today to the children afflicted with the disease. In a more medically aware society, it's difficult to comprehend that kids are still targets of ridicule, isolation and even rejection by some uninformed adults. Cases of reprimands or even school suspensions for simply wearing a hat indoors are not uncommon. Some schools place young victims into special education classes or abandon them in "behavior groups." The psychological damage the hair loss can and does cause a child is sometimes more permanent than the disease itself. Imagine growing up in a neighborhood where other kids won't play with you because you have no hair. Siblings have even been ignored because their brother or sister is bald.

As children interact with others, their identity is formed. This identity is expressed in how they wear their hair and in what activities they participate. For children with alopecia areata, adjustments often need to be made to help them to participate in social activities. Being able to participate is an important part of growth and development. For instance, if they wear a hairpiece, is it secure enough to stay on during sports? What happens when they go swimming? The chlorine in the pool can be very damaging to hairpieces. Should the child forgo the hairpiece and face questions from peers? These are only some of the issues that children with alopecia areata must face in addition to the developmental tasks of their age group.

I've witnessed not only groups of children but also adults who ridicule a fellow human being because of a physical difference. Kids are easily led due to their innocence and peer pressure, whereas some grownups would rather be followers of the misinformed majority. The same rationale applies when people don't fully understand the unknown, like alopecia areata.

It is my contention that the most mistreated or taken for granted portion of the human anatomy is hair. I've always been amused by the countless cosmetic innovations man has devised over the years—radical hairstyles, chemical dyes, etc. The scalp, being the most visible area, has always served as a focal point for self-expression and individuality. The importance placed on hair, body image and beauty in our society is reflected in magazines and other media. An individual's sudden loss of hair can signify to others the presence of a contagious or life-threatening disease, thus bringing about fear of associating with them. This is not a new phenomenon. In early years, some people with alopecia areata were institutionalized and segregated from others in society for fear of contagion. Thompson and Shapiro (1996) reviewed the importance of hair throughout history dating back to biblical times. Hair ornaments have been found as far back as 8000 BC; Samson in the Bible lost his strength when his hair was cut. Hair styles over the ages have changed and are often a part of how one expresses her/his identity. We've seen this in the long hair of the hippie generation, the colored, spiked hair of the punk rockers and the dreadlocks/cornrows of the Afro-American community. It's certainly not my intention to attack the hairstyling industry, but I wonder how many professionals, during the course of performing their hair magic, give thought to the physical aspects. The majority of all human hair used in the making of wigs comes from poor or third world countries abroad, mainly because their growth is by far the purest. I make this comment only to call attention to health issues, not to start a new hair movement or anti-hairdresser campaign. After all, mankind's vanities must be served.

The scalp normally contains 100,000 hairs, and the average number of them shed daily is 100. Hair protects the head from sun; eyebrows stop moisture from dropping into the eyes; while eyelashes and nasal hair keep dust away. Healthy human hairs are classified in three phases of growth: Anagen hairs are growing ones; Catagen hairs are those undergoing transition from the growing to the resting stage; and Telogen hairs are resting, remaining in the follicles for variable lengths of time before they either fall out or are removed, such as by a hairbrush. Contrary to popular belief, neither shaving nor menstruation has any effect upon hair growth rate.

The disease is characterized by the loss of hair in one or, more often, several round or oval patches, usually on the scalp. The hair loss is initially always patchy in distribution; however, cases may present a diffuse pattern. During the regrowth stage, the hairs are downy and light in color. Later they are replaced by stronger and darker hair with full growth. I went through those phases many times, which naturally brought tremendous joy when I saw the new fuzzy hairs. In my case, these periods would only be temporary as the years went by. To some patients, there is progression of the disease, with the development of new bald patches, until there is a total loss of scalp hair known as alopecia totalis. This occurred just prior to my teenage years. Those were the most difficult times in my relationships with the other boys and probably the most stressful period for me.

Although the disease alopecia areata was labeled many centuries ago, its cause is still unknown, but in recent findings as an autoimmune disease, genetic susceptibility is strong. Nearly 25-40 percent of patients have a positive family history. There are reports of twins with alopecia areata. The disease draws no lines, and all races or age groups of both sexes are equally affected. When hair has been lost over the entire body, including the scalp, the designation is alopecia universalis. It was during my early twenties, while married and attending art school, that the complete phase of the disease took its toll.

Since then, I've never sat in a barber chair, nor had to concern myself with hairstyles or having to shave daily. Thus, contrary to satisfying adult vanities from a barber's chair, I sought sanity instead on a psychiatrist's couch. The physical effects of alopecia areata are often only part of the nightmare. The psychological wounds can be deeper, especially for young victims, and sometimes never heal.

Although the direct cause of alopecia areata still remains a mystery, there have been treatments approved for other diseases which have had positive results. Yet it is not known why some patches will regrow in a few weeks without any treatment and others will completely resist all forms of therapy. The literature is replete with data from studies using various therapeutic approaches, none of which is clearly superior to another. No one treatment works well for everyone, but spontaneous remission is common. This is presumably why some treatments in uncontrolled trials give high response rates. It is only when patients are in a poor prognostic category, such as pre-puberty onset or a history of other autoimmune diseases, that the prognosis is chronic or life-long.

Midway through my twenties, I would no longer have to deal with the unsightliness of the hairloss. Full hairpieces of the '60s, although not perfected as they are today, would give me some comfort. The longer hairstyles of the '80s and '90s made it somewhat easier for me to disguise my baldness. In any event, the first wig I wore made the affliction much easier to deal with.

My head no longer was the attention-getter, although in certain situations I remained somewhat uncomfortable (i.e., with strangers). It was continually in the back of my mind that someone would discover that I wore a wig and the ridicule I most feared would begin once more. But with today's technology, the styles and various types of foundations available make all hairpieces practically undetectable.

Research is ongoing and support groups are available; however, some patients still report lack of support when newly diagnosed with alopecia areata. When the first symptoms occur, many patients describe having their condition being incorrectly diagnosed by their primary physician, with the cause usually attributed to stress and few treatment options provided. Through education coupled with research, it is hoped that alopecia areata will be viewed differently and patients will receive accurate up-to-date information.

In addition to psychological issues, there are practical concerns for patients with no or little hair. The following are only a few that alopecia areata patients face regularly. But most will tell you that a sense of humor helps.

Should I wear a wig? What kind of wig? Synthetic or real hair?

How much will the wig cost? Can I afford it? Is it covered under the medical plan? Wigs or hairpieces may be covered by the medical insurer if it is called a cranial prosthesis and the patient is provided with a letter explaining that it is for a medical condition. Legislation is changing. Check with the National Alopecia Areata Foundation, wig makers and medical insurance companies to see if a hairpiece is covered.

Keeping a wig on so it won't fall off. There are many methods of keeping the wig in place, from suction cup designs to special double-sided tape.

Make up. How can I disguise the fact that I have no eyebrows or eyelashes?

Finding a hairdresser who can give a good cut to cover up the bare areas.

When dating, do I tell him/her or not?

Should I have children? What is the likelihood of them

having alopecia areata?

Nail polish. Can it be worn if nails are pitted, which is a common trait in alopecia areata victims?

Do I participate in sports? If so, how do I disguise my condition if I do not want it known?

For those who are experiencing alopecia areata, let my true story, *WALLS*, serve as a testament to survival. The disease was a major crisis in my childhood, but it also gave me the inner strengths one needs in life. Alopecia areata, at the outset, had been a shock to me, but it's not a death-dealing disease. There are many other crippling infirmities far worse than the loss of a head of hair. I eventually learned to consider myself fortunate to be impaired only with baldness. My friends and acquaintances today accept me for the person I am, not the malady I have. But closest to my thoughts are always the children that alopecia areata strikes. To the parents, teachers and grownups in their lives, I simply say, please don't turn your back on them because you don't understand. They need your strength, comfort and support. Counsel yourselves with a qualified dermatologist and learn about the disease. Then, most important of all, take the time to educate the others around them, especially your child's friends.

There remain many unsolved mysteries surrounding alopecia areata and other autoimmune diseases. To every victim of this genetic phenomenon of nature, there is one simple truth: Consider yourself lucky. There's no comparing the loss of 100,000 strands of hair to being handicapped, hungry, poor, homeless or dying from illness and senseless wars. Besides, in this day and age, "Bald is beautiful."

Research

Andrews' Diseases of the Skin: Clinical Dermatology. Eighth Edition, Arnold, H.L.; Odom, R.B.; and James, W.D. W.B. Saunders Co., Philadelphia, PA, 1990; Ronald Domen, M.D. (former Miller Memorial Blood Center Medical Director); Nina MacDonald, B.Sc.N., R.N. (Nurse/Manager, Vancouver General Hospital Skin Care Centre and University of British Columbia Hair Clinic); Jerry Shapiro, M.D., F.R.C.P., and Harvey Lui, M.D., F.R.C.P.C.

References

National Alopecia Areata Foundation
P.O. Box 150760
San Rafael, CA 94915-0760
www.NAAF.org

Dermatology Nursing, 1999, Volume II, Number 5
Jannetti Publications, Inc.
East Holly Avenue, Box 56
Pitman, NJ 08071-0056

Recommended Reading
Alopecia Areata
Understanding and Coping with Hair Loss
(Thompson & Shapiro, 1996)

Recommended Website – www.NAAF.org

A FINAL THOUGHT

Humankind's worldwide community of families is society's
foundation.
Thus, may today's caregivers nourish our young with love,
kindness,
truth, guiding discipline, and compassion—
for today's children are the hopes for Mother Earth's
tomorrows.

Will Lonardo – 2012

Our Molly -
She truly represented the
meaning of unconditional love.